Blurb

THE WEIGHT OF THE JOURNEY BY KEN BYERS

THE WEIGHT OF THE JOURNEY

Ken Byers

September 2012
Copyright Ken Byers 2012
ISBN 9780983224211
Lloyd Court Press
Portland, OR 97212

ACKNOWLEDGEMENTS

It has become a cliché to say it takes a village, but indie novel writing is as apropos a use of the phrase as any. I wish to thank all of the following for their contributions to this work. Tom Haley for encouragement, energy, knowledge, and buying my books to give to friends. Rae Richen for her continuing encouragement and judicious use of a blue pencil. Harvey Gurman for the "eagle-est eye" in his detailed reading of the manuscript to find the invisible-to-me mistakes that haunt manuscripts like this. I wish he could have had the last look. Bill Renfroe for creative energy and local knowledge. Jay Harris for his enthusiasm and wonderful imagination and insights into the act of creation. Rick York, Jean Haley, and Marybeth Stiner for reading and sharing their feelings and ideas. This book began life twenty years ago as a different story in the same setting. Without the help of John Pendergrass it would not have happened at all. A special thanks to Bob Sorge of Josephine County, Oregon, forester, fire fighter, and gold miner whose stories and knowledge led to much of the local color. As always, a special thank you to my wife, Meg Mann, who patiently watched me stare into space and while I constantly forget to do the simplest things. Thank you, my dear.

FORWARD

Banner County, should it really exist, would do so in a world slightly larger than this one where more fell into the realm of the possible. This is the world of *The Weight of the Journey*. Many things are different over there. The United States Forest Service is not quite as observant there as it is here, and the National Weather Service operates a little different. My apologies in this world for what happens in the other. The same is true for various state agencies. My *mea culpa* is the pursuit of a good tale. For Oregonians, don't go rushing to your atlas looking for Banner. It's not there. From my point of view, I wish I could drive there and look around. But I can't so the book is the next best thing.

Ken Byers
November, 2012

THE WEIGHT OF THE JOURNEY BY KEN BYERS

Part I: Broken Images

The Fire

The lightning bolt streaked out of the midnight sky. It struck a rock shelf in the Siskiyou National Forest in California, twenty miles south of the Oregon border. The strike splintered the rock and shattered the bolt into sparks, some of which ignited beetle kill debris littering the forest floor. The smoldering quickly grew into flames. Other nearby lightning strikes started other fires within minutes of the first strike in what would later become known as the Siskiyou-Banner Complex fire. The lightning ignited a heavy fuel load primed by a hot, dry summer, and intensified by Douglas Fir-beetle kill. The five smaller fires it started all went unnoticed because of other, larger fires burning several states away.

Within minutes of ignition, the winds from a high pressure zone off the Pacific Ocean shifted toward a low pressure front moving south out of Canada. The winds picked up speed and pushed the fires inland toward the tinder-dry slopes of the Pacific Coast Mountain Range. Sixteen miles south of Gasquet, California, the five smaller fires met. The combination of fuel, wind, and an upslope provided the ideal components for the birth of a monster.

By the next night, it had spread to eight hundred acres. It remained unnoticed.

The Weatherman

Meteorologist Mitchell Ellers pulled two tables together and spread out his print-outs. At this time of night there were few customers in Coffee Rings to complain about his hogging tables. He put his "Favored Customer" away cup emblazoned with the Coffee Rings logo, a steaming cup of coffee with a donut for a cup holder, on a corner and pulled up a chair. He arranged his papers to replicate the display of his five monitors at his National Weather Service workstation that wouldn't be his for another five hours when his shift started.

The first set of papers showed the Earth's surface from a computer-adjusted-height of twenty-five miles that focused on an area covering the Southern Oregon~Northern California coastline from Bandon to Crescent City, and eighty miles inland from Grants Pass down the Interstate 5 corridor to Yreka. The printouts were twelve hours old, and on the depiction of that remarkably clear August day his attention focused on the smoke from a new forest fire burning along the border of the two states. The area obscured by the smoke was as close to the middle of nowhere as you can get. If it weren't for satellite imaging the fire would grow to a dangerous point before anyone on the ground would recognize the threat. Ellers placed the flat of his hand over the fire's location. He closed his eyes and tried to imagine its spread by the time of the next satellite pass. He sighed in frustration, and rapped the table with his knuckles.

"What's wrong, Weatherman?"

Ellers looked up into the face of Dewey Farrell.

"What brings you to Coffee Rings at two o'clock in the morning?" Ellers asked. "The usual?"

"Yeah. Can't sleep and I don't watch television."

It was their usual exchange. They'd met two years ago at a support group for men whose wives had died. The meetings, held in the basement of a church, were dreary things bracketed before and after by AA meetings. The first conversation between the two men consisted of observations on the similarity in the facial expressions of their group with the recovering alcoholics. Neither man went regularly, so they didn't bump into each other often enough to become friends. It wasn't until they saw each other at Coffee Rings a couple of times that they exchanged "hi-how-are-ya's." The third encounter led to a shared table and confessions about the support group. Both were there under false pretenses. Farrell's wife had died, but his primary reason for being there was to get clearance for a return to work. In Ellers' case, his wife hadn't died, she'd left him, but he said it was enough like death to make the time worthwhile. It took a year before they traded even the most rudimentary details of their lives.

On that occasion, Farrell already sat alone with his coffee when Ellers came in. They sat in silence, Ellers with his back to the door. When Farrell acknowledged the arrival of new customers, Ellers looked around in surprise since he'd never seen Farrell acknowledge anyone. He saw two uniformed cops standing at the counter.

"So it's true that cops eat donuts?" Ellers said.

"Caffeine and sugar. Hard to get through the night without them," Farrell said.

"You're a cop?" Ellers asked, picking up on the surety of the tone.

"For the moment," Farrell answered.

"What's wrong?" Ellers knew as soon as he'd asked that he'd gone too far.

"Gotta go," Farrell said, and stood. He left without a nod or a word to Ellers or the cops.

It was months before they met again, and this time Ellers was careful to stay away from Farrell's personal life, although he was curious. He suspected that Farrell was at least ten years younger than the fifty plus his haggard face suggested. There was still a bounce in his step that Ellers possessed in his forties and now missed. That meeting came at a another middle of the night session with Ellers covering two tables with weather print outs.

"What are these?" Farrell asked, surprising Ellers with the curiosity.

"Weather charts. I'm a meteorologist."

"What channel?"

"No, I'm a real meteorologist. I work for the National Weather Service."

Most people follow that lead with comments about how much it rained in Portland, but Farrell nodded and drank his coffee.

Afterwards, they encountered each other a couple of times a month at various times of the day or night the way of single men lacking structure in their lives. Eventually, they got around to trading business cards with names and phone numbers. Ellers saw that Farrell's card introduced him as a consultant to police departments on technology issues, not as a Portland cop.

"What's wrong?" Farrell asked again, pulling Ellers back to the present.

"Sometimes my day job gets in the way of my real love."

"Which is?"

"Wildfires. Specifically, forest fires."

Ellers saw Farrell close his eyes and shudder. Still sensitive to his earlier experience, Ellers asked, "Did I say something wrong?"

Farrell looked at him silently over his cup as if making a decision. "My father died in a forest fire."

"I'm sorry. Let me gather these up," and he stood and pulled the weather charts toward him. As he did it uncovered the papers below. Farrell glanced at the newly revealed sheets, then cocked his head and picked up the top sheet.

"If we hadn't been bumping into each other for the last couple years," he said, then tossed the paper on the table, "I'd say you were setting me up."

Ellers looked at the discarded sheet, then said, "You know where that is?"

"Yeah. I was born there."

"You were born in Banner County?" Ellers asked, then rocked back in his chair. "You mean for the last two years I could have been learning about Banner from you?"

"Why would you want to?"

"Are you serious? The cloud, or as you natives call it, the Cloud," his emphasis creating the capital 'C.' "There's no place else like it in the world!"

"I couldn't help you," Farrell said, "I haven't been back in over twenty years."

"Is that where your father died?" Ellers asked, his enthusiasm overriding his caution.

"Yes, but I haven't been back for other reasons, too."

Ellers tried to salvage the conversation, but true to form once Farrell felt intruded upon, that was the end. He stayed long enough to finish his coffee, then stood.

"See you tomorrow night?" Ellers asked, the question was their traditional parting line.

"Going fishing for a few days," Farrell said. "No coffee up there. See ya."

"I hope so." Ellers wanted to see Farrell again soon.

When Ellers finally reached his workstation, he checked to make sure the USFS was receiving the same feed he saw. During fire season, the Forest Service supplemented their satellite images with those from the National Weather Service. They also called if they needed more precise forecasting for a specific, smaller location. He checked his email and found nothing new from the USFS. The new fire was still off their map.

He clicked his mouse, and his screen reset to the view 100 miles above the earth. He saw two blemishes on his otherwise clear screens: one was the smoke from the new fire, and the other was a small patch of cloud fifty miles northeast of the fire. He knew the cloudbank's irregularly shaped contours added up to precisely seven point five square miles with an average depth of 1200 feet. He knew because it had been exactly the same for the thirty-one years he had worked for the National Weather Service, and God only knows how long before that. In the beginning he didn't have the tools to make measurements that precise, but since they'd become available, the "Inter-Coastal Mountain Anomaly" as he'd named it, had been there day after day, never changing. There was no manmade way he knew of to create the cloud. He even had a private name for it: The Banner Mystery. It was a mystery because he knew very little about what lay hidden from his lofty view, and what he did fed his voracious need to know more.

The cloud covered the top and upper slopes of a mountain with no recorded name near the southern border of Banner County. The mountain, whose elevation reached to 3,103 feet, had not been explored for a simple reason that drove Mitchell Ellers crazy. It was one hundred percent on private property; it was surrounded by private property, and the owners had rejected every attempt he'd made for twenty-five years to explore what lay inside the cloud. He considered going in without permission, but the region was widely known for a level of violence that kept him looking behind his desk and down through a satellite image at the impenetrable cloud. That was why he needed Dewey Farrell.

He wasn't the only one who wondered what the cloud hid. DEA wanted to know. Southern Oregon and northern California were known for very high quality marijuana grown in that band of hills that flanked the Pacific Coast range. In the last ten years, the National Geographic had made at least a half dozen attempts to determine what topological features could produce a fog bank the same size every single day for years and years. Their every effort had been denied.

Every year on his vacation he made trips to Banner County to see what he could legally see. He still felt the excitement of the first time he saw the cloud-shrouded peak from the ground. Until that moment he hadn't ruled out a technological glitch, the electronic equivalent to a figment of the computer's imagination. If the view of the mountain right in front of him excited Ellers, he was the only one. The locals didn't notice it anymore. It had always been there like the sun always came up in the east.

His years of visits had produced no meteorological reason for the anomaly. The surrounding hundreds of square miles were dense forests of Douglas fir. On the mystery mountain, the trees could be old growth, centuries old, and trees that old were big. He'd heard rumors of redwood trees, giant redwood trees like those found on the northern California coast. That was possible, if not likely. Giant redwood trees need approximately five hundred gallons of water a day per tree. Most of that water came from moisture-rich clouds rolling in from the Pacific Ocean and taken in through the trees' upper reaches. But his Banner Mystery sat many a dry air mile from the coast. If those redwoods were there and they relied on atmospheric watering, the water wasn't coming from the ocean. The possibility made the mystery deeper and more compelling.

Ellers reached for his Banner Mystery log. He turned to the first blank page and wrote the day's date, then "No change."

Dewey Farrell

The condo where Dewey Farrell lived when Thatch McPherson's phone call came sat near the end of a short street lined on both sides with newly planted trees and condo complexes each with their own style. The styles ranged from colonial with faux columns and names that ended in Village, to art deco with the tacked on touches, and names like 'The Broadway' written in slender san serif fonts with bulges in the O's and P's. The lack of hominess on this street of thrown-together styles fulfilled Farrell's top priority when he down-sized. A condo would be a superficial place to live, but would never have the substance of home. Farrell had given up on home. He had no more family and had no interest in pretending that he did. Home had noise, living noise, not the artificial sounds he pumped from digital screens via coaxial cable or wireless feeds. Home had the cooking smells of meatloaf and marinara sauce, not the stale odors of a single man. Home had a semi-attached garage where he stowed his fishing gear on the wall. In the condo he packed his fishing gear up two flights of stairs and jammed the rods in the corner of a closet behind his winter coats. Condos housed people stranded in life: people transferring from careers and economic stations; people alone, people retired, people left unhappy by unexpected detours, and people who had given up. People like Farrell.

After his wife, Diane, died, the house across town had become too big. Too much room for memories. Too much work that took too much time that he had too much of. He sold it. On his last day, he walked around with the new owners showing them the secrets of the house it had taken him years to discover. He had tears in his eyes and made no effort to hide them. As he prepared to back out of the garage for the last time, he placed a hand on the corner of the house and wished it better luck this time.

At the moment he entered the condo after four days fishing at Badger Lake, the condo had what he wanted – a shower. The lake, less than a hundred miles east of Portland but remote enough to seem part of another continent, had left him gritty. He felt tired, too. More so than the last time he'd made the same trip. More things reminded him that he now pushed middle aged at forty-one.

He opened a beer from the fridge, turned on the air conditioner against the August heat, and headed for the shower. He glanced at the answering machine as he passed. The blinking light announced two messages. He almost left them for later, but stopped and pressed the button.

"Hi, Crash, old pal. Probably too much to ask of you to recognize the voice after all these years, but still – "

He recognized the voice and the nickname. The voice made Farrell think of laughter and always had, and the nickname came from his long ago youth in what now seemed to be a faraway land. The voice belonged to Thatcher McPherson.

" – old friends aren't supposed to forget their asshole buddies, are they?" The voice paused. "Do you think 'asshole buddies' sounds vulgar in men our age? I guess we're not kids anymore. It sounded good back then. How long's it been since we had a beer together? Fifteen, sixteen years?" Twenty years, Thatch. Almost half a lifetime. "Whatever, hope you can get a few days off. I need to see you. If they bitch, whoever they are, tell them to stuff it because you're about to become independently wealthy. That got the cop's curiosity stirring?" Thatch paused. When he started again, there was a new intensity in his voice. "Hey. Asshole buddies never bullshit each other? Right? Same rules, old pal."

Now there was a slight catch in the voice.

"Meet me at the Middle of Nowhere, that roadhouse we always wanted to sneak into when you were - what? Ten? I'll be there tomorrow night, Tuesday, from about eight until midnight. I'll have a beer on the bar for you. Tomorrow night's best, but if you don't show, I'll be there the next Tuesday and the beer will be flat. Same time. There's no place you can call me." A longer pause but Dewey heard breathing. "Hey, Dew, how come you never came back? It can't be because Pearl kicked your ass out. I'd really like to know why before I die."

The call had come yesterday.

"By the way," Thatch said, "here's a sweetener for you. Tess is here. She might even be at the Nowhere if you make it tomorrow night. She says she has an insight into your mother, if that means anything to you." Another pause. "That's all true, man, but it's frosting. Anybody wants to know where you're going, tell 'em you're chasing down a pot of gold. Like the end of the rainbow. Oh, one more thing. Pack your six-shooter and keep it handy. This really is the Wild West. Dewey, things have changed. Please. I need you for a friend more than you ever needed me." Need and please were strange words from the mouth of Thatcher McPherson. "Honor the old friendship, and then we can make a new one. You know, start over, have some laughs, drink some brewskies, maybe play some Bingo like the good old days. See ya tomorrow night."

Thatch was the oldest by a year. When he graduated high school he abandoned Dewey and went off to college. After that Dewey had received nothing more than sporadic phone calls, like this one. Thatch had never left a callback number. Dewey knew that Thatch had lived around the Pacific Northwest for years, but his pride kept him from tracking him down. Thatch's disappearing act had hurt. It still hurt enough not to get back in the car and drive five hours just because he'd called. Besides, Dewey had a life and couldn't just drop things and hit the road.

The second message started.

"Farrell, George Sturbridge. How about putting the program off a couple a weeks? Got a few scheduling problems. Sorry for the short notice."

So much for a life. Sturbridge was chief of police in Ellensburg, Washington, and a client. Since Farrell had "retired," he consulted with small police departments around the Northwest, introducing new networking practices and technology to cope with budget cuts. The three week job was supposed to start Thursday.

Dewey dialed the Ellensburg PD main number, asked for the Chief and got his voicemail.

"Chief, Farrell here. In the meantime, don't fill those two openings. We can work around them and with the savings you're a quarter of the way to your budget cuts. Call me when you're ready."

Even with no conflict, Farrell still didn't want to meet Thatch. He stood at the window and looked at the parking lot. Bringing up his mother rankled. He used to care who she'd been. She was dead, and had been since he was four or five. Any cares he might have had about her were long gone.

"That card doesn't work anymore, Thatch. I know who I am now."

He thought about Thatch while he drank his beer. They had called them their asshole buddy rules. In his call, Thatch had invoked the rules as if they still mattered. Then there was the bit with the gun. He'd made it light, calling it a "six-shooter," but Farrell had heard the tension. He owed Thatch and Tess. At a time when Dewey's life was surrounded by uncertainty and mystery, the McPhersons were clarity.

Their friendship had a dynamic: Thatch told him what to do, and he did it. Like when they played football, Thatch was the quarterback and stood there while Dewey went deep, running his ass off, bumping into cars, trees, and people until he earned the name "Crash." The name stuck when Thatch saw it was the way Dewey attacked most of his life. Head on, his body running ahead of his brain. The name disappeared along with everything else when Dewey left Banner.

Then there was the whole gold thing. They'd dug holes along creek beds when they were kids and pretended any rock they found was a nugget. Thatch was convinced there was still gold "in them thar hills." He tried to drag Dewey into some of the many caves of Banner County by calling them gold mines, but Dewey would not go. He hated the claustrophobic darkness. Thatch said Dewey hated the caves because they reminded him of his being alone. Dewey said he hated them because they were dark. He remembered one argument when Thatch threw his arms around him and told him if he ever felt lost in a cave not to worry, because he would be there.

Farrell stood in the shower until the hot water ran out. He knew he'd spent his life since he'd left Banner County trying to prove he didn't care about Thatch and what he'd left behind. There were times he felt his life was no more than a shadow of the promise he'd been born with. Now a widower and out of steady work, he'd downsized more than his house. After he got out of the shower and dried, he dumped the bag with the dirty fishing clothes on the bed, and repacked it with fresh t-shirts and jeans.

He hauled his bag down to the car, and put his .45 automatic back in the quick release holster under the front seat. He could tell from the weight the fifteen round clip was full, plus the one in the chamber. His fingers found the safety and he made sure it was still engaged. As he steered his Cutlass into the street, he adjusted the rear view mirror as a moving truck pulled out of a driveway behind him and cutoff his view. He looked forward and wondered where this new road would lead. He was going for Thatch and the rules, but Tess was there too, and that was another story. But Pazer, and Banner County, were nothing but other stories – the stories of his childhood.

He gassed the car, visiting with a clerk he knew who'd been robbed the previous week, and reloaded his "Valued Customer" jug at Coffee Rings where he lost minutes because he'd held the door for a woman who ordered four coffee drinks with froth and shaved chocolate and other things that required explicit directions to the barista.

Fifteen minutes later he was on Interstate Five heading south listening to classic rock. The music filled the car until the top of the hour when the news started. The first story was about the fires burning along the Oregon and California border. Two of the largest burns were predicted to soon join south of Banner County. When that happened the region was looking at a hundred year event.

When the second story featured Pazer, the county seat of Banner County, the coincidence caught his attention.

Banner Timber Products was headed for more litigation. The State Supreme Court had ruled against Banner's argument that logging private property was exempt from environmental and land use laws. The story said it was all theater because the real issue was Banner's attempt to extended their tax exempt status with the state, an arrangement that stretched back to the founding of the county more than a 150 years ago. Pearl Banner, CEO and sole owner of Banner Timber Products, would appear before the state legislature when it reconvened in January.

Farrell shook his head at the mention of Pearl Banner. When it came to names from his past, none, not even Thatch's or Tess's, carried more baggage.

"Get out and don't come back!"

Three hours later when Farrell left Interstate 5 at Grants Pass he'd tired of the air conditioner and opened the window. He crawled through the town's summer evening traffic while the hot, gritty air from the fires now only sixty miles south wafted in. As he crossed the Rogue River he saw a spectacular sunset colored with the deep-hued oranges streaked with black that looked like a dirty thumb print smeared across the sky.

The dashboard clock read ten-thirty before his headlights lit the sign for Pazer. For the first time he felt confident he'd reach the Middle of Nowhere before Thatch's midnight deadline. The closer he got the more anticipation he felt. There was no one in his life he'd known longer than his old friend. Thatch had wanted to know why Farrell had never returned to Banner County. Farrell would soon tell him he never went back because he feared the questions he ran from were still waiting.

He would be there in minutes. He felt dread born of naiveté. Traveling from the world he'd lived in to the world he guided his car toward was never that easy. The dread acted like a slap in the face. Banner was minutes away.

THE WEIGHT OF THE JOURNEY BY KEN BYERS

Johann Prus

"Why do you pleasure me so?" the young woman asked, lying at his side, sweat drying between their bodies, daylight pouring through the wall of glass high above the fantasyland-like world of Dubai City. "No others give me such pleasure, highness. It is as if you drink from me." "Perhaps I drink from the fountain of youth," Johann Prus said, wiping his mouth on a sheet, "and I drink your youth."

"Then drink your fill. Whatever you seek I will gladly give if I can."

He placed her hand on his spent masculinity. The one thing he wanted most at the moment he could not buy with all the money in the world, and no amount of drinking from her font would change that.

"You are human, not a machine," she said, misreading him, then brushing him lightly with the back of her hand. He heard how carefully she selected her tone, not an ounce of offense intended. He appreciated why she commanded the fees her handlers charged. "Tell me what you want."

"Your question is sincere?" he asked.

"Please, highness." He felt sure it was a term she extended to all who could afford her. Probably right more often than wrong.

"Humans are simple creatures," he said. "Their tastes are rarely exotic. They want to live a long time and achieve their dreams. I am no different. But unlike all but a few, I will achieve mine."

"Your secret, highness?"

He looked at her nineteen year old body, sleek, golden, and glowing with youth. "I know they all want your health, your youth. As will you one day when it leaves you. On that day *you* will pay *me*."

"Is this a powerful secret?" she asked, disbelief in her voice that a time would come when she would grow old.

"Oh, yes."

"Why?"

He loved her sweet curiosity found only in the young. If it were for sale he would buy it. If it were not for sale, he would steal it or take it by force.

"Do you truly wish to know?" he asked. When she nodded and arranged her hand to do its maximum good, he said, "Today you have everything in life. That is the wealth of the young. But you spend your wealth one day at a time. It doesn't seem like much and draws little concern."

He moved her hand away from his delicate member and turned to shield it from her. He stroked up her stomach toward a breast until his thumb and first finger surrounded a nipple then closed on it. He pinched her bud as if to pick it. Instantly, she arched her back.

"What if your every waking moment was filled with such pain?" he asked, pressing still harder. "What if your pain grew with each passing day worsening on your road toward death? What would you pay to find release? Anything, yes? Do anything?"

He released her nipple.

"As such pain leaves your body you would savor the return to life." He watched her face as the pain left and she became a wounded animal. Next came anger before she caught herself, and when she did she resumed her pliant role. She tried to speak, but he put a finger on her lips.

"Such pain is the fellow traveler with age." He kissed her forehead in apology. "The most valuable power in the world, more valuable than gold or oil, is the power to extend a pain-free life. I shall own it."

He lay on his side now and felt the stirring of an erection. There is no greater aphrodisiac, he thought, than the promise of greater wealth and the giving of pain. He knew it was a false promise, but she had proven her value and he lay beside her content in the moment.

His bedside communicator hummed.

"Yes?" he said, his voice activating the machine.

"A thousand pardons, sir, but the reports from America are here. You instructed me ~ "

"Arrange transport for the girl. I will be there in a moment."

He closed his eyes. All this talk of pain, and his own kept in abeyance by the girl's distractions, now reclaimed his body.

"One day," he promised himself, "one day soon I shall own such power."

Dewey Farrell

It had taken dynamite and diamond-tipped drills to slash a path for the pass. Farrell drove the winding road on the strength of his high beams as they cut tight funnels alternately flashing bright reflected off the rock and black as the headlights shot twin streams into the night. They created a strobe light effect. He felt an invisible membrane block his journey as he crossed the summit and tear with an explosive rip as he burst into Banner County.

"Welcome home," he thought.

With no moon and no town for miles, Dewey was sure the night was deeper than city-dwellers ever saw. A curve suddenly opened onto a large valley discernible only as a deeper darkness than the surrounding hills. He saw the neon light of the Middle of Nowhere's sign five miles away and a thousand feet down the mountain. The only other light was the flashing red beacons of a radio antenna north of the Nowhere's sign. The clock said ten fifty-two. Plenty of time. His beer wouldn't even be flat.

He lowered both front windows in the hope of cool air. The road hugged the edge of the mountain, but Dewey kept an eye on the Nowhere's sign as it came closer.

Even two miles off the first gun shots sounded as crisp as surgical incisions in the stillness. Their echoes ripped across the valley floor. They overlapped, and the echoes confused the direction but he knew they came from the island of light in the darkness. The tight mountain curves kept him with a foot on the brake despite his urge to stomp the accelerator and launch into space aimed at the Middle of Nowhere. He pounded the wheel in frustration as the shots continued, but now they had a different timbre, like there were new guns being fired as well. The sound of the gunfire seemed a freak of nature taunting him and underscoring his impotency. He could hear the shots above the wind whistling in the open window, and above the shriek of the tires on the road and do nothing.

When he reached the bottom of the hill, the road lay straight to the roadhouse. He milked the last ounce of horsepower from the Cutlass.

Despite the roar of his engine he heard the echoes of the shots bouncing off the hillsides and the black reflective surface of the night. His sense of anticipation vanished, replaced with dread.

He held his breath during a long silence, but when single shots replaced the bursts, their finality sounded more terrible. He counted seven, then an eighth deliberate shot. Dewey recoiled from each as if holding the weapon himself, feeling it jump in his hand.

Headlights came on near the roadhouse sign and slowly turned away. The murderers were escaping, then more shots sounded. Two cars of killers? The vehicle took its time even as Farrell cut the distance.

He took his right hand off the wheel and reached under the seat for the .45. He aligned the wheels for the center of the graveled parking lot and slammed on the brake before his car left the pavement. When it hit the loose rock, the rear end slew around.

He saw two men leave the roadhouse. One man dragged a leg and leaned on the other while using the butt of a rifle as a cane. They made for a pick-up truck near the door.

The men saw Farrell's car. They separated, the wounded one dropping to a knee, as their rifles came up. Farrell tromped the brake and pulled the wheel putting the right side of the car between him and the guns.

Their first shots crashed into the right front quarter panel and shattered the windshield. Glass sprayed his face.

He stuffed the gun between his legs and used his right hand on the wheel, and left to open his door. He grabbed the gun as the centrifugal momentum of the still moving car dumped him on the gravel. He felt the gravel cut into his bare elbows and forearm, and his pant leg tear at the knee. The backend swung away leaving him several feet from where he hoped the killers expected him. He kept rolling and came up at the rear of his car. Clearing cover, he aimed for the closest shooter. His target appeared to be changing clips. Their eyes met as Farrell's finger closed on the trigger. Just as Farrell prepared to fire, blood from the glass cuts dripped into Farrell's eyes. He fired and the gunman spun as if shot in the shoulder instead of where Farrell intended. The other man had limped to the truck. The deep throated growl of the truck's big engine sounded.

The man Farrell had hit launched himself over the side of the pickup bed before Farrell could wipe his eyes and get off another shot.

The truck gained traction. Its backend fishtailed as it aimed at the already wounded right front side of his car. Farrell got off three shots at the driver's half of the windshield. The oncoming truck swerved slightly, but still delivered a glancing blow to the Cutlass that drove the car back on its springs and knocked him to the ground.

Over the top of the truck came rifle fire with the selector on full automatic. Farrell hugged the gravel until the shots ended as the truck raced into the night.

Farrell's ears rang as he stood. He brushed his clothes creating clouds of dust. He saw trickles of blood from gravel, glass, and debris on his arms and on the back of his hand where he had wiped his eyes. The pin pricks of pain dotted his arms and face. Adrenaline ebbed, replaced by a sense of dread. His chest heaved and his pulse raced. He heard the sound of upbeat country-western music from inside the roadhouse.

Farrell took a deep breath and went in. Shell casings littered the floor near the door. He picked one up. 5.56mm ~ M-16's. The shooter he'd seen reload held it by the pistol grip. The weapon was light enough to hold in one hand.

Taking a deep breath, he looked around the room. The first thing he saw was the Budweiser sign ~ the round, lighted one that revolves as the horses pull the wagon in their perpetual circle. It was the sign that hangs in half the saloons in America, but only the top half remained leaving horses without legs, and wheels with no bottoms. The wagon-master smiled on. Some of the fallen glass lay on the bar and the rest on the floor. On both bar and floor some pieces were streaked in red while others floated in red pools.

Farrell closed his eyes again and groped for something to lean against. His hand found the jukebox as the song ended leaving only the whirling of an unseen fan lost in the gloom of the room. No moans, no stirrings, no signs of life. Bonnie Raitt broke the silence with the opening notes of *Nick of Time*. The irony of the song's title enflamed his raw feelings.

Light came from scattered ceiling fixtures in canisters sunk in the drop down ceiling. Each light did no more than create an island in the heavy shadow that still filled the corners and nowhere other than near the bar could the light be called good. The air hung heavy with the acrid smoke of gunfire. The fan created eddies alternately revealing then obscuring Farrell's vision.

"I'll be waiting at the bar," Thatch had said.

Twenty feet away it waited for him. Bullet holes stitched the wood below the bar top. They formed a jagged line, evenly spaced except for a break above the contorted body on the floor. The man lay on his stomach, head turned away, right hand draped over the bar's brass foot rail.

Farrell touched his slick skin on the bare shoulder exposed by a tank top. The man must have been standing at the bar when the killers came in. He would have turned and seen them with their guns. He would have been afraid, but the fear wouldn't have lasted. The first shooter would have started with the bar in case a bartender had a weapon hidden below the countertop.

Farrell's hand slid down over the shoulder and turned the body.

Twenty years, half a lifetime, didn't stop Farrell's knowing even before he rolled the body. He pulled the still form toward him.

Thatch's eyes were closed and there was a smile on his lips. The ironic kind that Farrell remembered; the one that made you sure Thatch knew something you didn't, and pissed you off until you found out what it was. The kind of smile Thatch always had in his voice whether anything was funny or not. Farrell hoped the smile was for what Thatch saw ahead rather than behind.

He let go of the shoulder. Thatch rolled away. Farrell's hand moved down the body's arm to his hand and held it tight. Flecks of blood dotted the hand, but blood smeared the ball of the right index finger. It was the hand that had been draped over the foot rail.

The wood paneling of the bar was dark. The blood markings were darker. He leaned closer and the light improved. He looked up and saw the broken Budweiser sign turn his way. With the additional light he made out *B22*. Even in death Thatch remained enigmatic.

Farrell examined the body and found the chest and arms heavily muscled. He remembered Thatch thinking muscles were mundane. Also out of character for the Thatch from their childhood were hands callused from hard labor. Lower, there were wounds in both legs. The back of the right leg had an entry high in the thigh that exited through a gaping hole over the knee. The left leg had one too, the entry lower and the yawning exit straight through. Thatch must have had his right foot on the rail.

He looked at the stitching along the bar paneling again. It went from one end to the other. The bartender must have been out of sight so the shooter sprayed it all. That was why Thatch had taken it the way he had. He must have been the first one hit, and why the shots hadn't killed him immediately as they would have if they'd hit higher. And why he'd had the chance to leave the message.

There was another wound ~ the killing wound. Powder burns against the shirt over the left shoulder blade. The exit was a gaping glimpse of the slaughterhouse spilling Thatch on the floor.

Stepping carefully around the shattered chairs and tables, he walked into the dimness of the room. The center of the room depicted chaos in still life. Five of the dead lay in proximity to a round table upended by flying bodies and bullets, the table top shattered by automatic weapon fire into slivers and shards. Two of the bodies were roughly dressed men who either held handguns or had one at their side. They flanked the body Farrell purposefully avoided looking at. He dropped to the floor and sniffed the barrels of both weapons. They had returned fire which explained the wounded man and spoke to their skill. They would have had very little time to draw and shoot. They bore a resemblance to each other. Both had narrow, hatchet shaped faces and sandy hair which was harder to see in one than the other because of the blood. They had slender builds and long tapered hands.

Finally he could put it off no more. The front of Tess's white t-shirt was flooded with blood. Three bullets had hit her; one in her stomach, another in her right breast and the last near the shoulder. A kill shot created a fourth hole, this one over her heart. She was already dead when the gun was held against her. No blood surrounded the last, powdered-ringed hole.

Tess's eyes stared at him, and her hair spread wildly underneath her as the shots had knocked her backward and onto the floor sending her chair flying. He tried to gather her body into a semblance of dignity ignoring the experience of years of never touching a body at a crime scene. Tess was not a "vic." She was a person and no indignity could deprive her of that. He looked under chairs and behind nearby tables for her purse. He didn't find one.

He felt tears on his cheeks and retreated. Tess and Thatch aside there was work to be done, and if he didn't do it now, the locals would take away the chance away.

It appeared four men shared the table with Tess. The two bodyguards, Farrell was sure that's what they were as they flanked her and both were able to return fire before dying, wore dusty boots worn at the heels. Of the group's two remaining bodies, one was a man who wore white canvas sneakers, Levis, and an open black sport coat. The left side of the coat lay pulled back and the empty, inner breast pocket bulged suggesting something thick had been removed. The label on the coat said it came from New York City. The dead man's features, stature, and coloring were Hispanic. The one remaining victim of the group was male, young and well-dressed. He looked out of place with his khaki trousers, a tucked-in short-sleeved shirt with a button-down collar, and highly-polished shoes. His hair, what was visible around the kill shot to the forehead, was short and freshly barbered. He was clean-shaven and his hands were soft and clean. Farrell didn't go through the body's pocket to look for I.D.

He found two more bodies with shots to the head that were superfluous. Nobody survives three or four upper torso hits from high-velocity rounds. The kill shots were performed because the killer liked the feel of putting a gun to someone's head and pulling the trigger. He thought of the dark stains on the shirt of the man he'd shot.

He walked to the two bodies apart from the group. Both men were long haired, one in a pony-tail, and wore dirty work clothes. The boots were well-worn and the knees of the denim pants had done hard time.

Dewey crouched and looked at their hands. Both sported calluses and ground in dirt. They looked like Thatch's hands only dirtier. They had wallets where Thatch had none.

Dewey looked around the room. Bullets had pocked-marked the walls with broken plaster, splintered wood, and shattered neon signs reading FULL SAIL ALE and MILLERS GENUINE DRAFT. Only one table still sat on four legs, the others all lay on their sides and none of them had escaped the strafing. Most of the chairs were tipped over. One chair sat upright directly under a light canister, aloof from the horrific blood spattered chaos surrounding it as if nothing in the world was wrong.

Dewey walked behind the bar. No one. There were some loose bills at one end. He counted twenty-one dollars. None of the bodies were likely candidates for the bartender. The floor behind the bar was littered with broken bottles, dark brown shards stuck in the wooden slats of the slip-resistant grating. Picking his way carefully, he moved to the other end of the bar. The back mirror had splintered like everything else and his reflection came and went as he moved. Near the end of the glass was a photocopied sign stapled to the wall. It read THIS ESTABLISHMENT CAN NO LONGER OFFER PAPER PRODUCTS. WIPE YOUR ASS ON A SPOTTED OWL. The paper was yellowed with time and untouched by either spatter or bullet like a message just arrived from another time zone.

The flap at the end of the bar lay open. He walked through to a hallway that led deeper into the roadhouse. The first door on the right read SQUATTERS. He pushed it open and the stark cleanliness of the bathroom suggested it was the alternate reality that had sent the owl message. He let the door swing closed and moved to the next one. POINTERS. He leaned a shoulder and pushed.

Even the carnage in the front room failed to prepare Farrell for the body stuck in the window. The man must have been standing at the urinal when he heard the shots and screams. He knew he was dead if he went out the door so he tried the window that was much too small. His panic wedged him tight into the casing, and that was where the shooter found him, feet probably kicking as he heard the door open behind him. The trigger man had used too many bullets. There was no way to count them, other than by the ejected brass. The blood had streamed down the wall to pool at the base with other evacuated body liquids.

Farrell reeled away, hitting the door frame and gasping for breath. His years in homicide were of no use for this. His uneven steps became wobbly as he entered the front room. He saw an untouched glass of beer on the bar, out of place in its normalcy, looming over Thatch's body.

"There'll be a beer on the bar for you," Thatch had said.

He looked away and reached for the phone behind the bar. It had taken a direct hit and was dead.

He went to his car and tried his cell phone. Not enough signal, so he walked around the parking lot with the phone in the air looking for bars.

"God *damn* it!" he yelled, into the night.

Near the neon sign he found a signal strong enough to the call the Banner County Sheriff's office.

"Name's Farrell," he said, when the phone was answered. "I'm at a place called The Middle of Nowhere. You have nine people shot dead out here."

"This some kind of joke," the male voice finally answered.

"Nope."

"You say nine dead, all shot?"

"That's right. If you don't believe me, try calling the place. The phone's dead. Doesn't prove anything, but adds a little credibility."

"I know you ain't callin' on that phone. Zeke never paid a phone bill in his life. So, how are you callin'?"

"Cell phone."

"You must use Verizon. They're the only carrier that works and you're standing in one of the few places in the whole valley you get any bars."

Another pause.

"You get calls all the time about mass murder?" Farrell asked. "How come you're so calm?"

"I can't decide whether to believe you or not."

"With the heat and the right wind, you'll figure it out soon enough."

"Yeah." Another pause. "Okay, shit! Sheriff's gone home for the night, but I'll call him. Night cruiser's on the other side of the hills, too. Might be awhile. You gonna hang around?"

"Yes. I'll be here. Who's the sheriff?"

The deputy was preoccupied enough to answer. "Buck Fulsom. What's your name again?"

"Farrell, Dewey Farrell. Say hi to Buck for me."

"Yeah. I don't suppose you did it."

"No," he said, breaking the connection.

He walked back into the roadhouse, and stared at the bar.

There were only two things along the ruined stretch of wood that looked like they belonged there. One was an empty beer glass to the right of Thatch's fallen body. The other was the full glass no doubt waiting for him. He walked to the bar. He picked up the empty glass in one hand and the full one in the other, then knelt next to Thatch's body. He ticked the rims together and drank. He set the glass next to Thatch McPherson and patted his shoulder.

In the cordite crusted air and amid the violence of death, Farrell placed his hand on his friend's heart.

"I'm sorry, my friend. I promise whoever did this will pay. And I promise to find what you wanted to share with me."

Johann Prus

He came from money so old the only depiction of its birth would be in the fifteenth century paintings and woodcuts of Holbein the Elder or Jan Van Eyck, although their scenes were many miles west of the rock valleys of eastern Poland where the Prus family found salt. The difference between old money and the other kind was that old money owned land while new money sat in banks in either cash or stocks, or owned man-made objects. Land was in limited supply and all the good land had been owned for generations, if not centuries.

The salt mines that carried the family name until the early years of the twentieth century gave the family six hundred years to build a wealth that not even he knew the full extent of. By 1920, between war and rebellion, the Prus name had faded into the obscurity of the very wealthy. It had become mobile with the advent of international banking. As the money moved around the world, so did the family. Now, due to good fortune and a vicious disregard for others, he alone remained.

Long bloodlines were not always strong bloodlines, and he exhibited most of the weaknesses. His frailties taught him an appreciation for his strengths, the most important his ruthlessness. So much of what he wanted was not for sale that to obtain it required innovative and bold solutions.

His desk faced a wall of glass that looked down from his top floor perch and across a great urban expanse that disappeared into the haze of this sun-drenched land. The windows did not open and there was no balcony. Part of great wealth was that he could bring the world to him. When it didn't come o him, he traveled in limousines that parked in underground garages and took him to private jets that awaited him inside private hangers.

He tapped the pages in the blue binder that held the long awaited report. Even though the pages held disappointing news, they came as no surprise. NO PERCEIVEABLE CHANGE and DISINTEGRATING VALUES appeared throughout. The twenty pages were filled with graphs and tables and paragraphs with long words that only a few months ago meant nothing to him. Now they carried meaning. He drummed his fingers ever faster. It was a tick he indulged. It kept him focused. He imagined his diseased blood coursing faster, absorbing more oxygen and washing away fatigue.

The report said that the results he sought could not be reproduced in a lab or even in soil not native to the plant. The last two pages made it clear that while not all approaches were fully explored, the end he sought seemed unlikely.

He smiled. He understood. Just as the salt mines of his ancestors could not be moved, so it was with this. But as salt was vital to sustain life, his new desire was vital as well. If it could not be reproduced elsewhere, then the course was clear. Once the goal was attained he would have a two-fold triumph: he would be the sole source, and his old blood would be renewed.

He thought of the exquisite creature that had just left him. He would see her again one day when her fruit of youth had withered and fallen to the ground.

"I want any news from America as soon as it arrives," he told his assistant, then resumed his dreams of youthful vigor filled with boundless energy to pursue any fancy of his imagination and the will to know he would always do whatever it took to get what he wanted.

Dewey Farrell

Farrell knew the time before the sheriff's people reached him would be his best chance to find anything. Before he re-entered the roadhouse he went to his car and tossed his gun on the front seat. He placed his wallet on the seat next to it and made sure his carry permit was visible. As he opened the Nowhere's screen door the jukebox began Nat Cole doing *Stardust*. The jukebox's irony lamented the loss of loved ones from years gone by.

Inside he turned slowly in the devastation. He wondered what could have motivated the slaughter of nine people. The kill shots delivered to each victim bespoke of deliberation and a military-like precision that broke down at the point where excessiveness set in and made it blood lust. The body in the men's room was simply sadism. The professionalism broke down again in the parking lot when Farrell had raced in. But even then the shooters were sensible. They ran. They didn't waste time in a situation they couldn't control.

Giving the killers credit gave the shootings an even more chilling air. How many were supposed to have died, and how many simply because they were there? Would the killers have murdered twenty or thirty people if there had been that many in the bar? Probably not. It would have been a control thing.

Walking around the room again, Farrell focused on the group. What were the five doing here and how did Tess fit in? More importantly, why did she need bodyguards? What had she known that he would want to know about his past? He felt guilty thinking of himself. What had been in the Hispanic's pocket? Had the contents been part of the motive? *The motive?*

Nat Cole sang, *When our love was new, and each kiss an inspiration . . .* although when Farrell's infatuation with Tess was born there had been no kisses.

The last Farrell had heard she was an anthropologist. If that was still her calling, what was an anthropologist doing in Banner County and here in The Middle of Nowhere with bodyguards?

Of the dead at the table, four, including Tess, were Caucasian, and the fifth Hispanic. The round table made prioritizing the seating arrangement at it problematic. Farrell guessed that Tess and her bodyguards were together, but who the young clean one that looked like a lab assistant was with could go either way. The Hispanic's turned out pocket suggested he had brought something. Judging by the gaping pocket, the killers knew what they were looking for and who had it. It was the first solid sign of premeditation, although Farrell had assumed it from the beginning.

Returning to Thatch, Farrell patted down the pockets and found his keys. He sorted them on the bar and found two with GM logos. At least he wouldn't have to try every car in the lot.

He tapped the bar top with the keys and started toward the door but the money on the counter caught his eye. Twenty-one dollars. Maybe the bartender had left and the patrons were on the honor system. If so, some had died honest men.

In the parking lot, the second GM product he tried opened with Thatch's key. The door had been unlocked. It was a ten year old GMC Silverado with a crew cab minus the backseat, a Warn winch mounted over the front bumper, and four wheel drive. The tires were new with a distinctive tread design. Whatever Thatch wanted to haul, he had plenty of room and power to do it.

He opened the door and the dome light came on. He looked under the seat. A few rags, a beer can, a Snicker's wrapper that reminded him of Thatch's sweet tooth, and a large black six cell flashlight. He climbed behind the wheel and slid across to reach the glove box. It was locked. He used the other key and opened it. He found a flashlight, some loose papers, and a loaded .38 Chief's Special.

He found nothing belonging to Tess. He sat in the front seat and thought back to his childhood. From the time Dewey was twelve until he was fifteen, Tess had owned his fantasies. Tess at fourteen, two years older than Dewey, wandering through the house in a bra and half-slip. Farrell remembered Thatch's smirk as he stared. It must have been no big deal if it was your sister, but to a boy who lived in a world without women it was a seismic event.

Twisting in the seat, he peered into the empty crew cab space. He saw a cardboard box near the back window. Other than the box and a pair of wadded up coveralls, the space was empty. He took the mud-crusted coveralls out and felt the pockets. He found a rag in a back pocket and used it wipe his dirty hands.

Through the side windows he saw headlights. They wound down from a higher elevation, stopped and went dark on the side road well before the intersection with the Nowhere on the southwest corner. Farrell's impression before the lights went off was of a van, or a pick-up with a camper. He tried to remember what lay up that road, but it had been too long. The antenna with the red aviation warning lights lay in that direction, but he could think of nothing else.

Keeping low, Farrell opened the front door and took Thatch's revolver. He reached for the rectangular cardboard box in the back of the cab. The flaps were tucked in, and a rag covered the top. He pushed his hand in. Near the bottom he found a book.

He opened it. It was a journal. The first date was four months earlier. The last date he found was ten pages before the end and over two months ago. Tucked in between the pages was a folded piece of heavy paper.

Dewey unfolded it and saw a map. The map had no name, no legend, no features identified, but was divided by a hand drawn five by five grid. He scanned the map then moved on.

Feeling a bulge at the back of the book, he found a plastic pocket taped to the inside of the cover. In the pocket was a small address book. He pulled it out and it opened to the middle. The M's. At the top of the page was written "Tess" followed by a phone number and an address, both in Pazer.

He heard a roar then saw flashing blue and red lights blinking brightly in the dark. He closed Thatch's truck, put the journal and the gun inside his ditty bag in the trunk of the Cutlass, and waited. He watched to see if the lurking van would move away. He saw nothing, but suspected it still lurked.

The cruiser slowed as it neared the parking lot. The search light mounted near the driver's window came on. Farrell shaded his eyes with both hands letting the driver see they were empty. The spot moved over the length of his car, then to the front of the roadhouse. The logo and print on the driver's door announced Banner County Sheriff.

The top lights went off, and the door opened. The man who got out stood tall and wide. He wore Western style boots. There was a razor-sharp crease in the uniform pants and the shirt sported a portable radio fastened to the epaulet. He wore his gun belt Western style riding low on the right hip. The gun in the holster was a revolver, not an automatic. The man turned and stooped to reach into the car, and came out with a Stetson styled with a gently curved brim and flat top. He settled his gun belt and was ready for business.

Farrell heard a long sigh before the man said, "Still can't follow orders, can you Crash?"

"Nice to see you too, Buck. I wasn't sure if you were still sheriff."

"Sheriff as long as Ma'am says I am." He stepped closer. "You look like shit."

"Thanks."

The sheriff played with his hat again as he stared at the roadhouse. "I expect you remember her even if you can't remember she told you to leave and never come back."

Farrell said, "Never's a long time. Besides, that was before she ran things."

Sheriff Buck Fulsom settled his gun belt again.

"Your old asshole buddy in there?"

"What makes you ask?"

"He shows up a couple of months ago after twenty years, then here you are."

"He's in there." Farrell said.

Fulsom walked around Farrell's car, looking in the windows.

"You're lucky to be standing there," he said, looking over the roof.

Yes."

"You stay right where you are until I see things my way, then we'll talk." There was no drawl, but he spoke slowly.

I'm in no hurry."

Another set of red and blue lights entered the valley from the same direction as the first.

Tell Roy to wait, too," the sheriff, said before he went into the roadhouse.

The second car slowed like the first, but when the driver saw the other cruiser, he accelerated and pulled in on the far side of the lot, the two cruisers bracketing what was left of the Cutlass. The door opened. The driver got out and walked quickly toward Farrell. His uniform was wrinkled like the end of a long shift sitting in a hot car. He was neither tall nor short, heavy nor slim. His hat was more rounded and the curve on the brim more severe than Fulsom's.

"Sheriff inside?" he asked.

"That's right. You Roy?"

"Yep. He said to tell me to wait out here, didn't he?" Roy asked. "Always the same. Wait outside until he's done."

"How come?" Farrell asked, making small talk.

37

"Just the way he likes it," was all Roy said, but it was clear it wasn't all he was thinking. "Got some ID?"

"On the front seat."

"Get it."

Farrell picked up his wallet, pulled his driver's license, and held it toward the deputy who didn't take it until he had his notebook out.

"Everything on here current?"

"Yep."

Roy wrote, then asked, "Occupation?"

"Consultant."

"Who do you consult?"

"Police departments."

He looked at Farrell, then back to the license. "About computers, right?'

Farrell nodded.

"Yeah, I got a cousin on the force in Yakima. How come you're here? Sure as hell isn't to consult with us."

"No. I was supposed to meet an old friend."

Roy's eyes moved to the roadhouse, then back to Farrell.

"Wanna tell me what happened here?" He pointed at the car. "Looks like you got lucky."

Farrell told him about hearing the shots on the road and what happened when he got to the parking lot.

"You think you hit them?"

"The left shoulder on one, and maybe the driver. The truck swerved when the shots hit the windshield."

The screen door opened, and the sheriff said, "Farrell, I count eight bodies. You said nine on the phone."

"The men's room,"

The sheriff went back into the building.

"Jesus," Roy whispered, "nine bodies?"

"They didn't tell you?"

"Just said there'd been a shooting, and there was a witness. Sheriff doesn't believe the radio is secure for more than the basic need to know.

'Specially now." Roy walked around the shot up Cutlass shaking his head. "Must be pretty bad in there, huh? Fulsom wouldn't miss something like that, 'specially since it ain't like he don't know the layout."

"Why especially now?" Farrell asked.

"Lot of media in town. How bad is it? In there."

"There's no way to prepare yourself," Farrell said.

Roy kicked some gravel and cleared his throat. "Seems my cousin said this consultant guy was an ex-homicide cop. That right?"

"That's right," Farrell said, looking closer at Roy.

"Kind of young to be an ex, aren't you?"

"Life doesn't always come up to expectations."

The sheriff stepped through the screen door.

"Roy, come over here."

Roy looked at Farrell, then started walking. Sheriff and deputy talked outside the door, both glancing Farrell's way. Finally Roy nodded, pointed at the Cutlass, and headed for his cruiser. As he passed Farrell, he said, "That car ain't street legal with all the damage."

As Roy drove away, Farrell saw where this was going.

"Farrell," Buck Fulsom called, "step on over and answer some questions."

As Farrell approached, Fulsom asked, "What were you doing here? Start at the top."

"I got a call from McPherson. He left a message yesterday, but I didn't get it until today. I was out of town."

"Where were you?"

"Fishing."

"So, you get home, listen to the message, and drive five hours to meet him. How long had it been since you'd seen him?"

"Long time."

"So he calls you out of the blue - it was out of the blue, right? - and you head south. You ever give a thought to being told never set foot in Banner County again?"

"Nope."

Fulsom shook his head before saying, "Should have stayed away. Recognize anyone else in there?"

"Of course."

"The sister."

"Right. Her name was Tess and you know it. Don't be an asshole, Buck."

Fulsom met his eyes and held them before saying, "You touch any of them?"

"Thatch. I turned him over to be sure it was him and then patted his shoulder."

"Touching. I'd forgotten you were such a sensitive guy. Probably why they called you Crash. You touch the Hispanic?"

"His coat was like that when I went in."

"Her?"

"Tess? Yes, I did. Straightened her hair. I don't know why. Sensitive I guess."

"There's a blood trail. I suspect it's not yours."

"Not mine."

Fulsom stood straight, centered his hat and settled his gun belt.

"Okay, that's all I need from you. You should have ignored McPherson and stayed away. Nothing's changed. Pearl Banner runs the show and I do what she wants. It's my job to hang on to the ideals the outside world seems to have lost. You can catch a bus for Grants Pass out by the sign in the morning."

"The car still runs."

"Not in my county. Shot up that way it constitutes a threat to public safety."

"Yeah, lot of public out here. I'm driving it out of here unless you want to get confrontational."

"I've waited a long time to kick the shit out of you." He played with his belt again. "This is just what I need before what's in there hits the fan."

His hands went to the thong on his thigh where his gun belt was tied. Next would be the buckle. Farrell sighed. He was three inches shorter and twenty or thirty pounds lighter than Fulsom, and the worse for wear after hitting the gravel.

"Sheriff?" the portable radio speaker on Fulsom's shoulder hissed. "Sheriff, Ma'am wants you to call her right now. She's called twice. Sheriff?"

Farrell watched the choices splash across the sheriff's face. He was sure if anyone else had wanted Fulsom to call he would have ignored it, but Pearl Banner, as he remembered her, expected people to do exactly what she told them, and that was when she was twenty and had exiled him for life.

Fulsom's eyes never left Farrell's face as he keyed the mike.

"I hear you. I'll call her."

"Sheriff? She knows what happened out there."

"Then she's ahead of me." He let go of the mike, and retied the thong. "Don't even think about leaving." He took the long way toward his cruiser making a wide sweep toward the Cutlass. He got closer, drew his gun and shot out the left front tire. He looked over his shoulder at Farrell and blew the smoke off the barrel.

Farrell laughed at him loud enough to be heard, then walked to the car and rested his hip against the door. He had a good view of Fulsom as the sheriff dialed the cell phone and close enough to hear what was said. Fulsom looked at him and tried walking away, but turned and came back because there was no signal other than beside the sign. He saw Fulsom stand straighter and guessed the call had been answered. The sheriff talked, listened, then glanced at Farrell.

"Dewey Farrell's here," the sheriff said. He listened again then stomped his foot. "Ma'am! I want nothing to do with this guy!" He listened. "I don't care if he's Sherlock Holmes, I don't want him anywhere near a dead body unless it's his own." More listening. "He won't need no room! He can sleep on the damn bus taking him back where he came from." Finally, after silent head shaking and foot stomping, "Yes, Ma'am. I'll tell him."

Farrell had heard enough and walked away until the sheriff finished. When Fulsom closed the phone, he threw it into the car and yelled, "God *damn* it!"

"Not supposed to kick the shit out of me?" Farrell said, with a smile.

Fulsom took deep breaths and went through his getting-it-together routine of hat and gun belt, then said, "Before you die laughing, you ain't going to like it either. She wants us to go back in there together. We're supposed to, as she put it, 'team up.' You're supposed to 'share the benefit of all your homicide experience' and I'm supposed to catch whoever did it. Before sunrise or sooner. Oh, and no matter what time we finish, she wants to see you tonight."

Dewey pointed at his car.

"Yeah, I told her the car didn't run. She's sending a tow out from town and finding you a room for however long you're here. Roy will be back to take you to her."

"How'd she find out?" I asked.

"Anonymous call," he said.

"You're right," Farrell said. "I don't like it."

"Word of advice," Fulsom said. "As long as you're here, do what she tells you. With your record it will be a test, but on the bright side if you're no better at it than you were the last time, well, it will make my day."

Johann Prus

He rarely slept more than an hour at a time, and then only when it couldn't be avoided. He exercised to maintain flexibility, but cared little for personal strength and appearance. He wanted his guests to see his face, especially his mouth that could be cruel, and his pale, blue eyes that radiated power. He had a man's chin, but his full lower lip suggested the mouth of a woman. The clash of his features left his guests uncomfortable. If he set his mind to it not even the splendor of his possessions could make them feel at ease.

One of the great benefits of wealth was the freedom to pursue any passion no matter how esoteric or extreme. His great passion was discovering what others desired most. He'd devoted years to perfecting his skill at reading these hidden desires. He found they fell into three categories: wealth, health, and youth. Even when health and youth were unattainable, people still sought them. He called these three desires universal needs.

He directed his managers to find products and promises that addressed these "universal needs." It took a while for his people to understand what he meant. As their understanding grew, more things appeared on the list. To make the list, there was one more condition that had to be met. There had to be a plan where Prus could control the market with absolute exclusivity.

He focused his forces to look for anything dealing with flaws to the human condition. These included defects in the genome, incurable illnesses, afflictions that stole life, and the unforeseen that plagued otherwise healthy humans preventing them from enjoying their otherwise healthy and privileged life. The work started slow. Part of the reason was that he had no investment base in medicine and medical research. They were both fields that resisted gross investment because there was already so much money in it. International pharmaceutical companies were second only to oil in terms of liquid wealth. He guessed he could buy a pharmaceutical company, but he didn't believe it would further his goal. Along with their stock would come a corporate culture that more or less played by the rules and had huge files with drug regulatory bodies worldwide. Not even Africa was a fall back plan for product failure. But most of all what an existing company did not have was the renegade frame of mind that would dream up the next major breakthrough. He wanted a cure for aging, while the existing companies were searching for the cure for cancer. He suspected the breakthrough he sought was only possible with something that carried a black market aura, something that was so effective it could not be approved officially for years.

Then two years ago, word came from America from a first time source. It had taken months to reach him. It came from one of the only markets that would complain about something being too good – illicit drugs. The product defied cutting and the high quality meant sales went down because the enjoyment lasted longer. The combination caught his attention. He didn't like the drug business, but with interests as diverse as his he didn't always know what corners his tentacles probed.

Slowly the question that captivated him emerged: "What if a chemical produced from a naturally occurring plant provided relief from pain and repaired the damages of Alzheimer's and other diseases leading to dementia?"

Initially, the "naturally occurring" part limited his interest. There would be profit from commercializing the process but once anyone could do it, what was in it for him? That the plant was illegal raised an eyebrow, but when he was told the plant could only be grown in one place in the world his interest began to burn brightly.

Dewey Farrell

Farrell and Sheriff Buck Fulsom stood outside the screen door of the Middle of Nowhere. Fulsom must have unplugged the juke when he'd gone in because the only sound was the whirring of the fan.

"Why would the killers call Pearl?" Farrell asked. "What did they tell her?"

"That there were dead bodies at the Nowhere."

"That's all? They had to say more than that!"

"Ask her yourself when you see her! If they said more, she sure as shit didn't tell me. My job would be a helluva lot easier without her skimming the flow of information." Fulsom wiped the brim of his hat with a handkerchief from his pocket. He folded it before he put it back. "But then I'd have no job without her."

"What if I don't want to see her?" Farrell asked, leaning into Fulsom's space. "What if I'd rather stand over there and wait for the bus?"

"Then I get to shoot you and she gives me a metal. People always do what she wants." He stepped closer, and said, "Personally, I think you ought to give the bus a go."

"I was just curious," Farrell said, then waved at the door.

"Just a minute," Fulsom said. "I did some checking on you after McPherson showed up. I thought you might not be far behind."

"I'm flattered. What'd you find?"

"Funny thing. No one said you got fired, but no one said they were sorry to see you go, either. I talked to a reporter. She said you had a code about the truth. Without it, nothing makes sense."

"The truth isn't easy to find," Farrell said, "and it's not always welcome."

"You hang on to that thought. Come on."

Inside, Fulsom asked him how he saw it. Dewey noted the sarcasm, but ignored it and started with the missing bartender.

"The bartender's name is Zeke," Fulsom said, interrupting. "He owns the place, and leaves early when he don't feel so good which is most nights. Folks are supposed to leave what they owe on the bar." He pointed at the twenty-one dollars, then looked around. "Killers must have been well paid. Crash, don't even think of looking for Zeke. That's my job."

"You're assuming I'm staying. What if Pearl tells me to get out of town?"

"You won't go."

"No."

Fulsom looked around. "How many shooters?"

"At least three. The two I saw and someone to drive the other car. The only brass I see is for the M-16, but there was probably more than one weapon. For the kill shots, the killer policed his brass. The entry wounds look like 9 mil. It's the group at the table that interests me." They walked closer to the five bodies and Farrell made a point not to look at Tess. "Look at all the wounds. The M-16's must have been on full auto with thirty round clips. With three guns they could have sprayed the whole room and not reloaded."

Dewey looked around.

"What they weren't ready for were the two men flanking Tess. Recognize them?"

"Vaguely."

"Their guns have been fired. They had to be fast to get a round off."

"You touch them?"

"No. My nose works. I'm guessing they were bodyguards and pretty good."

Fulsom looked closely at the men.

"Still don't recognize them?" Farrell asked.

"Nope."

"The shooters really liked killing," Farrell said, leaning over the bodyguards. "I heard three groups of shots before the well-spaced kill shots. The first bursts, then the second group had different weapons mixed in. Probably these two returning fire." He pointed as he talked. "The killers put those holes in the walls nowhere near a vic to start the panic, then they sprayed the room. I thought they were pretty good at first, but they were cocky. They didn't expect anyone to be armed, and one of them got shot. The next two bursts did the actual killing. Savoring it as they pulled the trigger. They would have set it up so the first guy through the door goes to his right for the bartender in case there was a gun behind the bar. The second goes for the target group at the table, and the third starts at the left."

"How do you know the target was the group?"

"You gotta better idea? Nobody but the Hispanic got turned out and the shooters didn't bother with the twenty-one bucks. The other possibility was Tess. Where's her purse? I didn't pat her down for car keys although I thought about it. But she's at the table, too." He looked around, and shook his head. "The shooters came to kill people. One guy might have acted on a thrill impulse but not three. This was premeditated."

Farrell forced himself to look at Tess.

"Where's her purse?" he asked, again. "Women always have purses or bags or something when they go out. Here she is, probably at a meeting, and she has no purse."

He knelt beside the body and reached for her.

"What are you doing?" Fulsom yelled. "Back off!"

"I want to see if her keys are in her pocket. If they are then it's easier to believe she came in without a purse. If she doesn't, that means she had a purse and it's gone. As far as we know there's nothing else missing. That makes her important and a place to start."

"Go ahead," Fulsom said.

Farrell patted all her pockets. They were empty.

"Do you know which car is hers out there?" Farrell asked.

Fulsom nodded and Farrell followed him out to a blue Road Runner. Fulsom tried the door. It was unlocked. The sheriff looked through the car. No purse, no bag. They went back in.

"What about the Hispanic?" Farrell asked. "When a pocket bulges like his it means something bulky came out."

"Like a big thick envelope of money," Fulsom said.

"Why give Tess money? If that's what it was. You know why she was in Banner?"

"Writing a book."

"You know that how?"

"Ma'am told me if she needed anything, to make sure she got it. Like an escort into some of the less savory parts of the county. McPherson was supposed to be able to go anywhere and talk to anyone."

"What was the book about?"

"No idea. She never called and I never talked to her."

"How along ago did she get here? She get here before Thatch?"

"Yeah, by three or four weeks. She'd been here five or six months."

Dewey opened his mouth, but before any words came out Fulsom yelled, "Enough! I hate this shit. I hate talking to you and I hate seeing your miserable face. I hated you and your buddy over there all the way through school. Shit! Twenty years," he snapped his fingers, "gone in an instant! McPherson was bad enough. Always thought he was so fucking smart. Then you showed up and the two of you started palling around. It was terrible. The day after you left for good we threw you a 'we're glad you're gone party.' Just now, I would rather have cut my tongue out than tell Ma'am you were here. If I'd known she was going to tell you to stay, I would have."

He went to the door, then called, "Get the hell out of here, Farrell. It's a crime scene and you're a nobody!"

In the parking lot, the two men stood twenty feet apart not talking. Farrell got his bag out of the trunk, then leaned on the boot as the flashing lights on Roy's cruiser came into sight.

"Stay in the car!" Fulsom yelled at his deputy as the door opened. "He's just leaving."

Dewey reached into his car and came out with his gun and two spare clips.

"That stays, Farrell!"

Farrell held the weapon and popped in a fresh clip. He put the gun in his belt and turned his back.

"You know why you ain't bleeding on the ground," the sheriff called, "but don't think it'll happen again. She won't always be there to protect you."

Farrell tossed his bag in the cruiser's back seat and got in beside the deputy.

"Jesus!" Roy said, as he drove into the night.

Farrell looked out the back window as the cruiser hit the pavement at the sheriff with the gun still in his hand at the end of the arm that hung limply at his side. The image got smaller as the car picked up speed.

Roy ran the cruiser's speed up on the road out of the valley, but slowed when it entered the tree line. Farrell knew the exact moment they hit the tall trees because the stars disappeared.

"The Sheriff may not be the easiest man to get along with," Roy said, "but things don't usually reach guns in the parking lot in under an hour. Another thing, I don't think a man would turn his back on Buck when he has a gun in his hand if he didn't know him."

When Farrell didn't answer, Roy said, "So how long you've known him?"

"I kinda grew up here."

"When did you leave?"

"When I was eighteen."

"How come?"

"Pearl told me to leave and never come back."

"Wow! Why?"

Farrell looked at him and said, "Long story."

"How'd you meet her? Unless things have changed, it's not that easy."

"I don't know if things have changed, but at the time she wasn't running the show. How come so curious?"

"I've been here six years and I've spoken to her once. You've been here a couple of hours and it's a meeting in the middle of the night at her house."

Farrell saw the doors of the vault that held his childhood memories swing wider.

"My father was a forester for Banner Timber. Weekends during the school year and all summer he would take me into the forest. We went all over the county, but mainly in the hills south of the Nowhere. I loved to draw so I carried a sketch book and drew what I saw. One day I saw her. She didn't know I was watching her. When she saw me, she asked what I was drawing and I said I was drawing her. She looked frightened and disappeared like magic. The next two trips into the forest I went back to the same spot but never saw her. On the third trip she was there. I got the idea she was waiting for me, and I wondered if she'd been hiding the other times."

"She want to see her picture?"

"Yeah, but I'll get to that. She asked me my name. When I told her Dewey she said it wasn't a proper name. I told her it was the only name I had and asked hers."

"You didn't know who she was?" Roy asked, surprised.

"I had never seen her before. She didn't go to the regular school and never went to any of the town events. Eleanora went sometimes, but Pearl never did."

"Eleanora was her grandmother?"

"Eleanora was Ma'am in those days. Ma'am. Just like the Queen of England. When Pearl saw her name didn't mean anything to me, she relaxed. We talked about the forest. She loved it, too, but we saw things different. Later I realized she saw board feet where I saw trees. I told her I loved to draw the trees. That was when she asked to see the drawing of her. I was embarrassed but she pushed so I opened the sketch book and handed it to her."

Roy braked and turned right.

"She like it?"

"She said it didn't look like her. I told her I'd finished it from memory because she'd disappeared. I said I could work on it if she wanted to sit, but she tore it out and kept it."

"And?"

"And she walked off through the trees and was gone."

The road opened as the trees were replaced by a white fence around gently rolling pasture. Bright lights appeared in the night.

"I guess I'll have to wait to hear what happened next," Roy said. "You gotta ride later?"

"You're going to be too busy. You have enough morgue space for nine bodies?"

"No, but that's up to Buck. He's pretty resourceful."

Roy turned up a driveway to an all-white house illuminated with floods.

The landscaping, even with night and the harsh white lights washing out the colors, stood out. Shrubs and low bushes lined the concrete driveway that led to the Banner house. It was not palatial, but it suited the family seat of a wood products empire. The single story house was all wood with a gently sweeping roof line. A wide covered porch, called a gallery in other parts of the country, fronted it. Extra wide double doors sat precisely in the center of the house. Farrell had been here before. He remembered the house was bigger than it looked from the front.

Roy swung wide to drop Farrell by the double doors. Dewey got his bag and wished the deputy good luck. He stood looking around and breathed deeply as the cruiser pulled away. The air acted as another trigger into his past. Banner County had always had a smell of its own. He tested the air and expected at least a hint of smoke from the fires to the south, but nothing spoiled the Banner air with its tinges of forest and honeysuckle although where the honeysuckle came from he didn't know. He'd never seen honeysuckle growing anywhere in Bannerland.

The Fire

Many experienced firefighters will tell you that wildfires, especially forest fires in the big trees, are driven by more than the whims of nature. They'll tell you they have minds of their own.

The fire that would be called the Siskiyou-Banner Complex fire earned that reputation in its sixty-third hour. It could have turned left and found itself starved for fuel trapped against the stone walled canyons of the Smith River. Instead, and contrary to the wind predictions, it turned right and struck a stand of trees dead from the Douglas Fir beetle that in forests this thick infested up to a hundred trees to a patch. The fire feasted on this vein of heavy beetle kill, both standing and on the ground due to the prohibition from clearing it in the name of protecting the forest. It grew in intensity, then coasted on bursts of fresh wind roaring in from the Pacific. Soon it would make its own winds and become a killer of humans as well as wildlife that already had suffered heavy losses. Historians would look back on that fateful wind that turned the fire right rather than left as the literal turning point in the fire's long and deadly life.

Fateful winds tend to even out. Within twenty four hours, the fired turned further inland instead of finding a series of canyons and steeply forested hillsides that would have aimed the fire at Brookings, Oregon. In previous years, fires had destroyed a town further north, Bandon, Oregon, and then decades later, threatened it with ruin again only to be turned away by humans and winds that worked against the desires of the fire. But that was yesteryear. This fire had other plans that held humans in contempt.

Dewey Farrell

The door opened behind him. He turned and saw Pearl. She wore a sleeveless silver gray blouse and pressed dark blue denim pants. Her hair was combed and her make up in place at two a.m. The last time he'd seen her she'd been naked. She had been on her knees on the bed, fists pounding the mattress and screaming at him.

"Get out! Get out, damn you! Never come back!"

Now she said, "Twenty-three years almost to the day."

"Hello, Pearl."

She stared at him in the bright artificial light.

"You're a mess. Come in and clean up. I'll find you a fresh shirt."

She held the door. Farrell walked in and stopped. It was the first time he'd been through the front door. The foyer made it clear you were entering the realm of wealth. From banisters to floors, wood gleamed. The colors of paint on the walls played off the natural color of the wood. Small chairs and tables were to look at and not to use other than to drape a coat over, or for keys or mail.

She closed the door and stood next to him. She was four inches shorter than he was, and when she faced him, she had to look up. Her right hand went back and lashed out in an open-handed slap to his cheek. He didn't flinch.

"Goddamn, you!" she yelled. "I have no heir."

Her eyes, an intense blue-gray, burned into him. He couldn't decide if what he saw was rage and frustration, or a sense of irreplaceable loss. Her hands closed into fists and she beat her sides.

"I was never the only man in town," Dewey said, softly.

"If impregnation was all that mattered, there were lots of swans," she said, her eyes searching his face. "You never understood, did you?"

"I was eighteen," he said.

"I was twenty and I knew! How could you have been so dense? You dishonored your gifts when you left."

"I had no mother, my~ "

"Neither did I!"

"You had Eleanora! I had no family."

"You had me," she said.

"Did I? What did that mean?" He pointed over his shoulder. "That was the first time I ever came through the front door! If I had any gifts to dishonor, then no one else honored them either."

"It wasn't about social station, rich or poor," she yelled in the same voice she'd used back then. Then it softened. "It was about who we - you and me - who we are."

"Romeo and Juliet. That was what we said."

"What you said. The first time you said it I was sure you'd finally figured it out."

"It's a play by Shakespeare," Dewey said.

She rolled her eyes then walked down the hall. She opened a door into a powder room.

"Give me your shirt," she said, looking at the cuts on his face, then on his arms as he took the torn and bloodied shirt off. She looked at the blood on the shirt, then leaned closer and took his arm. "You still heal fast."

"No, I don't. Takes weeks for cuts to heal."

She turned his arm until he grimaced, but he saw the cuts from the gravel and glass had closed with only red lines and pinpricks remaining.

"How could you not get it?" She reached toward him then changed her mind. "This is where you belong. There is no happiness, no fulfillment, for you anywhere else. I'm surprised you're still alive."

He dwarfed her in the powder room and in his looming he softened his words.

"You know nothing about me," he said.

"Wife Diane, died of cancer two and a half years ago, no children. Early retirement for unspecified reasons, but rumor has it you were insubordinate and morose after she died leaving you a danger to yourself and others. Another source called you a burnout because you were tired of the bureaucracy, and what you saw as corruption others called compromise. Bottom line summed you up as a loner with no hope of

53

rehabilitation. You're in business, if that's what it is, consulting with police departments on technology issues, not human ones. Not a viable business. No friends."

Farrell stared at her.

"Don't let it go to your head," she said. "Wash the blood trails off your arms and face while I get you a shirt. Do you want a drink or something to eat?"

"Can I have both?"

"I'll meet you in the kitchen. It's down the hall."

"I know where it is," Farrell said. "I've been through that door."

He looked at his face as he washed. The cuts were healing fast. He'd been a fast healer when he was a kid, but that changed when he got older. By then he'd left Banner.

She's more beautiful now than when she was young, he thought. Pearl Banner, had she gone to public school, would have been the prettiest girl in school. Her straight back and erect carriage gave her a physical presence that had always intimidated him. It was what first drew him to her. She was as straight as the trees, and as proud. He looked to capture that in his drawing of her and figured that was why she'd said it didn't look like her. His was an idealized version and it was how he remembered her through the years.

Not that he thought of her much. He'd never considered coming back. It wasn't because she'd told him he couldn't, but he had nothing to come back to. Without the McPherson's he had no family, no friends, and no sense of belonging. He was the poor kid from nowhere, and she was the princess who would be queen. Not even when he decided to meet Thatch at the Nowhere, had he thought of her. Instead, he'd thought of Tess, the woman he'd never kissed, never seen in anything less than a bra and half-slip. Tess was safe, or so he'd thought. Not even when he'd heard Pearl's name on the radio had it occurred to him that he would see her, let alone stand in front of her and relive the most unforgettable moment of his life.

They'd both been virgins, and the first time had been in the forest on the banks of the river. They fumbled through teenage ignorance, struggling with the obvious this goes there. It had scared him more than he'd ever been scared when he'd penetrated her and she screamed and bled. She clung to him, wrapping her arms and legs around him, locking them together in an embrace that could have lasted a lifetime. She cried and he loved her with emotion untapped even when his father had died. When they finally stood, they walked naked into the river and washed each other with an intimacy people married a lifetime never achieve. It had always bothered him that level of intimacy had been unattainable with Diane. He and his wife were close and they loved each other, but it wasn't the same. Looking in the mirror as the cuts healed, he realized that if the aim had been achieving a closeness like he knew with Pearl, Diane never had a chance outside of Banner.

He walked shirtless into the kitchen where Pearl sat on a stool at an island. She hesitated a second while she looked at him, then tossed him a pullover golf shirt with the Banner logo over the heart.

"I don't cook," she said.

"I'll manage. Wanna drink?"

"No. Tell me about the roadhouse and why you were there. I expect it has something to do with Tess."

"Thatch, actually. Where's the bread?" She pointed, and he made a sandwich as he talked. "He left a message on my voicemail. He said he needed my help and used please. He never used either 'need' or 'please' so I came. He said he'd meet me at the bar if I got there before midnight."

"Thatch McPherson is one of the dead?" she asked, both surprised and tense.

"Yes. Tess was there, too."

Pearl's face went white. "Oh, my god!"

"What was she doing in Banner?"

"Writing a book. She was an anthropologist."

"Fulsom said you'd told her she could go anywhere."

"Yes. It was time for a comprehensive history. Was her laptop with her?"

"No. Should it have been?"

"She never went anywhere without it. This is bad." Pearl's face closed down into what Farrell thought was probably her 'Ma'am' face. "How many know?"

"Buck, me, the deputy, the dispatcher, and you. I'd be surprised if the sheriff's in any hurry to tell anyone."

She stood, and pointed at his sandwich. "Eat up. I'll be back in a minute. We're going out there."

"Pearl, hang on a second. Why would Tess need bodyguards?"

"Not now. Grab your stuff and let's go." She stopped in the doorway. "If you come with me, we do it my way. Can you do that?"

"I don't know, but I'm going with you."

"That's not an answer."

"It's the one I have."

She drove a white Banner Timber Products pickup with its green logo of four firs each taller left to right above the words *Trees forever*. It was the same logo on his shirt. Her intent stare through the windscreen invited no conversation. As the truck entered the valley and the Nowhere's light lit the night, Farrell defied the stare and asked, "Why the bodyguards?"

"I thought it was prudent. This can be a rough place."

"You hired them?"

"They were there because I asked them to be. They were family men."

"Do you mean all of Banner is rough, or specifically the Nowhere?"

"Outsiders have a hard time here."

"Did she always travel with bodyguards"

"Not always."

"What kind of book was she writing?"

"Family history. I don't want to talk about this now."

"We have to talk about this. Who was the Hispanic guy at their table?"

"I have no idea," Pearl said.

"I think she is the reason nine people are dead. If you know anything, it's time to tell Buck."

"I don't know of any reason why someone would want to kill her. If she was the reason, then she was doing more than I'd asked her to do."

He doubted he heard the whole truth, but he changed his tack.

"Who called you about the shootings?"

"Why?"

"Because I want to know who killed my friends." When she didn't answer, he said, "Don't go all pissy on me, Pearl. You can't throw me out this time. I'm staying whether you or Fulsom wants me to or not."

She didn't say anything, but the truck slowed. "The caller was male. No accent. Not educated, but not illiterate, either."

"What time was it?"

"Do you want me to tell you or interrupt?" she said, with an edge.

"I want what I need to know," Farrell responded. "I want to know what time the call came, and how it reached you?"

"Why? This isn't the way I work."

"It is the way I work, and my way is more important when there are nine dead. The caller was either one of the killers, or someone who set it up. The time will help establish which. The number they called reached you fast. That can't be easy. Just as important, cell phone coverage is spotty at best. Cell phone or land line narrows who made it and where it came from."

She stopped on the shoulder of the road.

"The call came at eleven-thirty through the office switchboard. We do business all over the world so it's always staffed. After hours, they route calls to me at their discretion. This call got forwarded when the man told Doreen if she valued her job she'd find me. Doreen tried to put him off but the man asked her if she knew how easy it was to kill someone. She put him through. I don't know if it was a cell phone or not.."

"What were his exact words?"

She thought for a moment. "He said, 'There are dead bodies in the Middle of Nowhere. This is just the beginning unless you follow orders.' He hung up."

"What does that mean?"

"I don't know."

"Pearl?"

She whipped sideways in the seat and pointed a finger. "Don't you dare push me! Nobody pushes me and nobody questions me!"

"How about if I never do it when anyone else is around? When they are, I call you Ma'am, and bow and scrape. But you need help, and somebody has to question you. Buck would love to be the one, but 'Yes, Ma'am' comes easy and he likes his job. Whatever's going on, you're in the middle. If that part is right, then Tess was there representing you. Thatch was there because he called me. One way or the other the McPhersons are dead because of you and me."

She'd turned back and gripped the wheel with both hands. Her jaw still jutted.

"Who and why people kill each other is what I've done since I left here. Why add something like this to your plate?"

"I don't know what the caller meant. I assumed I'd find out soon enough." She sighed, and her profile softened. "Remember I told you not to let my checking on you go to your head? I checked because I was going to call you. For help. That ought to tell you how much trouble I'm in. I would have said please and need, too."

"Then I showed up."

"Yes. I wasn't even surprised when Buck said you were here." She steered back on to the road. "These goddamn hills are still running us, Dewey."

Even after two decades away, he knew what she meant.

A refrigerated van with its compressor running sat with its rear door backed up to the Nowhere. Buck and Roy carried a body bag out and handed it into the van. Pearl parked the Banner truck to the side. Buck looked up as he wiped his forehead. He didn't look happy. He settled himself and walked slowly toward the truck. He had to detour around Farrell's car.

"No need for you to be here, Ma'am," he said, his once-fresh uniform now stained with sweat and blood.

"There is, Sheriff. I've told Mr. Farrell that I expect his help with this."

"That's not necessary, Ma'am!"

"Have you captured those responsible?" she asked.

"No, but he won't be no help to me and my men."

"Because you don't need it?" she pressed.

"We got all the help we need on the way."

"Who?" she asked.

"The State Police are coming from Grants Pass and bringing their Forensics Truck."

"You made that decision without asking me?" Pearl said, and Dewey couldn't tell if she was surprised or angry.

"You trust me to watch out for your interests. We got nine dead. Word is going to get out. I don't have help for a number like that. You'd be accused of covering up."

"I see," Pearl said, and gave Fulsom a nod of what Dewey took as approval. "How much do they know?"

"Only that we have a multiple homicide. I ain't putting any details on the radio."

"Good. When was the last time the State Police were invited into the county?"

"Not in my time," Buck said.

"You have invited the state of Oregon into my county at a very inopportune time," she said. "You know that, of course."

"Tell that to the dead," Fulsom said.

"You've covered my accountability. Good. Now there's even more of a reason I want this cleared up and the state out of here. Farrell stays and between the two of you make this go away."

Both men took the news and nodded.

"Do they know you've moved the bodies?" Farrell asked.

"We took pictures and chalked them. The truck with the bodies is going to the morgue in Grants Pass. Ma'am, I want to get the building buttoned down ASAP. We don't want news people out here when there's anything to see."

"Go about finishing, Sheriff, then we'll talk. I'll have Mr. Farrell show me around inside. We'll stay out of the way."

Farrell followed Pearl toward the roadhouse, but they stopped to look in the truck. Farrell counted six bags on the floor.

Inside the Middle of Nowhere, crime scene tape blocked off the blood trail of the wounded killer. Body removal had started with the bodies closest to the door. Thatch and the group at the table were gone. Fulsom and an ashen-faced Roy moved one of the two bodies apart from the others into a body bag. Farrell pointed at the face in the bag that would soon disappear behind the bag's zipper.

"Ma'am, do you recognize him?" Farrell asked.

Pearl looked at the body, then quickly away. The *coup-de-gras* obscured part of the victim's face. "No, should I?"

"Sheriff?" Farrell asked.

"I seen him around. He chased color. Him and his buddy." Fulsom pointed at the body as Roy pulled the zipper up. "Farrell, how about giving me a break and helping Roy with that one?"

Dewey took the foot of the bag and backed toward the door. He watched Fulsom close in on Pearl. When Roy and he got outside they hoisted the body onto the bed of the truck.

"How you doing, Roy?"

"I got sick," he said, and leaned into the refrigerated air in the truck's box. "I tried to get ready, but you were right. It's not in the head. It's in the stomach. I made it outside, though."

"Fulsom said these guys were chasing color. You got many gold panners working here now?"

"The price of gold keeps going up and they keep coming."

"Weed growers, too?"

"Yes, mostly out of state interests. Not many family plots left."

As they went, Farrell figured he'd given Fulsom enough time to make his case with Pearl, but the sheriff wasn't done. He stood with his arms spread, and hands upward in supplication. From Pearl's face Dewey didn't think the sheriff was making any progress. Pearl saw Dewey and cut Fulsom off.

"Buck, you finish with the bodies. Mr. Farrell can bring me up on what happened, then, when you're ready, we'll talk about what we're going to do. If the State Police arrive before we talk, I want Mr. Farrell involved."

Fulsom tried to swallow what, judging by his expression, was a bitter pill. When that wasn't enough for him, he stared a look that made it clear how he felt.

"Who sat where?" she asked, turning away from Fulsom.

"Tess was there," Farrell said, pointing. "Her bodyguards on either side. She would have seen the killers come in, but I doubt she recognized the threat. The guards did and got some shots off."

"It happened fast?" Pearl asked.

"Yes, very fast. Everyone would have taken at least one hit from those first bursts. It may not have killed them all, but one hit is enough to put a man down long enough to finish him on the next pass."

She looked at him and said, "You sound as if you saw this all the time."

"I've never seen this level of violence on so many people at the same time."

They watched Buck and Roy carry an empty bag to the Men's room. They'd saved the worst for last.

"Can Buck do this?" she asked. "Find the killers."

"Buck is your man. He knows what he's up against, and he had the sense to call the State boys. They're pretty good, and they'll get more help from Salem."

"I'm counting on you."

"I'll do what I can."

The swinging door to the Men's room slammed. Roy staggered then dropped his end of the bag. He raced for the outside door. Farrell picked up the end of the bag and met Fulsom's eyes as he lifted the body that had been stuck in the window. They carried the last body to the door, then hoisted it into the truck.

"Sorry, Sheriff," Roy said, wiping his hand across his mouth.

"Get them ready to travel, son."

Pearl had followed them out and pointed to the hills. Red and blue lights swooped down toward the valley floor.

"I'm sure both of you gentlemen know what I expect," she said. "I'm going home."

She started toward her truck, then called over her shoulder, "Mr. Farrell, if you would please."

As they walked away, she said, "Not exactly 'do it my way.'"

"Pearl, I'm no good at following orders."

She looked at him, her eyes scanning his face.

"Have the sheriff give you a ride back to the house. I'll leave the truck with the keys in the ignition out front. Use it until your car is fixed."

"Yes, Ma'am. Thanks. I'm trying this question again, because it's the starting point. Who wants you to fail?"

"There are a few, but they'd use money not guns." She turned to look south, toward the hills and the mountain with the Cloud. "It has never been more important for you to discover who you are. The answer is here if you can find it."

The Fire

In its fourth day the fire crowned for the first time. Crown fires are common in Australia where eucalyptus forests emit a flammable haze near their tops in summer heat. Crown fires in the Pacific region rely on beetle kill in fir forests to pull the flames off the floor through the trees' hollowed out insides. The trees act like roman candles shooting the flames into the canopy. The hard, hot summer that blanketed the Coast Range had depleted water content in the trees leaving volatile hydrocarbon-based terpenes behind to stoke the fire roaring in the crown. The hard to access coastal mountain ranges where the fire raged, had not been cleared of dead foliage in years, years marked by beetle infestations.

That first crowning came up a windswept draw as the rock walls reflected the sun and amplified the heat. After a nova-like ten minutes, the inferno burned out its fuel supply and found itself hemmed in by rock.

The rugged terrain that complicated human access also created wind tunnels that focused the frolicking erratic gusts. When the wind tunnels met the flames, the fire's average temperature jumped from fourteen hundred degrees Fahrenheit to two thousand degrees.

As the fire spread and found even more ideal conditions, the temperature continued to climb.

Dewey Farrell

Farrell stayed out of the way while the State Police talked with Fulsom. He saw Fulsom looking at him a few times wondering when he was going to step in. Historically, Banner County with its peculiar status of being privately owned did not play well with others. It kept its troubles to itself and in turn expected to be left alone. Farrell couldn't remember a single incident when someone from Banner County came to Portland to collect a prisoner. As a cop, when he thought of Banner, he thought of it as a foreign country without extradition. He had never seen a BOLO for anyone from Banner.

He paced as he waited. When his steps took him beyond the Nowhere's bright sign it was easier to see into the night. He saw the blinking lights of the radio antenna, and that reminded him of the van he'd seen parked on the side road. He looked at his watch. It would be getting light soon.

"Still a couple of hours before the bus," Fulsom said. Dewey hadn't heard him come up behind him even on the gravel. "I thought she told you to get involved."

"Are you disappointed?" he asked the sheriff.

"No, but curious."

63

"Buck, you and I have to get along to catch the killers so let's divide it up."

"You do whatever you want, and I do the rest?"

"Pretty much. Even so, tell me that doesn't work for you."

"As long as I don't have to see you it does, but I've got to know what you're doing because she's going to ask."

"How often do you go up in the hills?" Dewey asked. When Fulsom started to argue, Dewey raised a hand and asked to be humored.

"How far up?" the sheriff asked.

"Into the Cloud."

Long silence, before Fulsom said, "I've never been inside the Cloud. She doesn't expect me to, and I don't."

"Nothing's changed. The boogeyman – the Turners – still live in the Cloud. Right? You see anything any different lately? Maybe people going in and not coming back, or maybe going in and *coming* back."

"People have always disappeared in Banner, especially around the Cloud. When we were young it was ex-GI's out of Nam chasing color and packing M-16's, and hippies growing pot and armed with anything they could get on the streets. Trespassers on the wrong side of that invisible line still get vanished."

"But not a lot of problems for you," Farrell said.

"Relatives don't come around asking questions, and Ma'am keeps her policy. Stay out of her way, don't shoot at any of her people, and she leaves you alone."

"You ever wonder why she keeps it?"

"I always thought it was expediency," Fulsom said, "but there were a few times in the last couple of years I thought it might be something else."

"Like?"

"I don't question her. She still knows more about what goes on in the county than anybody."

"If the killer's trail leads into the hills, I'll go. Tell her the truth and you'll hear from me when I call."

"Not too many have gone in and come back," Fulsom said, "but I'll tell her."

"Good. Can you spare Roy to give me a ride back to her place." Dewey saw the question pop into Fulsom's face, and added, "She's giving me the pickup until my car gets fixed."

A few minutes later, he rode with Roy out of the Nowhere's parking lot. As they left, Farrell watched the blinking red lights off to the north.

The blinking red lights outlined a tower behind a house that became visible as dawn pushed westward. The antenna looked like that used by a radio station. The property sat atop a knoll that looked down the throat of the valley that included the Middle of Nowhere. The green house needed a fresh coat of paint, but an attached double garage looked better-tended with its white walls and doors. The gravel driveway ran straight from the road to where concrete replaced it thirty feet in front of the roll-up doors.

To the south, in the soft morning light of false dawn, Farrell saw undulating fields stretching ten miles to the foot of the hills. When the hills started, they quickly became steep. They joined a higher range not visible from where he sat that included the perpetual cloud-covered peak that lacked a name. The valley was twice as long as it was wide. To the east and west, the road between Grants Pass and Pazer divided the valley in the middle.

Dawn was still a few minutes away when the house's outside lights blinked three times. When Farrell did nothing, they blinked again. This time he got out of the truck and walked toward the house. A man in a wheelchair rolled down a ramp from the back and waited on the concrete. His long hair with a lot more salt than pepper streamed over his shoulders and blended into the straight salt of his beard. He held a steaming cup of what Farrell hoped was coffee.

"Hope you take it black," the man said.

"Right now I'd take it on my knees."

"That wouldn't get you a lot of sympathy around here. Keep your feet and come in."

The man wore denim pants, a worn white t-shirt with the sixties peace symbol on the front, and slits in the sleeves to facilitate his bulging arms.

He wore wire-rimmed glasses surrounded by his Jesus hair. He was pale, but not to the point of pasty.

The ramp led into a kitchen broad in the middle and shelves built low enough for him to reach from his chair. The counters were front edge loaded.

"Grab the coffee and have a seat," he said, pointing at a wood table with chairs at both ends and open in the middle. When Dewey sat and the man rolled his chair to the table, he said, "Well, well. Dewey Farrell. You don't remember me, do you?"

"Give me a minute. I've seen you before." He snapped his fingers. "You were at my dad's funeral."

"Right. I saw you a few more times when you were older, but you were pretty tight with the enemy."

"The enemy?"

"She who now must be called Ma'am. In those days she was just Ma'am-to-be, but that still packed a lot of power."

"Why would Pearl be your enemy?"

"Yours, too, if you only knew it."

Farrell pointed at him. "Cat!"

"Good for you, boy. That's what they call me. Before you ask why, it's for my incredible agility and lightening like reflexes. Or, it might be for all the lives I've survived."

"You drive a van?"

"You mean the one parked more or less out of sight near the Nowhere? Yeah, that's mine."

"Your hear the shots?" Farrell asked.

"Shots, even that many, by themselves do not draw much attention out here on the front line."

"So what did get you moving?"

Cat pointed at the vacuum pot of coffee and then at his cup. Farrell poured for both of them.

"Before we go there, what's your role in this?" Cat asked.

"Thatch McPherson and his sister, Tess, were two of the dead. I came to meet Thatch." Cat nodded. "So call my interest revenge."

"That all?"

"I wouldn't need more, but yes, there's more."

"Ma'am? The truck was sort of a tip off."

"Are you asking if I'm cavorting with the enemy? If so, I'll tell you no."

"That's a distinction that's not too important right now. Let's start with what is. Like the name I was born with. Charles Andrew Turner." When Farrell didn't respond, Cat said, "The Turner isn't suggestive?"

"Forty miles up the road in Grants Pass nobody gives a shit about the Turners and the Banners. I'll bet you more people there know about the Hatfields and the McCoys."

"What're you saying? It's good to be ignorant?"

"That's a little harsh. It's more like what's important here isn't important up the road."

"How old were you when your dad died?"

"Fifteen."

"And you never knew your mom, right?"

"Why?"

"Because I'm trying to figure out if you've always been this dumb, or if being gone all those years addled your brain."

"Unless you're ready to explain yourself, let's change the subject. I'm out of patience with people who expect me to know stuff because I lived here before I escaped."

"So you 'escaped.' Where'd you live here?"

"Pazer."

"Before that."

Dewey looked at him and tried to think.

"Nowhere really. Mostly in the forest. My dad moved around a lot."

"So you don't remember. Awkward."

"Not really. I tell people I was born in Banner County but my birth certificate got lost. People shrug as if what else could you expect."

"Funny, ha, ha. Are you baiting me into explaining myself? Explanations, dear boy, can get real expensive in a place that would so easily lose sight of who and where you were born."

"What's important to me," Dewey said, "is who shot six people and what I have to do to find them."

Cat snorted. "A little test to see how much I know? Nine died and I know because I capture every radio and cell phone call made in that valley."

"Just the valley?"

"Meaning the Nowhere's valley. Most of the hills, too, but Pazer and beyond are out of my reach."

"The Cloud?"

"Why would you think anyone's in the Cloud in the first place, and in the second, if they were, why'd they have cell phones?"

"I was a cop for a long time and every now and then I'd encounter a world class liar. That might sound like an insult, but it's not easy to spin a good lie, as I'm sure you're aware. The big thing is to know a lot about what you're lying about. Somebody once told me a good lie is eighty percent true."

"Sir, I believe you're calling me a liar. Why would you do that?"

"There's a lyric quality to a great lie that offers up an intriguing possibility that's usually true, and then in the next breath tears the possibility down with a lie. In this case, wouldn't it be exciting and romantic if people lived in the Cloud, but, if they did – I mean, how silly can you get, right? ~ they sure as hell wouldn't have cell phones."

"So you translate my lyric lie to mean there are people in the Cloud and they have cell phones."

"That use your tower."

"Kind of makes me an important player if I'm lying . . . an old guy like me in a wheelchair."

"Don't forget you're a Turner."

"There is that. More coffee? Some breakfast?"

"Seeing as how you're such an important player, maybe I should make some for both of us."

"I've got bacon, eggs, pancake mix and Jack Daniels. Pretty much the breakfast of champions."

While Farrell followed directions, and then cooked stooped over the stove, Cat talked.

"I heard the shots a little after eleven, maybe eleven fifteen. I might have misled you earlier when I said shots don't get my attention. I don't remember hearing bursts like that since Vietnam. I wasn't feeling good so I didn't do much at first." He shuddered. "Then came the single shots. They scared me enough to get moving. You heard those? I knew people were dying. I sort of panicked. It takes some organizing to get me out the door, and panicking doesn't help. While I was still working on it, I heard the next round. You mixed up in that? Okay, so now I'm rolling. I play it safe, because I'm curious not suicidal. I see you going through McPherson's truck, and don't know who you are. Pretty soon Buck pulls in and you both talk. Then Roy. So I peg you for a good guy, or a bad guy with a ton of balls."

Farrell dished up platters and moved them to the table. Cat wanted the Jack Daniels, but Dewey passed. They both ate.

"You said you heard all the radio and cell phone calls made in the valley."

"I said I *capture* all of them."

"Did you listen to any of the calls made from the Nowhere?"

"When I got back. Your call to the cops after you found the bodies. I got interested when I heard your name."

"Why?"

"I never doubted you'd come back. I just wasn't sure it would be in my lifetime, and, now that you're here, you're going to need me."

"That calls for an explanation."

"That you ain't going to get. Then I heard Buck talking to Ma'am. The man was pissed and he doesn't like you. So you went to her place? Never been, myself."

"All one floor," Dewey said, "you'd approve."

"Okay," Cat said, "you're turn. How do you fit in and what's your plan?"

"You're right. Probably going to need your help. I saw the killers drive off. The first vehicle didn't know I was going to be a problem so it didn't try to hide where they turned. I'm not sure they saw me."

"Where was that?"

"They turned south on the dirt road."

"Headed for the hills."

"Right. The second vehicle, fresh from the shootout with me and still trying to outrun my shots, took the main road east. Maybe because it was paved for speed, and maybe because they didn't want me to know where they were headed."

"So you're going to chase them into the hills?"

"Somebody has to. Fulsom stops where the road ends. Says he's never been in the Cloud."

"Have you?" Cat asked.

"I suspect you know I have."

"What do you remember?"

"Not much. I was maybe four or five. It was before we moved to Pazer when I was eight. I remember the fog going to the ground and how wet everything was. People in long coats, sort of like dusters, and wide brim hats walking slow through big trees, all the branches dripping with moss and water."

"We're they using cell phones?"

"If that's supposed to mean this is bullshit memory stuff, it could be. Every kid in Pazer believed the boogeyman lived in the Cloud and he'd carry them off if they weren't good."

"You tell the kids that story about the fog and rain?"

"I don't think so. As I remember it, the Cloud was never anything to joke about."

Cat focused on his breakfast. He finished three fingers of Jack Daniels, then leaned back in his chair and wiped his mouth on the back of his arm.

"You want to go into the hills, Dewey, I'll be your guide."

Farrell pointed at the chair. "From that?"

"More than one way to show you the way. When do you want to hit the road? Tonight would be good."

"Not yet. I've got a few things to do first like sleep."

"To quote the bard, time enough for sleep when you're dead."

"I think that was Raymond Chandler or Ross McDonald."

"They're my bards! They would understand this world."

The Weatherman

It took the gigantic Yellowstone Park fires of 1988 to whip Mitchell Ellers' interest in wildfires into a passion. Two thousand square miles of wilderness burned in the National Park until cooler weather in the fall brought rain. He knew he was hooked when the fire reached firestorm status after crowning and generating its own weather system complete with lightening that started more fires. He had read about firestorms and their effect on the weather, but this was the first time he'd experienced it so intimately.

He studied the fire for hours every night until he became one of the most authoritative experts on what was happening, although he had no official status and no one used what he learned. He studied every twist of the fire. He used the precise topological maps generated by the National Park Service to appreciate the role of elevation changes on the speed of the fire and on the winds that whirled it out of control and snatched victory away from the firefighters when they had their hopes up. He poured over weather maps for an eight state region plotting the high and low pressure zones and how they impacted conditions that initially fed the fires and then perpetuated them.

He examined the strategies of the firefighters and the decisions made by the commanders in the field. There were sensationalized accounts of ineptitude in the media, but the fire was fought with a plan that ultimately worked. No firefighters lost their lives and no significant buildings were destroyed. Even the loss of large mammals was minimized. It took almost ten thousand people battling the blaze, including four thousand military personnel, to protect priority sites, and in Ellers mind their efforts were a success. Conditions existed before the fire that made the fire possible, and from there you had to deal with what you had.

After the Yellowstone fires, he spent every fire season glued to his monitors. He took his vacations in August so he could travel to hot spots and observe first-hand firefighting methods and visit local weather stations where his growing expertise was welcome. By the dawn of the new century, he had his reputation as the Fire Demon.

In 2001 he launched his Fire Demon web page. It started with archived data on fires starting with Yellowstone, and in the next two years added evaluations of firefighting techniques. His breakthrough to fame came in 2003 when he started his fire season forecasting service. When he made his knowledge available as an advisor on firefighting strategies that included micro forecasts on areas down to a square mile, demand almost cost him the job that made it all possible.

When he met Dewey Farrell a couple of times a week over a cup of coffee, and eventually learned Farrell was from Banner, his hopes for solving his biggest, non-fire related mystery soared. Later, when Farrell mentioned he'd been inside the Cloud, Ellers almost hyperventilated. What Farrell could tell him of distant childhood memories convinced Ellers the Cloud was a type of pyrocumulus cloud fed by a heat source, but capable of forming moisture. If he was right, there were unique volcanic forces at work in that mountain under the Cloud. He would do anything to see it for himself.

With his vacation rapidly approaching and already scheduled to visit the area where the fire could easily reach, he felt a curious mix of elation and fear. Elation at the promise of seeing the Cloud for himself, and fear that it would be destroyed by the fire.

He had to do something. If the fire turned toward Banner he would volunteer his services. The trick would be not to wait too long. He looked at the card in the top drawer of his desk with Dewey Farrell's phone number.

Dewey Farrell

From the day Frederick Banner laid out the town of Pazer he envisioned four mills. He put them at the points of the compass, each three miles from the center of town, and left the middle for the people to live. At that time, unlike the teeming cities of the east loaded with immigrants from Europe, people were precious in Pazer. Each family had had their way paid west by Banner and given the promise of a place to live and a job.

The purpose of the original four mills changed over the one hundred and fifty years since Banner's first plan. Now the mills were a scaling operation to the south where logs from the forests were sorted and then moved on either to be sold abroad or to one of the three other Banner mills. Banner had never sold a high percentage of trees abroad, but some were sold to solidify working relationships with foreign markets. The pulp and paper mill with its sulfur smell sat at the east point, while the plywood mill with its soaker vats steaming at all hours occupied the north. To the west was the saw mill.

Before driving into town, Dewey made the circuit of the mills. He saw from the empty slots in the parking lots that none were staffed to capacity. From there he drove the tree-lined streets of town not as a trip down memory lane - although a certain amount of that was inevitable - but to see if word of the shootings had leaked out. The sleepy streets said Fulsom still had a lid on the killings.

Things hadn't changed that much in Pazer. Unlike most places, whole blocks had not been razed to make way for steel and glass, and he saw neither signs of a Starbucks nor fast food restaurants. The mom and pop cafes and lunch counters still lined the streets.

He found the house where, if Thatch's address book was correct, Tess had rented. He breathed easier when there was no police car in front. As he started to consider where the best place to break in might be, his cell phone rang.

"Where did you sleep last night?" Pearl asked.

"I didn't," Dewey answered. "Any ideas on how to break into Tess's house?"

"Use the key under the back door mat. I own it."

"Convenient. I just drove through town and it doesn't look like the press knows about the roadhouse."

"No, but it can't last. What are you doing there?"

"Looking for her laptop, or at least her notes. This has to be about her, or maybe her and you, so until I know what she was doing, or you tell me the truth, I'll just plug along."

Pearl hung up.

Dewey estimated the size of the house to be less than a thousand square feet all on one floor. He walked around the house through the yard rather than using the drive way on the other side. He saw no signs of forced entry. The yard was well tended, but dry from the summer heat. The yellow house had faded to an unflattering shade of cream. The window frames were white and they could use paint, too.

The key was not under the mat, but the door was ajar. He took the gun out of his belt and held it at his side as he pushed the door open with a foot. He heard nothing. He looked through the open kitchen to the living room. The house had been ransacked. Every drawer had been emptied and every cabinet door stood open. The flour and sugar canisters were upended on the kitchen counter.

It took a few minutes to see past the mess, but when he could, Dewey saw the house in layers. The walls and windows and floors with neutral colors and worn appearance were what he expected in a rental. The next layer was Tess. Even in the disarray, Dewey saw her presence. A spice rack leaned next to the upturned flour canister near the range. Both were bright, and spoke of use by a cook. The glass herb containers on the rack were not ceremoniously arranged alphabetically or with their labels facing out, but each faced any which way and various levels of their contents spoke of use. He decided Tess had known how to cook and enjoyed it. There were no dirty dishes in the sink or on the counter.

He walked slowly into the eating area. Two place mats faced each other across a wood dining table with four chairs. A candle in a cut glass holder marked the middle. Matching salt and pepper shakers stood at attention to one side. He saw no other signs of Tess and moved on to the living room that fronted the house.

Dewey felt sure the characterless furniture in the room came with the house. Bookcases lined a wall. The shelves were three-quarters occupied. Most were paperbacks, but quality trade paper sized books. He took a few from the shelves. All dealt with the history of the Pacific Northwest published by university presses. Given what Tess was doing, it made sense.

The inside of the front door was on a flip lock that didn't permit tampering. It looked new. He went back to the kitchen and found the same thing on the back door jam. It hadn't been set because she hadn't been in the house.

A small bedroom shared the front of the house with the living room. The bed had been ripped apart. He looked in the closet and found a woman's wardrobe that consisted mainly of outdoor and casual wear. There was one dress. Shirts were both long sleeved and short and most would not have been opposed to dirt if she'd had to crawl in the forest or in a cave. Four pairs of shoes were aligned on the floor. Two were outdoor wear only, another pair could have gone either way, and the fourth was what she would have worn to visit Pearl in her home or office. Dewey didn't remember what she'd been wearing when she died. He saw no boxes in the closet.

Drawers had been searched, but not dumped. Two drawers split the first layer of pullouts. Panties and bras to the right, and casual jewelry and scarves in the left. Her underwear was mostly white and functional. At the bottom he found a black lace bra and two pairs of colored panties, one black and the other red. They added up to a working trip with little time for seduction.

He went down the short hall. The first door was a bathroom just large enough for the short tub and shower combo, plus a toilet, a sink and a hang-on-the-wall shelving unit for the necessities. A small, in-the-wall medicine cabinet opened over the sink, that held only the usual.

The last room, the second bedroom, had no bed. Instead a large desk faced the wall. The room wasn't the mess the others were because the

THE WEIGHT OF THE JOURNEY BY KEN BYERS

drawers had been emptied and carried off by the searchers. A standard keyboard sat on the desk, but the USB cord sat unfulfilled. A mouse to the right suffered the same fate. He suspected her laptop traveled with her, and the killers took it at the Nowhere.

He found it hard to believe a woman with her accomplishments didn't back-up her work. Her generation, his, too, didn't believe cloud back-ups were secure, and if they did use them, they also used a physical device.

On a corner of her desk he saw a tin ashtray. He picked up a fragment of charred paper and sniffed. Marijuana.

He opened his cell phone and called Pearl.

"I'm busy," she said.

"Did Tess give you a thumb drive or anything as a back-up?"

"She gave me a progress report with a partial first draft."

"Can I see it?"

"No. It's confidential. Why?"

"Her house – your house – has been searched. None of her work is here."

"Who would care about a history of Banner County?" Pearl asked.

"Exactly," Dewey replied.

"What's that supposed to mean, Crash?"

"That means there's a lot you're not telling me."

There was a delay, but Dewey couldn't tell if she was thinking, pissed, or being interrupted. "I can't talk about this now." She hung up.

Dewey took a last look around the room. If Tess had hid something as small as a USB drive he would have to be smarter. She would been practical, like give a back-up to her brother for safe keeping, or perhaps to Pearl who, just because she said Tess gave her nothing, didn't make it so.

The ransacking of Tess's house firmly established her as part of the motive.

Johann Prus

He had never held a business stake in street drugs beyond a modest interest in marijuana driven more by its medicinal potential than its short term profits. He almost lost his interest entirely during one of the periodic drug wars that left men in his distant employ dead, and the authorities in both Mexico and America looking for the money behind the explosion in illegal drug trafficking. Had it been easier to abandon, he would have. But the drug trade was a vital cog to a subsidiary of a subsidiary that had cash flow and money laundering problems. He finally quit worrying because his desire to withdraw from the enterprise had nothing to do with laws and ethics, or right and wrong. His concern was based entirely on the possibility the problems might escalate and become a distraction.

Then he heard about Banner. What he heard about the giant size of the marijuana plants as well as their properties made the claims seem fantastical. The reports claimed the hallucinogenic aspect was startling in the depth of its "trip." Not a user himself, he had to accept the claim, but he had no reason to doubt their veracity. He wanted to know why. What was the difference between Banner marijuana and that grown else where. Finally, displeased with the vague and unscientific information he received, he directed his people to find a source of supply in Banner. Five months later when he looked for progress, he was astounded to see there was none. First his emissaries had been rebuffed by growers in Banner. Then they tried to plant and harvest their own crop. These efforts were met with a level of violence that caught these men who lived in worlds where violence was common place unprepared. They tried to respond with their own violence, but found resistance so great that even in the unlikely case the crop could be harvested, it wouldn't be worth the trouble. Banner protected its own.

Again his curiosity led him to look much closer at this obscure corner of the western United States.

While time passed, he learned of new research in one of his interests. He discovered Dr. Tess McPherson.

Her book on environmental influences and their role on human development interested him keenly. The topic was hardly the stuff of best sellers. She posited that each human was the product of not only what they ate, but where they lived. Not earthshaking left at that, but she went further tying the traits of recessive genes to places, and what environmental influences could drive some recessive genes further down the gene pole while spiking others, even lifting them out of their status as recessive. Simply stated, she wrote that radical environments can rewrite genetic code, and in some cases rewrite it in a single generation. He learned that her colleagues all felt her work too unbelievable to grant her speaker status at national and international meetings.

The subject carried deep implications for him. The Prus bloodline had thinned through the centuries largely due to inter-marrying. Fourteenth century imperfections were given the chance to take a stranglehold as the practice of marrying for position and power outweighed any interest in love or natural attraction. Five hundred years later a healthy child that lived more than fifty years had become a statistical improbability. He was the third of three children. He'd helped one to an early death, but the other brother died at forty-two from the effects of "wasting away." No amount of money could stop his brother's death. An autopsy on the brother whose death he'd hastened, revealed a series of genetic frailties any one of which would have killed him. The forensic specialist's report said there was no chance he would have lived past fifty.

At forty-six Johann already possessed traits found in his brothers. He had no over-riding issue racing him to his death, but historically, dying young appeared to be unavoidable. It wasn't fair. He considered himself much too powerful and wealthy to die before he was at least eighty.

When he became interested in Banner, he'd had extensive appraisals made of Banner Timber Products, including the personal strengths and weaknesses of Pearl Banner. Much of what he read offered little insight. Then he heard that Dr. Tess McPherson was in Banner. He learned she'd been born there, and had come back to write a history of the Banner family.

He didn't buy the "family history" premise. An anthropologist and geneticist writing a family history in the place where a plant with amazing properties was grown with perhaps incalculable impact on one of her prime interests was not plausible.

He tried to discover her true purpose. He tried subtle, and he tried direct, but none of them got him what he sought. He found a small entrée into the fanatically closed world of Banner when he heard a call had gone out to medical specialists whose fields covered a variety of blood related issues. Hemophilia, a condition that prevents clotting in blood, was on the list. Hemophilia had killed many of his ancestors and been a personal fear of his through childhood. The call had also gone to a clinic in San Francisco where he held an interest. Instructions were sent to insure one of the clinic's specialists participated. When he learned Dr. Belinda Blake, a hematologist whose specialty was blood proteins, had made the team he was thrilled. He made sure he was copied on all her work, and had programs added to her computers that would give him access to her research without her knowledge.

He was disappointed to see that her participation kept her in her lab. He'd assumed she would make several trips north for first hand study. Instead she was receiving samples collected by others. She complained, but her protests got her nowhere. When she persisted, she was told to accept it or resign.

Even secondhand, the information she received stimulated him. When he read about the "Banner Effect" the implications excited him to the point where he felt light headed and had to lie down. He sent word through the clinic's administrator that "corporate" wanted all the information she could get by any means on the so called "Banner Effect."

The six weeks he waited for more information seemed endless. When he received the thumb drive with Dr. Blake's findings, he told his staff he was not to be disturbed. He spent thirty-six hours reading the data, making phone calls to other experts he owned, and came to a conclusion. The effects he sought could be obtained only if he lived in Banner for an extended period of time. Since Banner welcomed no one and the entire county was owned by Banner Timber Products and Pearl Banner, he would have to buy her out. Feelers were sent. They were rejected. The speed of the rejection indicated they had not been considered. He decided to redouble his efforts to learn her financial vulnerabilities.

The analysis forecasted Pearl Banner could survive at least another ten years. He didn't have ten years. If there was a market downturn it would hasten the decline, but even that was too slow. He demanded more detail and was told that because Banner Timber Products was a privately held company they had to do no filing with the SEC or anyone else other than the IRS. They paid taxes to the federal government that raised no eyebrows and subsequently had never been asked for additional information. This in-depth study revealed Banner's arrangement with the state of Oregon. He'd never heard of such a thing and decided to pay Banner more attention. He also wondered if her arrangement could be passed to a new owner. Make that new occupier.

The first clue as to an immediate weakness was a third quarter federal tax payment that required a great amount of cash. It was a delayed tax event looming on her horizon. Analysis showed that she had tried to gain a more liquid position and failed, hence the extension. He told his people he wanted to know how she planned to meet the need. Once again he waited.

While he waited, a small book found in a used book store in San Francisco arrived by courier. The author was unknown, but the title intrigued him: *The Possibilities for Extending Life and Virility.* Though the description of place was vague, Prus immediately leaped to the conclusion the setting was Banner County. Again he demanded more. The only thing he received was a cryptic email that sent his pulse racing: *very possible the author is Frederick Banner about ten years after he was rumored to have died.*

On Johann Prus's forty-seventh birthday, on a day he'd been forced to bed for no explainable reason beyond listlessness and fatigue, he decided he could wait no more. He instructed his top aides to form plans for what amounted to a hostile takeover of Banner County, Oregon, United States of America.

Dewey Farrell

He knew he'd made a mistake with his approach to the already searched house of Tess McPherson. Anything there would have been found by the first searchers. Instead, he should have considered her.

She and Thatch had been close. They hadn't fought beyond minor sibling scuffles, and had always talked to each other. As the elder sibling, Tess had led the relationship. As kids, Dewey felt sure Thatch had told her of his infatuation, because right after Dewey confessed, she disappeared when he was around. Then a month later, not long after he'd told Thatch he'd wished he'd never said anything, she put in the occasional appearance. On the rare times Tess talked to him, he found it hard to breathe.

Now he ran a glass of water from her kitchen tap and sat at her table. He wondered if she ever brought the laptop to the table and wrote here. He liked the open feel of the three rooms better than the small bedroom that served as her office. His mind wandered. The fatigue from a sleepless night settled into him. He finished the water and let his head fall forward on his crossed arms.

His cell phone woke him. As he opened the phone, he saw he'd slept three hours.

"Where are you?" Fulsom demanded.

"Tess McPherson's."

"Did you break in?"

"No. I have the landlord's permission, but someone had already searched the house."

"Did they find what they were looking for?"

"I don't think so. The whole house had been turned." Fulsom didn't answer. "Why'd you call?"

"The State cops want to see you at the Nowhere. They weren't happy my witness had left."

"Did that break your heart?"

81

"No, but they're wasting time until you go out there. I only wanted their forensics, but they want to play detective, too." He paused. "They don't go looking for work, so find out why they're still here, would you?"

"I can tell you without asking. They got invited over the border into Banner County. They see it as carte blanche to do some poking. Given the tension with the state, the governor probably insisted."

"I want to know if there's more to it. If they're going to stay, they won't be any help and it could be dangerous. Do what you can to get them out of here."

"Right," Farrell laughed. "No problem. What are you doing?"

"I'm hunkered down behind my desk. The word is out. Just get your ass out there."

"Tess is part of the motive. If she isn't, why search her house? You get anywhere on the identity of the Hispanic?"

"No. The Staties have it now. They can reach out better than us."

"I'll ask."

"Yeah, good luck with that one."

"I'm very good at giving the appearance of cooperation."

"I noticed."

"On that straight line, I'm hanging up."

"Call me."

"If I can. I'm headed for the hills. I hear cell phones don't work too well up there."

"You heard right. Try to come back alive. If you don't, Ma'am will send us up there to find you. I hate the hills."

To Farrell's surprise, Tess had a local phone book and further surprised when he saw a listing for Turner, Charles A. He called the number and got voicemail. He recognized Cat's gravelly voice.

"Dewey Farrell here. Thought I'd come out and bring dinner. If you call in the next few minutes I can get steaks and trimmings. I have a stop to make first and it may take a while, so let's say sometime after six." He left his number.

He went out and left the door unlocked. He didn't have a key and there was no one left to lock the door against.

As Dewey started the truck, his cell phone rang.

"Get here before six," Cat said.

"Depends on the State Police," Farrell answered.

"Tell them you have a previous engagement."

"Cops don't always honor previous engagements."

"Make sure they do this time. We're headed into the hills. Tonight's Gold Night. It's your golden chance to meet the players. You'll get in with me vouching for you."

With news out about the slaughter at the roadhouse, media vehicles nosed to the crime scene tape like horses to a trough. Roy kept vans topped with satellite dishes out of the middle of the road so thru traffic could pass. Farrell turned the blinker on for a right turn under the crime tape. He saw the Cutlass where he'd left it. All the doors and the trunk hatch were open. He'd never see the car again without thinking of it as shot up and abandoned. It made him sad.

Reporters saw the Banner logo on the side of the truck and closed in on him before he could cross into the relative safety behind the tape.

"Who are you?"

"What does Pearl Banner think about the killings?"

"Is this the Wild West?"

It went downhill from there.

Farrell leaned on the horn and caught Roy's attention. Within another minute, he parked near the Cutlass. He couldn't get closer because of the wall of state vehicles. The forensics bus took the place of honor by the Nowhere's door. A large van backed up near the corner of the bus and techs in coveralls carried broken furniture out and handed it into the back. Farrell assumed they were collecting DNA evidence. He thought of the bodies loaded into the refrigerated truck fourteen hours ago. He would have been as thorough as the State Police were being because it was always good to look busy. Nine vics was a big number with a lot of blood and too many chances to get it wrong. Add all the media attention that the slow news days of August had turned into a high profile circus.

As he got out of the truck, a trooper wearing a flat-brimmed campaign hat and sweat dripping down his face held up a hand.

"Stay in the truck, sir," he called.

"I've got an invitation. Name's Dewey Farrell."

"Stay in the truck anyway. I'll check," he said, as he walked away.

"Tell them I'll be leaving in thirty minutes and we have a lot to talk about."

The trooper stopped and squared his shoulders. "You'll be leaving when we say so, sir."

"No, I'll be leaving when I say so."

"Get out of the truck," he said, omitting the sir.

Farrell did and the trooper grabbed his arm. He pulled him toward the Nowhere's door. It was the arm Farrell hurt last night in the parking lot, but he felt nothing more than a twinge.

The inside looked different. The broken tables and chairs were gone replaced by string and chalk marking where the bodies and other debris had been. He looked for a familiar face and found none. His escort announced, "This smart ass says he was invited." A worn face with tired brown eyes and turned down corners at the mouth met Farrell's eyes. It was the face Farrell had dreaded he would one day see in the mirror.

"Ah, the runaway witness," the face said. "Why'd you leave?"

"The killers were gone so no sense looking for them here."

"And that's your job?"

"I'll make a better job of it than you will." When that brought sparks of red into the face, Farrell held up his hand. "No offense."

"Because you're this hot shot homicide detective from Portland with your big city ways, and us Podunk shufflers can't detect a burnt out bulb."

"Ex-homicide detective. No, because I was born here and can go where no outsiders can."

"I thought you hadn't been back for twenty-five years."

"Twenty-three, but who's counting."

"You're still special?"

"Apparently." Farrell smiled, and relaxed. "Look, we can piss all over each other and amuse the people out there looking for fresh conflict, or we could be civil and figure this out."

"You start. Tell me what you saw."

Farrell did and was sure the man had heard the same story from Fulsom. Still, Dewey would have listened to the source's version, too. Even though it wasn't solicited, he gave the cop, whose name was Hamel, his belief that the crime was premeditated and that the group of five was the target.

"Any ID on the Hispanic?" he asked Hamel.

"Hector Elizondo. He has a sheet in L.A."

"Drugs?"

"DEA is very interested. Elizondo sort of disappeared a couple of years ago. DEA says they think he matriculated into the cartels as a procurer, but that appears to be less than a unanimous opinion."

"What's the other?"

"He was last seen in the East Bay – Berkeley and Oakland. Nobody knows where he was getting his goods."

"This came from you, didn't it?"

"Nice guess. Yeah, we know Hector. He was loose about which side of the street he worked. He dimed some competition."

"Weed?"

"Yes. Hector was ambitious. He was dedicated to the buck, but he preferred it came from an honest source. Kind of sorry to see him go. DEA knows more, but they aren't sharing without an invite to the party."

"That is the problem, isn't it," Farrell said, "keeping the players to a manageable number. Lots of issues. Constitutional ones, lots of legal murkiness, lots of coverage under very bright lights. All that, and you're playing on the road in Banner County."

"Complicated," Hamel agreed. "The DEA brings their own agenda and that would create more problems. The commandant called me before I left. He told me every decision I make, every line I cross, will be examined in the light of the national media, and will face state judicial review maybe as high as the Supreme Court. The last thing he said was good luck."

"If the legalization of marijuana passes next year, that change anything?"

"At the moment it's illegal. That's all I need to know."

"You wish. Legalized marijuana is already in the spot light in the alternative press, which may not mean much here in the middle of nowhere, but it does in a lot of places since California dropped the ball."

"Sounds like you're in favor," Hamel said.

The men paced side by side avoiding lines and string on the floor.

"It doesn't make any difference what I want, but we both know as cops we'd be better off if it passed. Frees up a lot of resources and takes folks like Elizondo and the cartels out of the picture. And that brings us back to Hector. What was he doing here, and for whom was he doing it?"

"We don't know."

"What does he have in common with an anthropologist writing a tell-all history of Banner County with Pearl Banner's blessing?" Dewey asked. "The only thing that comes to mind is frightening. Banner is interested in marijuana."

"That's crazy talk," Hamel said, "but let's say you're right. Who would want to make sure it never gets off the ground?"

"I don't know. This is Banner County. You want some advice on how to cover your ass?"

"If that means I'm not going to find the killers in the next couple of hours, then yes."

"Stonewall your bosses. All they want is to not see their names in the paper. Assure them you got 'em covered, and if you told them anymore you'd put them in jeopardy. The way I see it, your real job is to keep the media and your people out of the hills. If you don't, people are going to get killed. If a news chopper gets shot down up there it won't look good."

"You're joking," Hamel said, but his expression belied his words.

"Not really. More guns in the hills per capita than at a National Guard armory. There are caves everywhere above two thousand feet. Whole networks honeycomb those mountains. I said you were playing on the road, well, this is one hell of a home court advantage for the locals. Speaking of, I gotta go."

"Where?" Hamel asked.

"To the hills. I'm a citizen by birth."

"You sure about that free pass?"

"We'll see."

The Fire

No human saw the fire crown for the first time. Wildfires often burn in unpopulated areas, meaning details are sparse. The Siskiyou-Banner Complex fire was no exception. Smoke could be seen for miles had there been anyone there to see it. Fire spotters reported it, but a large fire burning near a populated area near Lake Chelan, Washington demanded resources normally available to the Klamath and Siskiyou National forests. Other fires from as far away as Colorado and New Mexico, further depleted the Forest Service fleet of fire spotting aircraft. Their budget was unlimited to save people, property, and habitat, but resources were always limited. The drain on resources gave the S-BC fire burning in the middle of nowhere free reign to feast on beetle kill and dead foliage. When reports came in from civilian pilots on the size of the fire, they were deemed exaggerated. No fire in USFS history had ever reached that level of involvement (measured in acres) without some effort made to confine it. By the time the first load of fire retardant was dumped from the air, the fire had grown to eighty thousand acres.

Credit for alerting officials to the danger posed by the fire went to Bill Renfroe in the Crescent City, California office of emergency preparedness. The emergencies Renfroe's office normally dealt with were tsunamis. No eastbound tidal wave in the Pacific missed Crescent City. After Renfroe received reports from people living along the Smith River, he drove across town to the office of the Forest Service housed in the North Redwoods Visitor Center. Questions were asked, and finally a plane was launched from Medford, Oregon to assess the fire.

The report from the plane was alarming. The S-BC fire would no longer be a secret.

Dewey Farrell

Farrell reached Cat's a few minutes before six. He pulled up the driveway as Cat rolled down the ramp alongside the house.

"I'll drive," Cat said, and pointed at the Banner logo on the door of the truck. "I'd like to get there alive."

Three minutes later, Cat sat behind the wheel of a decades old motor home dotted with rust and a cracked window in the side door, but powered by a motor that purred with a deep throated rumble. The driver's side had been altered so Cat could drive from his wheelchair. A lift had been installed on the passenger's side. Farrell sat behind him invisible from outside as Cat backed down the long drive.

On the road to the Nowhere, dust from Farrell's passage still hung in the still heat of early evening. As Farrell looked through the golden light across the valley, the Nowhere's sign came on. A minute later when the RV reached the intersection, cameras were rolling with the sign in the background and live reports were being talked into microphones.

"Imagine the philosophical hyperbole they're spouting," Cat said. "Almost enough to make me want to listen."

Cat came to stop, waved at Roy, and then started slowly on the road to the south.

"I'm just a local color kind of guy," Cat said, after they passed the roadhouse. "Roy won't give me a second thought. It's okay to sit up here now and enjoy the scenery."

Calling the shape of the valley an elongated diamond broke down south of the Nowhere. The terrain began to rise almost immediately as the tree line closed in. Along the side of the gravel road, the heat of summer had wilted the ferns and long stemmed grasses. Everything looked dull beneath their patina of road dust. The trees thinned near the edge of the forest where they touched the road. They had been harvested more recently, but life for a tree in the front rank was more difficult than deeper in the forest where shade moderated the temperature swings, and dew dampened the floor.

The road dipped to the west and when the RV came around the corner, Farrell got his first look in years at the Cloud.

"I know a guy," Farrell said, "who's obsessed with the Cloud. He's a meteorologist in Portland. He told me the Cloud hasn't changed one bit in size or depth in the thirty years he's been watching it. He can't understand it."

"That's not true," Cat said. "The Cloud has pulled back a couple of feet in the last twenty years. The Cloud leaves a measurable mark on the trunks of the trees like the water line on a bridge. The old marks on those trees are drying out, so the Cloud is lifting. Nobody knows why. Somebody suggested climate change, but I don't buy it. The Cloud's got nothing to do with the climate."

Their road continued to climb steeply with a sharp drop to the left that fell several hundred feet to the Salmon Jump River. Farrell had never seen a salmon jump in those waters. He knew the river started miles to the east where water poured out of the side of a cliff near a place called God's Finger. He and Thatch had gone exploring and never seen the water coming out of the rock, but they saw the dramatic rock promontory with a monastery perched on top of the rock. They learned later that was normal for late summer, but if they looked in March with the winter rain and the first snow melt of the season, they'd get quite a sight.

The higher they drove the greater the diameter of the tree trunks. When the road veered away from the drop to the river, tree branches arched over the road forming a tunnel. Cat turned on the headlights.

"How about letting me know what I'm getting into," Farrell said.

"Glad you asked. Let's start at the beginning. What we have here is a near perfect micro-economy. We have gold miners, strictly speaking they're panners since no one's digging mines. These guys have pulled enough gold out of the creeks to make a living since gold was six hundred an ounce. Now that it's sixteen hundred an ounce the profits are a little better, not that anyone's really getting rich. Call it a lifestyle choice. The big strikes, like a hundred years ago, were south and east of here, but that ain't stopping anyone from looking for more. How much do you know about gold?"

"It's heavy, looks nice, and can be a motive for killing someone."

"All true, but when you're taking it out of the ground there's more to it. The gold here is a high grade with traces of silver and platinum. The traces are called electrum and the silver and platinum make up less than five percent, typically about three and a half. It gets smelted out using a process called cupellation which has been around since man found gold and wanted it to be as pure as the driven snow. Cupellation will get it down to about 99.95% pure and that's close enough."

"Where do they go for the smelting?"

"Where else? The Turners. We've been smelting gold since we got to the mountain. It takes heat, and a few other things we happen to have on hand. We pour the gold into small ingots. It's fair to say the reason the gold culture grew so fast here is us."

"That, and there's gold," Farrell said.

"True. But without us, the guys would have to sell their gold in Grants Pass or Medford and lose a nice slice off the top in commission. They'd have to haggle over purity, too, not to mention the risks packing gold one way, and cash the other. We solved the problem."

"How do you get it out?"

"Ah-ah! Secrets are secrets." Cat drove through a series of S-curves then resumed his narrative. "Near the end of Vietnam, as more guys fucked up by the war chose to live in the wild instead of the cities, and more heads from San Francisco and Berkeley started moving in and laying out their weed patches, the woods got sort of crowded. Soldiers and peaceniks go together like fire and oil, so there were some shootings. The Turners stepped in. The dopers had cash, and the soldiers were digging gold and needed a buyer. All these guys needed was a little structure, so the Turners set up Gold Night. We took a small cut out of every transaction, and handled security. It grew from there."

"Usually the best armed run the security," Farrell said.

"That would be the Turners. Security isn't as big a problem as you would think given all the cash and gold. If you belong here, no problem getting close, but if you don't, that's a whole new blood spattered shirt. Last night kind changed that, though. Tonight, security is going to be tighter than a tick's ass and better armed than usual. Speaking of the Nowhere, what's the official thinking?"

"There's a lot more arguing than there is thinking. Agencies that have never had a footing here want a chance, and I'm telling them that's a real bad idea. They puff up their shirts and say they can handle Ma and Pa Kettle."

"What do you think happened?" Cat asked.

"Tess was in the middle. Either on her own, or with Pearl. What I really want to know is who profits if Pearl falls on harder times. I can't get a straight answer out of anyone. You got one?"

"The short answer is nobody around here. The status quo works pretty well. Just enough shootings to keep the riff raff out, and just enough lying about the gold not being found to keep most folk away. See, that's the beauty of Gold Night. The weed growers are masters at shipping small packages all over the country, so they spread their gold around. It keeps speculation down on where the gold is coming from." Cat pointed through the windscreen. "That's it dead ahead."

Farrell saw lights through the trees. The trees were so dense they elongated the light to give it the appearance of tightly barred windows. The flat road meandered through the trees until Farrell saw the set up for Gold Night.

In the middle of the huge circular clearing was a tent made of red and white striped canvas with pennants that hung limp from the tops of the center pole. Kiosks with brightly colored fronts radiated out like spokes from the tent. Kids ran, dogs barked, and men with long guns walked.

"Sort of a carnival feel to it," Cat said.

Next came a dozen smaller Airstream trailers. Surrounding them were big pickups with long beds and crew cabs.

"The trailers?" Farrell asked.

"Offices on wheels," Cat answered. "It's pretty big business around here."

"How big?"

Cat looked at him, then shrugged. "I brought you this far so no reason to hold back. A couple of million will change hands tonight. That's about seventy five pounds of gold at today's price which was $1,625.42 an ounce."

"Does the gold always sell?"

"Always to the highest bidder. When there's more cash than gold that can drive the price up. Some grower gets in a bind and needs to convert his cash when gold's running tight, then the bidding gets competitive."

"Who runs the auction?"

"The Turners, of course. This is our show. We take a very small slice, like I said, but the real bucks for us is we keep the silver and platinum we pull out of the gold during the cupellation. Everyone trusts us, well, they trust us more than anyone else, and if you think gold runs short from time to time, keep in mind there's always more gold than trust. These are hard, well-armed men who are handing their safety and livelihood over to more hard well-armed men. They wouldn't do it if there was a better way."

Cat steered the RV to a reserved spot where two men wheeled a ramp to the door.

"Pretty good service," Farrell said.

"I'm the Grand Poobah. The service had better be good."

Farrell leaned away and took another look at his chauffeur. "You're a regular Boss Tweed. You control the communication tower and here you are running Gold Night."

"I'm the public face of the Turners. Like I said, who do you think runs things in Banner County? It sure as hell ain't Missy Banner."

"You? You run Banner County?"

"Why not?" Cat laughed. "But you're being too literal. I'm a go-fer. Sort of a grandiose one, but still a go-fer."

"So who does run the show? Do I get to meet the king?"

"Queen. This part of the world is a matriarchy, and whether you get to meet her is up to her. You gotta earn the right. You know, be a good boy, do a big service, earn your knighthood, and you can drop to a knee before the Queen."

The door opened and the two men helped Cat down the ramp. Farrell stood out of the way, and watched the party-like atmosphere. Sodium lights on poles lit the festivities. The hum of generators provided low level background noise to the yells and screams of kids and adults. Attire ranged from work clothes to Granny skirts and tied-died shirts. Farrell smelled midway aromas like cotton candy, grilling onions, and hot dogs on charcoal grills that heightened the carnival atmosphere.

"Each claim or patch gets one representative in the auction," Cat said, "and usually that's the male although there are women who pan and others who run a patch, so don't be surprised. We're more Oriental in our approach than liberal or conservative. It's all commerce." He looked at his watch. "Hey, Caleb, first bell."

A stocky man wearing a red vest and a gun belt over faded dungarees climbed a ladder and struck a bell with a small hammer.

"That means ten minutes," Cat said. "You probably want to take a look around, but I don't think that's a good idea. No one knows you. You're this far because of me so stay close, and as long as you're right here, I could use a push through that flap."

Farrell pushed the wheelchair into the tent. He saw benches in rows to seat over a hundred people. At the front was a raised dais accessible by a switch-backed ramp. In front of the dais was a table with a scale, and a plastic dish on the weighing platform. The circular face of the scale was larger than any Farrell had seen before. A man worked at the scale adjusting the balance and the face to absolute zero including the dish, then verifying the accuracy with labeled weights.

"How long you been doing this?" Farrell asked.

"Long enough to be pretty good." Cat cleared his throat. "I hear twelve, do I hear thirteen, thirteen, thirteen, there's thirteen, looking for fourteen there it is on my right, keep it coming keep it coming now at fifteen," all said in the staccato cadence of an auctioneer. He used his normal, raspy growl to ask the man at the scale, "Ready, Little Bob? Okay, sign her off then."

Little Bob signed a book before handing it to Cat.

Two bells sounded.

"Five minutes. Miners can check weigh the scales to be sure they are perfectly registered. At sixteen hundred plus an ounce, you can say this is more than an ounce of prevention."

People started drifting in. A man in jeans held up by wide red suspenders and muddy boots put a measured weight on the scale. He put on a pair of glasses when he leaned in to check the weight.

"Good enough, Earl?" Cat asked.

"Give me the book," Earl said. He signed it and handed it back.

"That's the trade-off," Cat said. "Anybody can check weigh, but after they're satisfied, they have to sign. Anybody complains they can see who accepted the scales."

"Get many complaints?"

"Nope. This is a good deal, this whole thing, and everyone knows it. How about a push up to the seat of power?" As Farrell rolled him passed the scales, Cat said, "We're going to have to change to digital scales. Something that reads out to thousandths and maybe converts the price per ounce to the weight on the scale. The math these days is running to some pretty big numbers."

Farrell watched as growers and miners paraded into the tent. Even though they had to know each other there was little talk and fewer smiles. He thought of Cat's comment about business. Attire, for the most part, was utilitarian jeans and boots. The counterpoint was headbands and flowing, tie-died shirts. Farrell watched hands. He assumed miners would have harsh hands like Thatch, while the growers would be less calloused. If that assumption was right then attire cut to both sides of the aisle.

A bell sounded and everyone sat. Farrell took a seat in the corner near the ramp that left him a good sight line. Cat rapped a gavel and called the meeting to business.

Johann Prus

The date for Banner's large tax payment came and went, and the company paid its taxes on time. Prus knew where to look to find the logical sneaky ways to find cash, since he considered himself an expert, but found nothing.

He demanded more information. He sent people to Pazer to break into Banner corporate. The break was skillful enough to leave no trace to the unsuspecting. When he got the copies of in-house financial records he saw that there was a deposit of almost the same amount she owed on her taxes from a company in San Francisco. Prus had dealings with the San Francisco company as well. They were precious metals brokers – specializing in gold. It appeared that Banner had sold gold. He assumed the worst –they had substantial gold reserves and financial resources he had not suspected.

Gold in the ground paid no attention to lines on a map. Prus had interests in gold mining in various parts of the world and was well familiar with places where gold had been mined in significant quantities. He knew that the area south of Banner had been Placer mined in the early twentieth century. If there was gold to the south, there could easily be gold further north. Again he sent his agents into the field. They found no record of gold claims or licenses for gold mining in Banner County. He wasn't surprised. Pearl Banner owned it all. All she had to do was get a pan and go to work. Banner Timber was obviously astute enough to convert gold to cash when it became necessary. He wondered how she felt when she had to publicly sell gold to cover her cash needs. He was sure she'd hated the need. If he were her he'd do whatever it took to make sure it didn't happen again.

For a third time he had to revise his assessment of the company and its leader. He thrilled at the challenge. So few things in life surprised him because he underestimated his foe. He welcomed open hostilities with Banner. There were many ways to fight a war and his family had done them all, perhaps even invented a few ploys and gambits along the way. He felt his heart rate pick up, but he took deep breaths to get it under control. The weeks ahead would show if Pearl Banner had what it took to hold on to what was hers and deserved his attention.

Dewey Farrell

The hundred or so people in the tent for Gold Night fell quiet.

"You all know about the shooting at the Nowhere," Cat opened. "Any questions?"

"I heard Charlie Farr and Willie Duggan got it," said a man wrapped in a tie-died shirt and long hair. "Who gets their claims?"

There were a few groans, but others leaned forward.

"You all know the rules, and we ain't making no changes," Cat said. "You've all filed your GPS with the Turners, and we're the only ones supposed to know where you're looking."

If Thatch had followed the rules, Farrell thought, he would have registered his search, but Thatch and rules hadn't always gone hand in hand.

"We've already sent people out to check the Farr and Duggan claims and pick up anything loose," Cat continued. "Farr had a bag and it's on the docket for tonight. The proceeds will go to his next of kin. If there ain't none, we'll auction off the claim with the proceeds going to the trust. After our cut, that is."

"Goddamn Turners don't do nothing for free," came a grumble.

"I heard that," Cat said. "How many of you do something for nothing?"

There was silence until someone said, "Not on purpose."

"There you go. Anybody not happy can leave the county and go down the road to file a claim on National Forest land. BLM oughta get around to you in maybe ten years, then *if* you get a permit all the regulation will choke the profit right out of you. Anybody got anything else? No? Then let's open the bidding. Here's the magic number, so sharpen your calculators. Last month's gross to gold was 95.12%. For the benefit of my friend sitting there in the corner," he pointed at Farrell, "for every ounce of gold you put in you get .9512 of value. That's your ounce minus the impurities."

"By impurities," the same voice that had grumbled about the Turners earlier said, "he means silver and platinum."

"Mike," Cat said, and in the one word he packed a sentence worth of sarcasm, "you want to stand over the hot stove? Every damn month you complain, but every damn month here you are buying."

The room laughed, and Farrell saw this was part of the warm-up. Make light out of the ticklish issues and save potential problems from coming up later.

Men and one woman lined up next to Little Bob, the scale minder, who sat at a table with identical plastic bowls stacked up to his left. Little Bob placed an empty bowl on the scales, checked to be sure it registered zero, and the miner dumped the contents into the bowl.

"Number eight twenty-seven," Little Bob called, handed a receipt to the miner, and moved the bowl with its precious contents toward the scale. The bowl was always in sight of the crowd. Once he had three bowls lined up, Little Bob nodded.

"Buyers may inspect the first three bowls," Cat said.

Men came forward to inspect the bowl's contents. As they leaned over the table they kept one hand behind their back while the other held a magnifying glass. They took their time, and when each was done they returned to the benches.

Cat rapped his gavel again.

"Business is in session. Refining time is eight days. Market price for tonight is set at $1,625.42 an ounce, minus the impurities, makes it $1,546.10. Any seller here willing to settle for less than market, signify by raising a hand." No hand went up. "Okay, bidding will start at market price. Little Bob, weigh the first one which is . . . lot 827."

Little Bob put the dish on the scales. He watched the arrow bounce on the face until it stopped. "Three and three-eighths ounces."

Cat entered numbers in his calculator. "Make it $5,217.75. Who has the first market bid?"

Three hands went up.

"Fifty-three hundred?" Cat asked the bidders.

One hand remained and its owner came to Little Bob's table to exchange a stack of cash for a piece of paper leaving the Turners with both the cash and the gold. Farrell saw why trust was a mountain to climb and each participant had to make the journey. Little Bob took some bills from the cash then sealed it in an envelope. He pointed at the miner who'd given him the gold and paid him. The miner left, his transaction completed, while the buyer watched the gold disappear into a bag. After the third transaction, the bag with the gold left the tent.

After the fourth auction, two men came through the main flap carrying a cloth bag between them. The room's attention focused on the bag.

Cat hammered his table with the gavel.

"One per, gentlemen!" he called.

"We invoke the five pound rule," said the man, holding up the bag.

"Weigh it!" Cat demanded.

The two men were so close they appeared wedded at the hip until they turned to face each other in front of the scale. The man with the bag opened the draw string and upended the contents into the other's hand. A large nugget tumbled into the cupped, gnarled palm. Applause came from those close enough to see. Little Bob placed the nugget on the scale. The rest of the room took their turn to gasp as the dial on the scales swept past five pounds and bounced between six and a half and seven before coming to rest.

Little Bob leaned closer to the dial before proclaiming, "Six pounds, 13 ounces."

"Boy or a girl?" someone called, and the room laughed. Cat pressed keys on his calculator.

"The five pound rule says any claim with a deposit greater than five pounds may bring a second representative. Their offering moves immediately to the front of the line while there's a chance someone has enough cash to, shall we say, make a lump purchase. As with all nuggets there is an eighty percent deposit based on the market price because it's too hard to estimate the refined yield. Eighty percent of this would be $135,070. Any buyers with that kind of cash want to bid?"

Four hands went up.

"The bidding will be done in refined dollars making this nugget," Cat looked at his calculator and read, "a hundred sixty-eight thousand, eight thirty-seven. Any takers?"

All four hands went up again.

"One seventy?" and again all four hands went up. "Okay, boys, let's see who's got nuggets for balls. Two?"

Three hands raised and the room held its breath.

"Two twenty-five?" This reduced the count to two. Farrell wondered how often nuggets of this size hit the scale. If Cat's estimate that a couple of million dollars would change hands there was a ways to go without more nuggets.

"Two fifty?" No hands went up. "Two forty?" Still nothing. "Two thirty-five?" One hand went up. "Two thirty five it is unless Farmer Jack wants another shot?"

The man who was the last to drop out of the bidding shook his head.

"Okay, Rob, you need $188 grand for the deposit. As per our large transaction rule you fellows all go to the office and finish your paperwork so we can get on with our business."

As the miners left the tent they high-fived each other while many in the audience clapped until Cat rapped his gavel and Gold Night continued.

Farrell put the total value of the next few hours transactions over a million. There were more nuggets but none anywhere near the size of the six and three quarter pounder. Farmer Jack, the man who'd dropped out of the big nugget bidding found ways to spend his money.

From his vantage point, Farrell had the same line of sight as Cat. The rear flap came up and two men with guns raised came in and flanked the opening. One raised his weapon and signaled to Cat, who stopped in mid-sentence.

"Folks, we have a security concern. There is no need to overreact, but let's take a break while we see what's afoot. Gents with gold on the table retrieve it now."

The two men with guns came hurriedly forward before the audience could stand, and talked to Cat. Farrell couldn't hear it all, but he caught "intruders" and "guns" and decided that was enough reason for him to overreact.

"Listen up!" Cat yelled. "If you're part of the fire brigade report to your post now!"

Farrell slipped out of the tent and retrieved his gun from the RV. He saw people moving quickly around the clearing. The noise of having a fun night out disappeared, replaced with the quiet of serious purpose. Without warning the lights dimmed. He pushed his way through people leaving the tent and ran up the handicap ramp.

"Glad you're here, man," Cat said. "I sent my normal handlers out to their fire posts."

"What's going on?" Farrell asked, as he maneuvered Cat's chair to get it headed down the switch-backed ramp.

Before Cat could answer, a deafening *whump!* followed immediately by a fireball that ignited the tent. An acrid, petroleum odor assailed Farrell's nostril's and in the background he dimly heard screams from people still in the tent. Cat's hands went to the wheels and they started down the ramp.

Strips of burning canvas fell around them. Farrell heard the sighs and moans of the tent warning those still under it of its coming collapse. A flaming swatch fell on his shoulder. He took a hand from the chair to tend to his shirt, and lost control. Cat yelled, and then used his hands to attempt to get the chair back on course. Farrell could not have been off the chair's grips for more than a couple of seconds, but it was enough for the chair to pick up speed and head toward the ramp's edge. Farrell threw all his weight to correct the course without success until Cat did the same. The chair's outer wheel teetered inches from the edge. The ramp's height looked to be less than a foot, but it would still be enough to send Cat flying.

"Brakes!" yelled Cat, as Farrell jumped off the ramp, ran to get alongside, then leaned his still-smoking shoulder into Cat to straighten their course. Cat used the brake on the inside wheel to slow the chair and slue it toward the center of the ramp as they made the turn. Now they faced the wall of flame between them and the flap.

"Brake off!" Farrell yelled, and the chair picked up speed. Their only chance was to hit the flames with momentum and hope nothing derailed their flight.

Man and rider hit the fire. The flames instilled in Farrell a certainty he would die like his father, consumed by the blaze that left nothing but charred bits. He pumped his legs faster and wondered if his father had done the same, determined to outrun the fire before it scorched the life out of him.

As they raced through the wall of flames, the wheels crashed into something. Cat flew out of the chair followed closely by the airborne Dewey Farrell who had lost his grip. They sailed through the fire, then crashed to the ground, flames licking at them. They slapped at the embers, and Farrell felt a breath of cooler air. Cat's hair still smoked, and burn marks replaced hair in his beard. Farrell pulled Cat over the ground on his back trying to reach a margin of safety.

"Just a couple of more feet!" he said, leaning over Cat.

Gunfire shattered their relief. Farrell sprawled across the supine Cat. As he fell, he pulled his weapon out of his belt and looked around. The first sporadic shots could have come from any direction. Around them, chaos had grown into full blown panic as men ran looking for families, while united families huddled together. Moans of terror and pain filled the night. Farrell saw bullets impact one of the trailers thirty feet away, and a man spun throwing his arms wide as he crumpled. The Turners returned fire with a concerted volley.

Then defenders ran from cover toward the perimeter. The men fired as they ran, their rifles on full auto shooting into the night adding a sharper and more insistent note to the cacophony.

"Stay down," Farrell said to Cat, as he patted smoldering embers on the man's clothing.

"Ha, ha," Cat retorted. "Hey, if you don't get shot see if you can find me a wheelchair. I think the old one's toast."

Farrell patted his chest to extinguish a still smoking ember, stepped over Cat, and ran toward the trailers where one of them held over a million dollars in cash and gold. On the ground in front of the center glittering Airstream saw a man on the ground. The trailer's door stood open and shadows broke the light streaming from the interior. Farrell ran quickly, gun pointed at the door. From the corner of his eye he caught movement to his right. He dove to the ground, and rolled as bullets tore through the space he'd just vacated. He managed to bring the barrel up and get two shots in the right direction. He heard a grunt and scrambled to his feet covering the remaining distance to the trailer's door in seconds.

Inside three men crouched over a safe trying to open it.

"Just blow it!" yelled one man.

"There isn't time," came the reply.

Farrell stood in the doorway of the trailer and said, "No time at all, boys. Flat on the floor."

Two of the three spun with guns in their hands toward him. He shot one in the chest and the other in the leg as the man tried to get to cover in a space that offered none. The third man didn't move at all. His empty hands went up. The man shot in the chest didn't move as blood that had spurted now slowly seeped. The one shot in the leg writhed but posed no threat after Farrell kicked his gun away.

"Drop the gun," a voice demanded behind Farrell.

He did, and slowly turned. A man he'd seen inside the tent held a rifle pointed at him. He waved to Farrell to step out of the trailer.

"Shoot him, Monster," came another voice that added, "we have dead."

The rifle went to full cock as he stepped to the ground.

"Stop, you idiots!" came Cat's raspy roar as he emerged from the shadows carried between two men. With his hair and beard singed, and his clothes blackened by fire and soot, he looked like a demonic deity. "He saved my bacon while you were out there doing your headless chicken imitations. Who you got inside the trailer, Dewey?"

"One dead or dying, one wounded, and one surrendered," Farrell said, then pointed toward into the shadow. "There's another one over there."

"The safe open?"

"No. They were working on it."

"Busy night in paradise, eh?"

"Who you gonna call, Cat? State cops or Fulsom?" Farrell asked.

"Don't work that way here, mister," said the one who'd lobbied for Farrell getting shot. "You might say we manage our own courts."

"We'll take care of it," Cat said, then waved his arms in exasperation. "Will somebody please find me a Goddamn wheelchair! Who's coming in for our wounded?"

"Everybody," Monster said, "and there ain't no more wheelchairs."

"Yeah, okay. You guys get back on the fire lines. Come on, Dewey. Time for us to make our inelegant exit. Anyone got a truck?"

Keys were passed to Cat who handed them to Farrell. "I'm not so good in street-legal cars. Would you get my stuff out of the RV?"

As Farrell went to retrieve Cat's belongings, he saw the chaos had formed itself into a regimen. Intense spotlights shown into the woods where the shots had originated while armed men moved relentlessly among the trees. Other people, both men and women, grouped around elaborate fire hydrants unfurling thick hoses. Farrell didn't remember seeing the hydrants before. As he reached the RV, two men pushed around him carrying another hydrant. They stopped nearby, kicked dirt aside, and shoved the tip of the hydrant into the ground then twisted to lock it.

When he reached Cat's vehicle, it showed fire darkened spots overlaying the rust, but no additional body damage. Farrell retrieved their bags, and followed a Turner to a pickup and got behind the wheel.

While Dewey ground the ten year old Ford 250's manual transmission into reverse, he saw Cat talking to Little Bob and the one called Monster. Less than two minutes later the men had Cat in the passenger's seat and they were rushed out of the clearing and onto the road.

"Why'd you hustle me out of there?" Farrell asked a subdued Cat.

While he waited for Cat's answer, Farrell saw the fire burning behind them and was surprised that it appeared not to be spreading.

After a long silence, Cat said, "Fire is a cripple's worst nightmare."

The truck's old headlights kept their speed down on the unfamiliar road as Farrell struggled to drive around the sharp bends without power steering.

"How come the fire isn't spreading? I thought the woods were a tinderbox."

"We have our own systems. The clearing is huge so the fire had a hard time reaching the limbs, but we have men good at controlling fire. We have to."

Cat's eyes went out the side window as Dewey drove.

"Those bad dreams," Cat said, "the ones where I'm trapped in a burning building – or tent – started a few nights after I learned my legs were useless. I was in the VA in San Francisco on a ward of other crips who'd just taken the same bad news lying down I got. We all wanted to walk. Every one of us would have gone back to the jungle if we could walk again, and think we got a helluva deal." He laughed. "Most of us had said at one time or another we'd do anything to get out of Nam. It reminded me of the old joke about the black dude that gets a wish from a genie and says he wants to be white, up tight and out of sight, so the gene makes him a tampon. You gotta think those things through before you send them into the universe."

Dewey smiled as he fought the road.

"I figure you saved my life twice back there," Cat said, his voice barely above a whisper. "You got me out of the fire and then you didn't let me get shot. Thanks, man. I appreciate it."

"How much?" Dewey asked.

"How much do I appreciate it? Try me."

"Why'd you hustle me out of there? Who is 'everyone'?"

After a pause as Cat held on to the dashboard while the truck lumbered around a series of switchbacks, Cat said, "Couple of hundred feet up here there's a place to pull over." Cat gave a weak chuckle. "Yeah, right there. Turn off the lights, but keep your hands to yourself."

The moonless night was clear, and the stars did little to lighten the dark.

"You've known since the day your father took you into the Cloud there are secrets in the mountains. Tonight if you'd been there when 'everyone' made the scene it would have been awkward."

"Don't make me keep asking why. I feel like a three year old."

"There is a natural order of things." Cat slammed a fist on the dash. "Goddamn it! I don't know how to answer you! I feel like some bullshit soap opera that's stringing out the tension." After a long sigh, he said, "Okay, here's the best I can do. There is a natural order to what happens because that order is how we perceive and understand the world around us. Most of the world you live in doesn't deserve much in the way of second thought, but this one does, and more to you than most."

Farrell waited, expecting more, but when he realized there was no more, he said, "I saved your life, twice, and you feed me this 'I'd love to tell you but you'd never understand' bullshit! I'm not an idiot, but that's how I've been treated since I got here. When I'm not getting shot at, that is. How about I drop you out here and you walk home?"

Farrell instantly regretted his words, but Cat laughed.

"That's better, man. You gotta see behind the curtain, man. You're damned right that you saved my life twice, and, as you were told by me before the night went to hell, I am the Grand Poobah. For services rendered you get a Get Out of Jail free card from the Turners good for damn near anything you want."

"I want answers to my questions!"

"There's a detail about that card I haven't mentioned. It doesn't work on me. You can't use it on the giver."

"But once I get in the Cloud, I'm good as gold?"

Cat laughed again, "Beautifully phrased. Yes, good as gold inside the Cloud."

"Do I get to meet the Queen?"

"She'll hear of your service."

Farrell ran the night's events through his head before asking, "How about a couple of answers to questions that have nothing to do with me or my mysterious past?"

"The odds for an answer go way up."

"You said during Gold Night the Turners had visited the claims of the two miners who died at the Nowhere. How come you didn't mention Thatch McPherson?"

"You want to know this why?"

"Because I want to find out if you can answer a straight question with a straight answer! Jesus!" Farrell took a deep breath. "Thatch found something and because he did, he called me. He died with that information on the tip of his tongue. I can't do much for him, but I can find who killed him and whatever he meant to share. He doesn't have a family with Tess dead, so I guess I would be as close as he has to next of kin. I doubt that carries a lot of weight with the Turners."

"So the question is still why didn't I mention McPherson and his claim?"

"That's the first part."

"I didn't mention it because the claim was never filed. We don't know where it is."

"I'd hoped for more."

"Yeah, well, I'll give you this. The brother and sister McPherson were making themselves a royal pain in the ass. He kept showing up in places where he shouldn't. I know for a fact he got shots fired his way at least three times. No one wanted to hit him, but they sure wanted to send the message to get his ass out of where it had no business. He bugged miners and growers alike. He was like a pinball in a hot game bouncing off anything in his way."

"What about Tess?"

"Different, but still a pain. She was very good at wrangling invitations, and when she had access to where most people never get to go, she was adept at negotiating more than what people were used to saying. She had a reputation for honesty and persevering, so folk who met her professionally

THE WEIGHT OF THE JOURNEY BY KEN BYERS

chose to get their side in before someone else got in theirs. She had Pearl Banner's blessing, and that, in Turner World, made her unique."

"Pearl's blessing counts in Turner World?"

"More than you might think."

"Had Tess been in the Cloud?"

"I don't know for sure, but I think so."

"How could the Grand Poobah not know?"

"When it comes to the Cloud, I'm a serf. I'm like the cord between the bulb and the socket. Unplug me, and I'm useless."

"What's that mean?"

"Somebody else controls the cord. End of answer."

"What was she after?"

"Anthropologist type things. She wanted to exhume Turner bodies for as far back as they were buried on the hill. Touchy subject, but to my amazement the powers that be, the Turner powers, went along with it."

"Why would they allow that?"

"The Turners have health issues."

"What kind of health issues?"

"I'm not in the loop on that one."

"You're a Turner. Aren't you worried?"

"I have my own more pressing issues, and I don't live in the Cloud. My advice is to drop this line and focus on the roadhouse."

"Any chance Tess McPherson was trying to sell large quantities of weed?"

"Jesus! Where's that coming from?"

"The Hispanic guy dead in the Nowhere was an ambitious distributor. Selling here would be like taking tea to China. That leaves buying."

"It's possible, but I don't know where she would get it. Hard to hide big patches below the Cloud. She sure as hell wasn't getting it in the Cloud."

They sat in the dark until Farrell said, "Back to Thatch, if he didn't register his claim, any ideas where it might be?"

"Lot of room in Banner. Did he give you any clues?"

"His message said I should plan on getting rich."

"That's it?"

Farrell tapped his memory and listened to the message again.

"He said if anyone asked where I was going, I should tell them over the rainbow."

"So he'd found the pot of gold."

"Thatch liked to play with words. It was never a good idea to take him too literal."

"But that's all you've got?"

That's it." Farrell yawned before he could answer, and while he did he thought of the diary in his bag. He yawned again. "You gotta an extra bed?"

"For the man who saved my life twice? I'll even throw in a shower and breakfast all for the incredibly low price of driving me home and wheeling out my spare chair."

Within a mile of where they'd stopped, the road leveled and became straight. They saw the sign for the Nowhere in the distance and watched it get closer like a beacon guiding the weary traveler home. The crime tape was still up but the crowd had disappeared save one local sheriff's car and Farrell's shot up Cutlass.

"I guess I'm going to have to deal with my car myself," he said.

"Let Ma'am do it."

"I don't need to burn any favors on her with things I could do myself."

"Having second thoughts about the enemy?"

"No, and she's not my enemy. I don't know what she is."

After pulling into Cat's driveway, Farrell followed directions. As he pushed the backup wheelchair into the house, Cat asked, "You been shot at two nights in a row. You going to stick around, and go for three?"

Farrell didn't answer as he wished Cat good night. Before he got settled, Dewey went outside and called Pearl. It was two-fifteen and he expected her voice mail, but she answered on the second ring.

"Where are you?" she demanded.

"Near the Nowhere so my cell phone will work. I was expecting voice mail."

"Come over now. I need to talk to you."

"Sorry, but I've been up almost forty-eight hours and my brain has quit. I'm going to find a place to sleep and get some."

"You can sleep here."

"And people will talk. Got a wild guess how many news agencies have you staked out?"

"I will not change my life for them."

"You will not get what you want unless you do."

After a short pause, she said, "What do I want?"

"I don't know, but I'm working on it."

"Why did you call?" she asked, and her voice softened.

"To set a time to see you tomorrow. Pick a time and place and I'll be there."

"I don't have time until tomorrow night. That's why I don't want to wait. A lot has happened."

"Yeah, me too. What time's your day start?"

"I have an appointment at 8:30."

"Meet me in the Nowhere's parking lot at seven. It's cleaned out save for a deputy who looks asleep, and my shell of a car. You'll drag some followers, but it will look like you're meeting an employee since I'm still driving your truck. I'm going to bed."

He hung up, but she beat him. He went back in and found Cat with a drink at the kitchen table.

"I'll bet you didn't tell her you're sleeping with the enemy," he said.

"Get over the enemy thing."

"Old habits and all that. Besides, you saying she's not don't make it true."

"You know what I think?" Dewey asked, coming to the table with a fresh glass into which he poured a half inch of Jack Daniels. "They say animals can feel or sense an earthquake coming. I'm not an animal, and I don't know if it's an earthquake, but something's coming."

"Pray, Swami, do go on."

"That's it. Just the sensation, but I will say confidence is high and that's why I'm staying. All I have to do is stay alive long enough to figure it out."

"On that front, if you need more firepower there's a locker in the garage with about anything you'd want. I have a feeling, too. You're going to need to keep your ammo dry." He toasted Dewey again. "What's on your agenda come day break?"

"I'm meeting Pearl in the Nowhere's parking lot at seven."

Cat finished his drink. "Guess I'll have to make my own breakfast. Bummer. Then what?"

"I need to know what the McPhersons were up to."

Farrell arrived at the Nowhere before Pearl. The tired deputy still stood watch so Farrell parked outside the tape. Pearl arrived a few minutes later in a gray S-class Mercedes that purred to a stop ten feet behind the truck. Dewey got out, waved to the deputy, and as he opened the front passenger door he saw two news vans stop down the road. He got into the luxury of the car. Pearl wore a pearl gray blazer with a diamond pin shaped as the Banner Timber Products logo, a white blouse, dark blue denim pants, and black high heels. Farrell didn't know much about women's shoes, but he guessed the ones she wore were hand made outside the U.S. Her make-up was perfect and her composure firmly in place.

Farrell couldn't compete. His face bore the signs of his trip through the fire less than eight hours before, and not even two showers could get its smell off his body. Blisters on the back of each hand were quickly fading under the magic of Banner County. Even through the acrid smoke smell, he noticed her scent, something else he knew little about since Diane had rarely worn fragrances. He took another sniff of her sweet, musky scent. He found his hand moving across the seat toward her, and snatched it back. He knew she'd seen it.

"You've got Fox and CNN following you around," he said, to focus attention out of the car.

She didn't answer, and his eyes met hers after they'd roamed his face.

"You were on the mountain last night!" she said. "In that fire."

"I was."

"Tell me," she demanded.

"Or else what?"

She sighed and raised a hand. He saw emotions he couldn't decipher flash through her eyes. "Please."

Farrell gave her a sketchy version of Gold Night knowing she knew more about the tradition than he did. He doubted it could operate without her consent. He left out all the details including how he got there, but she called him on it.

"Charles Arthur Turner gave me a ride," Farrell answered. "I kind of knew him back in the day, but I found him after I left your place the other night. I followed the lights on his towers. We recognized each other. We talked and I traded him info on the Nowhere for passage into the mountains. At the time I didn't know last night was Gold Night."

"How serious was the attack? Could it have been faked for your benefit?"

"Why would they do that? I'm nobody. Just a guy hitching a ride with Cat."

"That's a gratuitous lie and you know it, but get on with it."

"It was serious enough to kill people. I don't know how many."

"We never will. The Turners deal with their own."

"So they said about the attackers we captured."

"You captured some alive? Who are they?"

"Three guys, two alive. They were trying to open the safe to get at the gold and cash. One was wounded and the other had the good sense to surrender."

"I don't know about that," Pearl said, "I'm sure they're all dead by now. Turner justice is quick and unequivocal. Would you think the three were some of the men who attacked here," she waved out the window toward the roadhouse.

"They were the same type, if not the same men."

"You think last night was a diversion?"

"A diversion for what?"

"I don't know why those men would take such a risk. What is there here that men would die for?"

"Last night there was a million dollars in gold and cash. That's a lot more than was here at the Nowhere."

"All surrounded by heavily armed guards. That's not the same as killing unarmed people in a bar." She looked at her watch on its jeweled band. "I have enemies, but I don't know anyone who would do what's happened. I have to go."

"Hang on one more second," Dewey said. "Can I get everything Tess gave you? Did she ever mention anything about where she kept her notes either paper or a flash drive?"

"Yes, and no."

"Can I use the yes part today? Is it at your house?"

"I'll call and tell Elsie you're coming. I changed my mind on showing it to you because I agree it's pertinent. She must have had notes, but she never showed them to me. Elsie will put the files on the table in the library. I don't want them to leave the house."

"Elsie is still working for you? My god! She has to be seventy!"

"Eighty-two. She worked for Eleanora, and when my grandmother died, she left Elsie in charge of me. She'll make sure nothing leaves the house, so don't even think about it."

"Oh, darn! I'll sacrifice myself and work in air conditioned comfort instead of the claustrophobic heat of the truck. Speaking of, you mentioned something about arranging for my car to get towed and fixed."

"Buck said it was part of the crime scene."

"Pardon me for assuming that you run everything around here. I'll make my own arrangements."

"Why are you so snippy with me, Crash?" she demanded.

Dewey knew she was right, but couldn't find the words to apologize and settled for making it worse.

"Because I can't put my role here into a frame I understand. I'm not working for you, but I am. I feel like I'm being manipulated by everyone because they know more about me than I do. I've been shot at and burned, both perfect reminders of just how far out of control I am in whatever it is I'm doing. I've killed at least one man and wounded three others. In my years as a cop I fired my gun three times and the most damage I did was wound a fleeing suspect. What bothers me now is that not only does my skin heal faster, so does my conscience." He knew he was evading the key issue. "But the most unsettling part is I get into this car and I want to hold your hand. Where does that come from? I notice your fragrance, and I can't tell you the last time I noticed a woman's scent."

"I hardly ever wear a scent to work," she said. She looked out the windscreen. "When I do it's never this one. It's made locally from natural ingredients by a hill woman who makes it only for me. This morning I put it on without thinking."

Farrell's hand started to cross the leather separating them, but he caught it again.

She reached for the ignition, then stopped. "How do you get along with Cat?"

He noticed she was now the one who ran."

"Interesting character. We seem to get along because it appears he wants as much from me as I want from him."

"What's he want from you?"

"He's about as forthcoming on my past as you are, but he wants something. He calls you the enemy."

"Maybe I am. Historically at least with the whole Banner versus Turner feud."

"You don't seem upset that I'm hanging out with him."

"I'm not upset. In fact," she faced him and her blue-gray eyes, now more gray against the blazer, pulled at him, "it may just be the right place for you."

The light headedness Farrell felt since entering the car now threatened to swamp him. Her scent seemed to fill not only his head but his chest. He remembered the lyrics of a song where the singer said she wanted to dive into the pool of her lover's eyes. He reached for the door.

"Will you be there when I get home?" she asked.

"I don't know. It depends on what I find." This time his hand made it across the seat and she took it. "If I am, we need to figure out if this is us, or your fragrance, or maybe it's your eyes beguiling me, or if there is some higher power using us as pawns." He felt her grip tighten and his did, too. "I . . . uh, I have feelings coming alive that I'm not used to. I don't know what to do with them. What is it you want?"

"I want to be a mother to a child, not a town and a business."

She let go of his hand and reached for the key in the ignition.

The Weatherman

On day five of the Siskiyou-Banner Complex fire, Mitchell Ellers had received no requests for additional information from the United States Forest Service. On that fifth day the weather pattern changed and took on the proportions of a firefighter's nightmare. As the low pressure pocket from Canada deepened, high pressure readings rose sharply over the Pacific. The combination would produce sustained winds to eighty miles per hour and gusts as high as one hundred.

The highest winds would miss to the south, but what scared him were the wind velocities that would screech through the canyons and winding gorges. When any of those slits in the mountains took a gust it would focus the wind like a nozzle on an air hose. When that happened, Mitchell anticipated the fire advancing as much as two miles in an hour. Firefighters thinking they were safe could suddenly find themselves trapped with only their aluminum sheets for protection. Aircraft fighting the fire would also be in peril from unpredictable up and down drafts accentuated by the heat of the flames over which the planes would be flying.

What Ellers didn't know was that the USFS had not yet assigned firefighters on the ground, nor aircraft to fight the explosive fire. The reason was simple. They didn't have any. The fires to the north and southeast were still out of control and the danger to person and property much greater.

The new fire had also taken on a sneaky character. With the mountains and tricky winds, smoke was not yet detectable to the more populous north as wind currents and eddies created by the mountain passes carried most of it to the unpopulated areas to the east. Towns and ranches remained blissfully unaware of their danger.

Johann Prus

He pushed himself to understand what he read about Banner County and its leader. He found it difficult to reconcile the pieces. Banner Timber Products was straight forward. The upsides and downsides were all things he'd seen before. Yet, Pearl Banner did not act like the leader of a large company suffering through difficulties. She acted like she owned the world, which she did, at least her world. He could see no peaceful way to dislodge her.

Before his family left Poland, they suffered every indignity known to royalty as one nation after another invaded. His ancestors became adept at not suffering. They understood there are goods and services that everyone needs, and if they met those needs they could ride out the comings and goings. The Mongols had been among the first so long ago his family were still serfs. After the Prus's became wealthy, everyone from the Swedes to the Lithuanians invaded, but the family had salt. Invaders did not want to devote manpower to the mining of salt, so they found it easier to appease than to oppress.

He possessed an arsenal of tricks and strategies learned from centuries of experience.

Dewey Farrell

Pazer had been laid out in a circle. As the town grew, so did the circle. The streets were straight, and the only time the circle was perceptible was from the edges or from the air. The circle had a greater diameter than Farrell remembered. When he was a boy the circumference edge had been the mills. The mills were still there, but newer houses pushed passed them.

Downtown looked pretty much the same. The school was the same; Main Street was still the highway between Grants Pass and the coast, and carried both locals and travelers through the heart of town. Retail stores still lined both sides of Main for ten blocks. After that parks and other non-commercial uses took over. What Farrell didn't see were franchise fast food outlets and chain stores. The main grocery store was a local company with its biggest store on Main and two satellite locations near mills. It had some smaller competition, but it wasn't from Seven-Eleven, but a chain called Insta-Shop.

Businesses filled side streets on either side of Main. There were Laundromats, dry cleaners, and all the support businesses people anywhere need. There were some smaller office buildings where the list of occupants included dentists and attorneys. All the buildings he saw were made of wood.

Some things had not changed at all. The grade school and high school still sat next door to each other. City Hall still looked like a municipal building built during the '30's except instead of stone it was wood. The police and fire shared a building that showed no signs of expansion despite the town being bigger.

The Timber Topper Café, a block off Main, served coffee in heavy, off-white mugs just the way it was supposed to be served. The booths all had diners so Farrell took a stool at the far end of the counter. As he worked on his second cup, he watched the journey of his breakfast in the arms of a woman who looked as if she could carry four more breakfasts without breaking a sweat.

"Here you go, hon," she said. "Over smashed, whole wheat doubled, home fries doubled, and a side of cakes. Think that will hold you?"

"Only if you keep the java coming. Oh, some Tabasco, too."

On her next trip to pour coffee, she said, "Nice burn marks."

"You'd think at my age I'd know not to play with fire. Better not get that coffee too hot."

During Dewey's slow journey through his breakfast, the café lost most of its diners. By the fourth cup, he was the only one sitting at the counter and only two of the booths still held people. He looked up and saw the waitress staring at him while she leaned against the stainless steel back counter. He dabbed at his mouth with his napkin and held up his water glass. As she came to take it, he saw her name was Ter. There was room for more letters, like in Terri, but Ter was all there was.

"I think I remember you," she said, putting down his glass. "If you're the same guy, you were a couple years ahead of me in school, but you were pretty cute. You go to school here?"

"I did, but no one told me I was cute."

"Not to your face. It's sort of a coincidence you being here," Ter said, stepping closer and lowering her voice. "Farrell, isn't it?"

"That's the name."

"Mine was Terra Northby. Now it's Atkins and I've gained weight. About ten pounds a kid."

"I remember. Blonde. Wore your hair long and straight."

"Small town makes it easy to remember. Yeah, blonde. Damn hippie parents, as if the name and style didn't shout it from the rooftops."

"So, Terra, what's the coincidence?"

She went down the counter and put water and coffee in front of a newcomer. He must have been a regular because all she gave the fry cook was a name, and came back to Dewey.

"You lived with the McPhersons for a while didn't you? That the reason you're here? Because they got killed?"

"I stayed with them for a year or two, and, yes, I'm here because of them. Why?"

"Tess usually sat right there," she pointed at a stool to Dewey's left. "She came in for breakfast or lunch. I don't work dinner. Not every day, but often enough for us to talk. I didn't know her in school. She was too old. But we talked. The last time I saw her, she asked if I remembered you and I told her you were cute. She laughed and agreed."

Dewey pushed his empty plate aside and leaned forward.

"She say why she wanted to know about me?"

"Not really. She said she knew you had a crush on her when you were too young to do anything about it. She made it sound like she wished you were older."

"I did have a crush, and I was old enough to do something about it although it would have lacked finesse, and I probably would have died of fright before anything happened. What else you guys talk about besides me?"

"She asked about my parents. You know, the hippies."

"Why'd she want to know?"

"She was looking for people who lived in the hills, especially if they'd lived there very long. When I told her how long they'd lived up there and where, she got all excited."

"Feel like telling me what you told Tess?"

"Maybe." She nodded down the counter. "I'll be right back."

"I might feel like it," she said, on her return, "if you came by after the kids were in bed."

"Single parent?" Dewey asked, and wondered what was going on. He couldn't think of the last time he'd been hit on.

"Single woman, emphasis on woman. There are some extra pounds on the frame but worth the ride."

"Terra, it wouldn't be a good idea, as gratifying as your offer is."

"Why not? You got something going already?"

"It's just not a good idea. This is a murder case."

"You a cop?"

"I was a cop, and I want to know why Tess and her brother are dead. Think you might find your way clear to tell me where your folks live in exchange for a generous monetary tip?"

She turned her back and went down to the cash register. He watched her go through her orders then looked away. He thought he'd lost his touch with women, then realized he'd never had one. He'd never been much of a flirt. When he saw an attractive woman he always noticed, but never knew what to say even when all he wanted was to say hello.

Ter came back and put down two pieces of paper. One was his bill, and the other was a map. She tapped the map with a painted nail. "You might not want to mention you're a cop. My phone number is on the back if you change your mind."

Farrell left a generous monetary tip.

Dewey knocked on Pearl Banner's kitchen door rather than the front. It was the door he used when he was young.

Elsie answered the door.

"Well, well, it seems a far piece since you darkened my doorway," she said.

"Hello, Elsie. You haven't changed a bit." And she hadn't. She was still slight, and still stood straight and looked you right in the eye, just like every woman he'd ever met in this house. She wore a print house dress, and glasses with plain frames.

"Liar. Twenty years plus worth of gray hair, but as I recall you were always smooth with the hi-how-are-yas. Come in. Thirsty, Dewey? It's hot out there."

"No thanks. I just had breakfast."

"Too bad. Cook doesn't get much to do during the day. She was thinking biscuits and pie when she heard a man was coming."

"If she doesn't mind waiting a while I'd hate to disappoint her."

Elsie led him to the library. Heavy drapes covered the windows and a green shaded banker's light lit a thick folder on a large wood table with a polished top that gleamed even in low light.

"Pearl said not to take anything."

Dewey tapped the top of the folder. "You count the pages?"

"Hundred and twenty-eight."

"Then I promise not to take any. You got time to sit and chat? Do you have any instructions on that?"

"None that say I can't. You sure you don't want ice tea?"

"I'd love a glass."

She left, and while he waited he walked the room. On the mantle he saw the family photos Pearl had shown him years ago. All the Banners shared a family resemblance. There was even a daguerreotype of Frederick.

The captivating one was of Eleanora. She stared solemnly out of dark eyes, her mouth unsmiling, but with her prominent cheekbones and strong chin that managed to remain feminine, there was no mistaking her strength of character. At the right end of the gallery was a picture of Pearl with Eleanora. He guessed Pearl was nine or ten making Eleanora in her mid-eighties at least. Both woman and child stood ramrod tall with chins up. Eleanora had her humorless look in place, but Pearl's mouth smiled at the camera. Farrell saw the family resemblance in the shape of their faces and around the eyes. When Elsie came back with the ice tea he held the picture of Eleanora and Pearl. After she set the drinks on coasters, he said, "They look a lot alike."

"They both look like Frederick," Elsie said.

Farrell compared the women to the stern founder of the dynasty. Eleanora had Frederick's eyes and forehead.

"Pearl was nine in that photo. She's more like Eleanora all the time." Elsie set the drinks down. "Dewey is not a proper name. It's not your first name as I recall."

"Recall? At no time in my life did I ever speak my first name aloud in this house or anywhere in Banner County. That means you got a look at the background check Pearl ran on me."

"How'd you know she did?"

"She as much as told me."

Elsie showed no signs of embarrassment at either getting caught in a small lie, or that she'd sneaked a peak at the report.

"I see everything that goes through this house. It's a privilege of tenure. I was born out there in the barn eighty-two years ago. I've worked in this house since I was six."

"Ever been out of Banner?"

"Twice with Eleanora. It was twice too often. How about if I call you Efram? It is your name."

"I might not know who you're talking to, but go for it."

"How's it feel being back in this house?"

"Well, I'm not a teenager anymore. Most days I feel like my life's behind me. Seeing you casts a few doubts on that."

"How come you didn't have kids? Anything wrong with you?"

Dewey took a sip from the glass.

"No, nothing wrong. It didn't work out. Diane, my wife, had internal problems. She said kids might be a long shot. We were alright with that seeing how I was a cop who had a way of getting shot at. Then she got sick. The hardest part was how we felt about being childless. Those are the toughest moments in life when you see the chances you missed."

Elsie looked at him and tapped her chin. He thought he heard her mutter, "missed chances," but wasn't sure.

"Tough. That was Eleanora," she said. "I know you met her."

"I did. She wasn't the kind of woman you met and forgot."

"I only saw her angry a couple of times. The maddest was when you left town. She said she was going to 'track you down and put you out of our misery.' She was clever with a turn of the phrase. I was surprised she didn't. Track you down." She drank from her ice tea. "Did you ever love Pearl or was she just bed company?"

Farrell didn't squirm and held Elsie's gaze. "She was my first. My wife was the second. I'm not much of a ladies man."

"Doesn't answer the question."

Farrell took a long time. "What I felt for Pearl then is something I've never felt since. Was it love? I've never had to find out."

"What do you feel now? You've seen her."

"I don't know, Elsie. I'm not a sophisticated man. I know violence and how to solve puzzles that wrack a person's soul. Why does it matter how I feel about her?"

"Because you just asked the damn question! You are supposed to know how you feel and why. She is forty-three years old and has no heir."

"She told me. She said it like it was my fault."

"Men! I swear to God!" Elsie shook her head, then leaned forward so she could rest her chin on the backs of folded hands supported by her elbows. "Push that folder aside. It doesn't have what you're looking for. I do."

She stood and headed for the door.

"I hope you have no plans for the rest of the day. I'll get cook going on food because you're going to need your energy."

"I'm not going to sit here if I have to listen to riddles I can't answer. I'm sick of playing that game."

"Then let's go straight to the answer. You are the only one who can make Pearl pregnant."

Forty minutes later a shaken Dewey Farrell sat at the kitchen table with Elsie while 'Cook' made a lunch that included hot from the oven biscuits and homemade chicken noodle soup. The air conditioner kept the kitchen cool. Dewey desperately wanted to ask about Elsie's stunning statement, but chose to be silent with the cook listening.

"Tess McPherson was an anthropologist," Elsie said. "I don't know if you can be one without being an historian, too, but Tess knew her history. She had a theory. She said Banner County imprints some of the people born here, but most aren't perceptive enough to recognize it. Circumstances play a big part in finding that perception. You with me so far?"

Farrell nodded.

"She came back here from time to time to test her theory on herself. She felt more alive when she was here, she said, and wondered how much of it was in her mind and how much of it was real. She found a measureable increase in her metabolism and other body functions when she was here. She healed faster, and could run further. Even her periods were different. They were more intense, but less painful. She told Pearl that was the first thing that made her wonder about Banner. She suffered terrible cramps and migraines when she wasn't here. Mental and emotional changes were harder to measure, but she was sure she performed better here than elsewhere. A few weeks ago, she said her work was flying because she saw things with a clarity she lacked elsewhere."

When bowls of soup and plates of biscuits were placed on the table, Elsie gave Cook the afternoon off.

"Tess first told Pearl her theory a year and a half ago, when the book was just an idea. She told Pearl because Tess wanted to use the Banner documents that go back to Fredrick. Tess was sure she'd find something she'd understand. She already knew there were times when the 'Banner Effect,' that was what she called it, was stronger than others, and it was much stronger in certain people."

"And Pearl went for it?"

"She did. Enthusiastically." Elsie paused, and pointed at another biscuit for Dewey. "That's what they said when I was in the room."

"What's that mean?"

"I don't want you thinking I'm talking out of school, because I'm not. My boss is still Eleanora, God rest her restless soul. Tess is dead and Pearl needs help. She isn't going to get what she needs until you know what the deal is. They were up to something, those two, and Pearl made real sure I didn't know what. It has something to do with what happened a long time ago. Something Eleanora did."

"What she do?" Dewey asked.

"You're the detective. Find out."

"Point me in the right direction."

"Eleanora had run things for sixty years by then. She was in her mid-eighties and still going strong. She lived until she was around a hundred and looked younger than I do. She wasn't the first Banner that had that kind of longevity – but most in the Banner family did not. The men didn't have it and some died down right young." Elsie watched Dewey carefully. "Eleanora had a habit of disappearing from time to time. Sometimes up to a month. She'd come back like she'd never been away and never say a word as to where she'd been."

"Where do you think she'd been?"

Elsie used her well-worn apron to wipe her glasses. "I think she'd been in the Cloud."

It took an effort for Farrell not to show his surprise. "What makes you think that?"

"She'd come back all chipper and raring to go. I've seen that so called Banner Effect most of my life and she had it." She held up a finger. "But she only had it if she spent some time away. Sort of like those women you see on TV that go to the spa, only this was some kind of super spa. You could get mighty rich if you could package what those visits did for Eleanora."

"So the feud between the Banners and the Turners is a lie?"

"Not always. What happened way back when really happened, but something changed along the way."

"When?"

"About forty years ago. About the time you and Pearl were born."

"What are you trying to say?" he asked.

"You're the detective. Figure it out. All I'm saying is that something changed."

Dewey ate some soup, dabbed at his sweaty forehead, and finished the biscuit on his plate. He'd just had a huge breakfast, but here he was eating like he was starved. Maybe this was part of his own Banner Effect. You ate when you could against the time when you couldn't.

"Tell me more about Eleanora," he said.

"Eleanora was born around 1900, but I think earlier. Records from that time are vague. She had a clear-headedness that gave her views others did not have. She steered the county through the end of the Depression, the second world war, Korea, the mass hysteria of the McCarthy years, and Vietnam. She didn't step down until she died during the Clinton years."

"What was she like?"

"She didn't make any mistakes when it came to the business. But life is more than business. About forty-five years ago, Eleanora went into the Cloud for an extended stay. I don't remember for sure, but say five or six months. Long enough for it to have been some kind of Moses-on-the-Mount moment for her." Elsie held a hand up and gestured toward Farrell. "Just because she went to the Cloud – if I'm right – doesn't mean she met up with any Turners. She owned the whole damn thing. It's important you get that distinction, okay?"

"I got it. But what I don't get is who's Pearl's mother? She told me back then her mother died when she was young and that you and Eleanora raised her."

"Her mother's name was Martha. She lived here for a couple of years after the baby was born. She disappeared every now and then – said she was going home – but she lived here. I never saw her husband. I asked one time and Eleanora said something that might as well have been mind my own business. Didn't ask again."

"What happened to Martha?"

"Word came that she'd died in a car wreck when Pearl was seven. We had a funeral and buried the coffin here in the family plot. Very convincing."

"You don't sound convinced."

"I've been around these powerful Banner women my whole life. They are God's gift to us, but they are mortal, and they do make mistakes. It's my job to make sure the mistakes aren't too bad. This is where you come in. There is a truth under all this, but I don't think we've seen it yet."

"You don't think this Martha was Pearl's mother?"

"She could have been, but she doesn't have to be, if you get my drift."

"If not Martha, who then?"

"Start detecting. When Pearl was an infant, Eleanora carried her on her chest, whispering to her, then from about six, Eleanora led her around for days on end. She talked to her, kept her by her side full time. Pearl was raised from day one to be the new Eleanora."

"Tie up the threads for me, Elsie. What did you mean about me being the only one who could make Pearl pregnant?"

Elsie busied herself clearing the table, then sat.

"Efram, you take my hands and hold on tight. What I'm about to say is going to raise your ire."

Dewey knew he couldn't leave without some kind of an answer even if it did 'raise his ire.' He allowed her to take his hands.

"It was unfair to say what I did, but you frustrated me. I told you an answer that guaranteed you would stay. Here you are. Call it motivation. The only way anything will make sense is if you, Efram, begin at the beginning. Consider this a puzzle to be solved. There is much riding on the solution."

"My ire is up!" he said, yanking his hands free. "I told you I'm a simple man. There is nothing special about me. I grew up, got married, and had a career. Nothing special at all."

"Nothing special?" Elsie yelled, as she jumped to her feet. "I called you dense before, at least inferred it, and I say it again this time in plain talk. You grew up without knowing your mother - sounds like an epidemic of motherlessness around here - your father died at a very questionable time, you stayed with people that piqued your curiosity, you met the most unapproachable girl in the county - ever wonder how that happened? - fell in love, or at least lust, ran off to what you think of as your life that saw your wife die young and childless, your career end suddenly, and circumstances free themselves to send you here at the moment the world prepared to change. Nothing special! Ha!"

Her explosion rattled in his brain like the crystals in the child's toy you shake, then put to your eye and see all the images from the last time lying there broken. Her explanation made sense standing in the Banner house. It would have been laughable at a bar in Portland having a beer. It would have been unthinkable sharing dinner with Diane. He saw his late wife as the place where he docked his life to reality, the reality most of the world lived in, but that dock and its world were gone now.

"Start at the beginning?" he muttered, standing half way between the chair and the door. "I don't even know where the beginning is."

"Then find your beginning where every life begins. With your mother."

Part II: The Face In the Woods

Cat's History of Bannerland

"When the Turners got driven out of Pazer, like the Jews out of Egypt, they all climbed the mount and hid in the Cloud. Their hegira was tantamount to the spreading of the red sea, nicking across, then watching the waves consume the pursuing enemy, only in this case the Turners hid along the road and picked off the posse chasing them one by one until it gave up.

"The Turners got run out of Pazer because, as the story goes and it's a good one, Jacob Turner shot Frederick Banner for messing with his wife.

"But before that could happen the Turners had to move west.

"The Turners came to Oregon in the early 1870's. By then the railroad had turned the four month trip into six days. They came because Fredrick Banner had a problem. He still owed the state of Oregon about a thousand people. Unless he came up with the rest of the 5,000 people he'd promised for the 650,000 acres, Oregon wanted it back. Frederick thought they were bullshitting, because who cared about all those trees, which was all there was on all that dirt. When gold was found along the Illinois River a few miles south of the Banner line, it seemed probable there was a lot more gold in Bannerland, a name already carrying some traction in the state legislature. The thought of gold interested Oregon whose coffers could use some color, but the threat of an invasion by crazy gold miners into unpopulated areas of his land scared Frederick more, so he decided to come up with the missing people.

"He had always relied on recruiters in places like St. Louis and Chicago for people to ship west, but the supply had gotten tight in part because Frederick was a good old fashioned Prussian racist and didn't want any Blacks. This was the end of the Civil War and there were a lot of white refugees from the South looking to relocate, so Frederick sent his recruiters to New Orleans. They came across one Victor Turner who said he could fill a couple of trains with family who'd love to live in Oregon even if they didn't know where it was. By 1880, there were a thousand Turners living in Banner County. No one knows how diluted the blood line was and no one cared as long as the heads got counted. Frederick didn't care about gold, if it was there at all, because he knew how to make lots of money on trees and they were in plain sight.

"Everything was going along just fine until randy old Frederick used the Spanish-American war to get Jacob Turner out of the way. Frederick had the hots for Jacob's foxy wife, so he drummed up one hundred strapping young lads, including Jacob, to go off and fight the Spanish. With the husband gone, he had his way with Jessica Turner, knocked her up, and to Jacob's amazement when he came home sooner than expected, he found a pregnant wife. Jessica spilled the beans, so Jacob picked up his Army issue Colt six shooter and used two of those six bullets on Frederick. One shot, as the story goes, in the balls and the other in the heart.

"One of the problems with the story is Frederick would have been about eighty and that was long before Viagra. Now he might have benefited from the Banner fountain of youth, if there is one, but it's easier just to write the whole thing off as a dramatization of the differences between the Banners and the Turners. More likely it was about wages since it's well known Frederick never touched a dollar he was willing to part with.

"Frederic Banner wasn't the only problem. The Turners had a few of their own. They came from a long line of drifters, and drifters frequently drift because they are pursued for a variety of reasons. After the Tuners arrived in Pazer, crime went up. Whereas crime against property had been pretty much unknown before the Turners, certain light fingered family members attempted to redistribute the wealth without chopping down a tree. When accused of their crimes, they attempted to drift, but found they were truly in the middle of nowhere.

"Some of the early Turners heard the gold stories and decided to go looking. Because Frederick owned all the land, the case can be made he owned any gold found inside his county. The Turners didn't have a problem with that. They didn't tell him they found any and he never missed it. Sounds all chummy, doesn't it?

"Obviously, it didn't work that way. Banner descendants, especially Eleanora in her early years, hated the Turners. Those years were the 1930's and things were tough. Rumors out of the hills were that the Turners were living high off the gold they found. Eleanora took that personally. She organized squads of bounty hunters to comb the hills and promised to pay one hundred dollars a head, literally, for a Turner. There were problems. Not the least of which is a severed head might have belonged to anyone and when god-fearing timber workers started disappearing the bounty ended. The other was the bounty hunters who gave it a sincere try had to go looking in the hills the Turners knew well. A lot of them didn't come back. Their heads might have, but the rest of them didn't.

"Eleanora was a tough, smart woman who learned from her mistakes. If the Turners could keep the Banners out of the hills, they could keep everyone else out, too. It worked for her to keep outsiders out of Banner because she was planning ahead. With thirty years to go, she had already started scheming for the day she would have to start paying business taxes.

"Part of Frederick's deal with the state was that he would bring 5,000 people to Oregon and give them jobs the workers would pay personal income tax on to the state. In return for this windfall, he would pay no business taxes for one hundred years.

"You might think the land would have been enough, but not Frederick. Originally, he had demanded a million acres, but Oregon said that was just plain greedy. Besides, the state couldn't find a million contiguous acres they were willing to part with that Frederick wanted. The 650,000 acres were what the state felt was just the right size, and Frederick liked the location. But he needed *quid pro quo* for the missing 350,000 acres, hence no taxes for a century.

"Banner still had to pay the feds, but this is a helluva long way from Washington, D.C. and I doubt Frederick declared much more than a pittance of his profits. In terms of personal wealth, he comes close to the robber baron status of Stanford, Hopkins, Crocker and Huntington. He remained pretty much in seclusion so his personal wealth is hard to estimate. There isn't a lot to spend your wealth on if you already own it all.

"So Eleanora saw her days of paying to the state coming. As the day drew nearer, she went to then governor Tom McCall who was a better politician than he was a governor, and told him she would pay the taxes to the state she deemed appropriate, and not a dime more. In return for being left alone and unaudited, she would ask for nothing back from the state. She maintained her roads, paid for her schools, had her own cops, and ran a nice, tight ship. She needed nothing from the state. She even went so far as to tell the governor he should consider the Banner model for other counties. Of course, there were no other counties like hers. McCall didn't take it lying down, but ultimately that was how it played out and Pearl is still playing it that way.

"Seems like a good deal, and historically there is no doubt it has been. But Pearl still has to pay for those roads, and schools, and cops, and all the rest of it. Those bills don't go down with smaller profits the way a tax bill would. Frederick and Eleanora's old deals are coming home to bite Pearl."

Dewey Farrell

For Dewey Farrell the beginning was not, as Elsie said, a mother he'd never known. The beginning was a phone call from a friend he'd found dead on the floor of the Middle of Nowhere. Dewey had arrived five minutes too late to have had a chance to save Thatch and Tess and maybe the others. He hadn't had the chance to promise Thatch he'd be there, and knew it was a messianic delusion to think he could have saved them all, but he could have tried. He'd stopped for a road cup and held the door at Coffee Rings for a woman that ordered four coffee drinks while he stood in line for an extra five minutes; he'd stopped for gas where he knew the people and chatted for at least five minutes longer than need be, plus decisions on the road that cost him more time. He could have arrived before the shootings as the killers got out of their trucks, and seen their guns. Maybe a witness, him, would have driven them away or at least forced a change of plans. If not, he was armed and he could have made a difference. Thatch and Tess could both be alive if he'd forgotten his manners or gassed at a station where he didn't know a soul. He hadn't tried harder to get to the Middle of Nowhere because he believed the days when anyone would need him to hurry were long gone.

Now Farrell stood in the empty parking lot of the Nowhere in temperatures near a hundred degrees. The crime tape was gone along with the reporters who now looked to the fire for their news. His car was gone, towed to Pazer where it was met by a gleeful garage owner who pictured his month getting better. He told Dewey not to worry because he had lots of experience with bullet holes. The hard part, he said, would be matching the paint, but he could do it. Oh, and he didn't take plastic.

A dark green VW bug that was old in the '60's snugged up to the Nowhere near the open front door. A Vietnam era peace sign decorated the car's passenger door. Dewey remembered the car from his youth. It belonged to Zeke, last name lost in the halls of time, the guy who owned the Nowhere. Zeke was Thatch's age, and stood across the street from the high school while he got loaded. It appeared he had the good sense to take over the family business since drinking and smoking were things he was already good at. Farrell was sure Fulsom had talked to Zeke, but that was no reason for Dewey to pass on him. Besides, Dewey had a plan.

Zeke sat in a plastic chair smoking a joint in the middle of a room empty other than the jukebox that at the moment played *Lunatic Fringe* by Red Rider. His legs stretched out and the toe of a boot bounced to the beat of the song that proclaimed every paranoiac's dream "we know you're out there." Zeke wore the years since Farrell had last seen him on his face. His body was still lean with sharp angles at his shoulders and wrists. The jeans he wore didn't hide knobby knees, and the boots were probably 12 A's.

"Man, don't stand in front of the light! It kills my fucking eyes."

Farrell moved and Zeke hit the joint. The heat in the building was stifling with no air conditioning.

"In case your pea brain can't figure it out, we're closed," Zeke wheezed as smoke leaked around the words.

"Still a smooth talker I see, Zeke."

"Who the fuck are you?" Farrell walked closer until a flicker of recognition sparked in Zeke's eyes, but dimmed just as quickly. "Well, well. Crash. Shit, what a thrill it is to see you."

Farrell smelled bleach lurking under the fragrant weed Zeke smoked. He walked behind the bar and began looking and touching. The taps were ready for customers and the refrigerated cabinets under the bar were stocked with glasses and bottles of beer.

"I need five minutes, Zeke," Farrell said.

"Tough shit. I need to get open."

"You help me, and I'll help you."

"Like you would do that for me."

"Maybe I have a reason."

Farrell walked into the afternoon sun. He moved to the magic spot with cell phone reception, and bullied his way past Pearl's interference.

"I need to get Zeke back in business at the Nowhere. I need him to answer some questions, but he's not interested without some motivation. Like getting open."

"Find out what he needs and call back. Your call will get routed. I know how to get money out of Zeke. He already owes me and I won't get paid unless he's open."

She hung up and Farrell went back in. Five minutes later he had a list pared back to what would get Zeke open without the wish list of items Zeke suddenly saw he couldn't live without. He made the call and was told it would be delivered in twenty four hours.

"Your turn, Zeke."

"I don't see no receipt."

Farrell waved his cell phone. "I can taketh away just as fast as I giveth."

Zeke looked around the empty room. Farrell wondered if he was envisioning it with fixtures and customers. "You really think tour buses will stop here?"

"Anything's possible. Tell me about Thatcher McPherson."

Thatch had shown up in the Nowhere somewhere between four weeks and four months ago. Farrell was quick to see that Zeke didn't do time, and decided to avoid the issue as much as possible. It had taken some sharp jabs to the memory to get Zeke to remember anything. When Tess entered the picture, Zeke's memory improved.

"Man, she was a fox. Always wore what showed what she had. Pretty nice, too. She asked me why I stayed high and I told her she should give it a try. She said she had and didn't like it. She had some bullshit reason, like it 'impaired her reasoning ability,' some shit like that. I told her that was the whole idea."

"How come you remember that?" Dewey asked, as he went behind the bar and opened the cooler where he'd seen the glasses. He took one out and filled it from the Mirror Pond tap.

"Leave the money on the bar," Zeke said.

"What did you and Thatch talk about?" Farrell asked.

"Beer. He liked beer, and working up in the hills is thirsty work."

"What was he doing?"

"Chasing color." Zeke snapped his fingers, although not loudly. "You know what? I think he found something."

"Why?"

"Who the hell do you think comes in here?" Zeke tried to roll a joint but his hands shook so hard he spilled more than found the paper. "I seen more color chasers than the average bear, and I know when they're feeling smug or toting a secret. Your buddy had found himself a patch of color."

"How long ago?" Farrell asked although he knew it would mean little with Zeke's sense of time, and took over the joint rolling.

Zeke shook his head. "I don't know. Awhile. Long enough for him to tell his sister."

"How'd she take it?"

"Not like I would have if my brother – if I had one – told me he'd struck it rich."

Farrell finished the rolling the joint.

133

"B22, Zeke," Farrell said, carrying it to the jukebox. He flipped through the song cards until he found B22. "Thatch wrote it in blood before he died."

"*Gold Dust Woman* by Fleetwood Mac. He had a thing about Stevie Nicks. Me too."

Farrell walked back to Zeke whose eyes had not left the joint.

"If my last act among the living was to scratch out a clue in my own blood," Farrell said, handing the joint to Zeke, "it wouldn't be Stevie Nicks. I'm pretty sure she didn't pull the trigger."

Zeke lit up. A brief flare as the paper ignited then settled into slow smoke. His closed his eyes as he drew on the joint.

"Ahh, Bingo, man!"

"Yeah, you're welcome."

"No, B22. Bingo."

Dewey put his shades on as he walked back into the glare of the afternoon sun that beat down on the Nowhere. He opened the door of the truck and found Thatch's book in his bag. After closing the door and laying a towel over the edge of the truck's fender to protect him from the metal's heat, he opened the book on the hood. He took out the map and stared at the grid.

He and Thatch had played Bingo when they were kids. It was always good for an argument in much the same way Monopoly or Parcheesi was. Unless Tess played. That was something else and Dewey didn't care if he won or not. He was too busy looking down her blouse or, if she wore a skirt, up it for a glimpse of underwear. He had felt guilty about it, but soon learned it was what preteen and teenage boys did, and he lost the guilt but still took pains to hide his lust from her. Later, he felt sure she knew because he caught that electrifying glimpse just often enough to keep him playing, but his mind off Bingo.

Dewey hadn't played since the last time with the McPherson's, but he was pretty sure standard Bingo cards did not have a B22. The B column only went to 15 and the number 22 fell below the I. Thatch and Tess hadn't always used standard Bingo cards. Tess, the smartest of the three, came up with a way to make the games more challenging. They all made a standard five by five grid with empty spaces and each column labeled across the top with the letters of Bingo. Then they made their own cards by writing a number between 1 and 75 in each box careful to avoid any repeats. Tess always made herself the caller because neither Thatch nor Dewey could be trusted not to be smart asses. In that version, B22 was very possible. Only Dewey would get the reference if he found something that could pass as a Bingo card with B22.

The other thing he had to do before the map made sense was to find the bigger map this hand drawn map in the book matched. With no names and no prominent features on Thatch's map Dewey didn't know where to start until he found it.

Thatch would have made plans for the Bingo card to be found, but Dewey doubted his friend had foreseen both he and Tess dying at the same time. If Thatch's contingency plan was to tell her then it would be of no help. Dewey drummed his fingers on the towel and remembered his friends. Tess had watched out for her brother, but as Dewey remembered Thatch hadn't confided in Tess. In Dewey's experience, those kinds of traits didn't change. The other thing was that Thatch had never been patient. The card would not be hidden where he had to go a long way to get it. Thatch was more of a Presto! kind of guy. He would want to wave a cape and there the card would appear as if from nowhere.

Nowhere!

Farrell walked back into the roadhouse. Zeke sat passed out in the heat, the roach smoldering on the floor at his feet. Dewey walked behind the bar and dropped to his knees. The refrigerated cabinets left a gap between their top and the bottom of the bar. Thatch could have reached over the bar and slipped his Bingo card in the slot ready to do his magic act at the perfect moment. Dewey put a hand in the space and it came out dusty. He went to the truck and got the flashlight from the road kit. Back in the bar, he shone it along the stainless steel tops of the cabinets. Near the middle of the bar he found an area with no dust. The space was about as wide as an arm wearing a shirt could fit. Dewey reached in. His fingers searched until he found a piece of stiff paper. He smiled as he pulled it out. The smile got a lot bigger as he saw the homemade Bingo card with a red 22 in the center box under the B.

He saluted Zeke as he left the roadhouse and thanked Thatch for not growing up. He would get a map from Cat and see if he could match it up.

In the parking lot he called Fulsom. "Where's Thunder Gap Road?"

After Fulsom told him, the sheriff said, "Go armed and don't take Ma'am's truck. That part of the county is sort of like sneaking over the wall into East Berlin, if there was still an East Berlin. Terrain is as rugged as any in Banner. Cliffs fall off under your feet, and canyons that end in boxes. You don't want to be there without someone who knows where they're going. If you're doing something you don't want anyone else to know about, it's perfect."

"Thanks for the tip. Tess McPherson interviewed some people named Northby and I'd like to know what they talked about."

"Good luck with the Northbys. Not real chatty folk up there."

Farrell drove to Cat's and pulled into the driveway. He went to the back door and knocked.

"It's open, and so's the bar," Cat yelled. "I was hoping I'd see you again today. I hate to drink alone."

"I'm not here to drink. Can I borrow the truck we drove home?"

"Too late. Junior dropped off mine and picked up his a couple of hours ago. To paraphrase the immortal Brian Wilson, 'Ma'am got wise to you and now you're thinking your fun is all through now?'"

Cat sat in a manual wheelchair with an open bottle of Jack Daniels within reach and a glass smudged from use.

"I've been advised," Dewey said, "not to drive a Banner truck up Thunder Gap Road."

"Good advice. Who you going to see?"

"The Northby's."

"Ah, and how is the lovely and perpetually horny Terra?"

"Friendly."

"Bless her heart. If I could walk again, and I would do anything to walk, I would walk to her front door like a real man and ring her bell. Why do you want directions?"

"Because I'm going there and don't want to get lost."

"What sends you off to visit her weed growing parents?"

"She sent Tess to see them. I'd love to know what they talked about."

Cat finished his drink and slapped his hands together.

"Alright, let's go. You're going to need some help with this."

"I'm not riding with you."

"Well, that's a fine pickle. Are you accusing me of inebriation?"

"Aren't you?"

"I am. Thanks for noticing. I'm still recovering from my brush with death. I guess I'll have to ride with you."

"That puts us in the Banner truck I'm not supposed to drive up there."

"An even finer pickle. Let me think," and he reached for the bottle.

Farrell got to it first and took it away. Cat tipped his empty glass back and mocked it being full.

"Oh, I've got it," he yelled with a hand in the air. "We'll put the portable pilot seat back in the Catmobile."

Farrell took a seat from the shed and bolted its frame to the floor behind the wheel. Cat's wheelchair took a position behind the driver and it, too, bolted to the floor. A few minutes later they were on the road. Cat called out the turns as the miles crept by. The first five were the same route they used for Gold Night, but a right turn took them away from the Salmon Jump River and into another arm of the hills that wound steadily up. As they climbed, the trees grew thinner as the Douglas firs gave way to scrub pine. The pine had been planted years ago as an experiment to grow faster trees to feed the pulp mills for newsprint. Dewey had left before he heard how the experiment turned out.

"That's it," Cat said, and he pointed to an unmarked road.

"You wouldn't have made it this far in the Banner truck," Cat said.

"You mean the lookouts?"

"You spotted them? That's pretty good."

"It's not like they're invisible. Are they always there?"

137

"No. After the last couple of nights folks are jumpy."

"So Tess wouldn't have had any problems getting here?"

"I guess she didn't. Slow down. The next right is a goat trail. There's a gate and it will be locked. Honk and someone will come down. Sooner or later."

They reached the gate and Farrell honked.

"How come you've been here before?" he asked Cat.

"Damn few places I haven't been if there's a road. I'm not too good on foot."

Farrell cranked the window down as the late afternoon sun got warmer.

"Ahoy in the truck!" came the call. "State your business!"

"My name is Farrell. Terra gave me instructions. I knew her in high school and I'm looking for information on Tess McPherson."

"That's Cat's truck, isn't it? He in there?" the man's voice asked.

"He is."

A couple of minutes went by then a man wearing overalls and an old fedora with a deep crease stepped out of the tall grass. He carried a sawed off shotgun rode over his shoulder. He unlocked the gate and pushed it open, then waved for them to follow him up the ruts that led over the crest of a hill. For a moment the man stood etched against the backdrop of blue sky before he started down the far side followed by Farrell and Cat. Overhead a Cooper's Hawk circled in search of prey.

When they reached the top Farrell saw a hillside of tall trees spaced far enough apart to allow sunlight to reach the floor. In the sunny patches grew tall plants with spiked leaves. Further down the hill, buildings painted green nestled inside the tree line of a dense stand of firs. He counted seven buildings including three glass greenhouses and a brick, bunker-like building with a metal roof taller than the others, and double doors high enough and wide enough to drive a medium sized truck through.

"Welcome to the sweetest pot farm in many a mile," Cat said. "These dudes know what they're doing."

Their guide pointed to a place to park. When Farrell got out the man had the shotgun in his hands.

"Leave Turner in the truck," he said, in a gruff voice. "State your business."

"My name is Dewey Farrell. I was a friend of Tess McPherson and her brother. I lived with them for a while when I was in high school. Thatch called me the day before he died and told me to meet him at the Nowhere, but I was too late. The least I can do is find who killed them. I'm here because Terra said Tess came to see you."

"How do you know our girl?" the man asked.

"I ate breakfast at the Tree Topper this morning. She recognized me and we talked. She liked Tess, and thought it might help me find why anyone would kill her if I talked to you."

The man stared hard at Farrell out of remarkably blue eyes set above a thin nose and a ten day beard. A Grateful Dead tee shirt poked around the edges of the coveralls.

"Midge!" the man called. "Man here says he was a friend of Tessie's."

A woman wearing a granny skirt and a tank top that exposed deeply tanned arms, and minimally contained deep set breasts that hadn't known a bra in decades stood on a porch. She sized Farrell up then waved to draw him in.

"Cat Turner's in the truck," the man called.

The woman considered the news. "He can come, too."

Farrell opened the side door of the RV and activated the lift that got Cat to the ground.

"What the hell is going on?" Cat complained. "I've been here before. They know me."

Farrell pushed Cat across the bumpy ground until he reached the porch. The woman stepped forward and extended a hand.

"I'm not sure if you're welcome, Mr. Farrell, but I'm Midge Northby. You've met my husband, Richard. I can offer you homemade blackberry wine."

"Yes, please," said Cat, with a smile.

Richard shook his head, then said, "Let's serve them and find out what brings them here."

They sat on the covered veranda around a farm table with raised wings. Farrell tasted his berry wine, not a favorite, but he knew what was expected of a guest. He was surprised at the full flavor and smoothness of the beverage.

"That's wonderful," he said, "thank you. I was a friend of the McPhersons." He told his story.

"So you're the guy Pearl told to leave and never come back, eh?" Midge said, looking at him. "I didn't know whether that story was true or not."

Farrell stared at her. "Tess told you that story?"

"Tess didn't. That's a pretty well-known part of the legend."

Farrell looked at Cat who was busy rolling his empty glass between the palms of his hands.

"You didn't mention anything about a legend," Farrell said to him.

"Got nothing to do with me," Cat said.

"Can we start at the beginning, please?" Farrell asked, looking at Midge.

"I thought we were," she said.

"How about when Tess came to see you. What did you talk about?"

Richard Northby held up his hand. "That, sir, is none of your business."

"Well, I think it is," Farrell said. "Banner County has been populated for more than a hundred and fifty years, so what makes this moment special enough to start all this violence? What does it take to motivate an anthropologist to get sucked in far enough to cost her life? You knew her well enough to call her Tessie, so help me out here.

When no one said anything, Farrell said, "Folks, I'm not here to pry into your private business. When I was thirteen my dad died in a forest fire and I lived with the McPhersons. I had a crush on Tess. My knees got weak when she was in the same room, and that was a lot. After she went off to college I got over it, but she was special. That's my personal business, but I'm not asking for anything like that from you. I need to know what took Tess to the Middle of Nowhere that could get her killed. I know she was writing a book and Pearl Banner approved, but that doesn't seem like enough to shoot anyone over."

"Maybe she was just unlucky," Midge said, "you know, wrong place and all."

"Nope," Farrell said, "she was with the target group meaning she was part of the reason for all the killing. So if it's not the book, what is it?"

The Northbys exchanged looks, then Richard waved at his wife to go on.

"She came by to hear our stories," Midge said, then looked to her husband. "Remember how she looked when she got here?"

Richard snorted, "I do. She told us we were exactly what she was looking for and that was before you two recognized each other."

"Recognized from where?" Farrell asked.

"She went to Stanford at the same time I was at UC Berkeley. We were both PhD candidates and even though hers would be in cultural and forensic anthropology, and mine in botany we saw each other from time to time. She didn't recognize my married name."

"So your daughter arranged it?"

"Yes. Terra called and asked if it was alright to give her directions," Midge replied.

"What kind of stories did she want?"

"Local myths and legends. She was attempting to substantiate some wild ideas."

"How wild?"

"Depends on the listener," Richard said. "You might find something hard to believe that Turner there never doubts for a second."

"For instance?"

"She thought there was something in the air or the water," Midge said. "Something that made her feel better than when she was anywhere else. You buy that?"

"The Banner Effect," Farrell said. "It's the same for me. Did you tell her anything that would lead her to the Nowhere?"

Farrell saw the looks the Northbys shared.

"I can use some help," he said, "if I'm going to get closer to who shot her and the others."

Midge waved him to patience.

"It's a long story. We've lived here for over thirty years. We moved here from Berkeley to find a better life and never looked back."

"What did you do there?" Dewey asked.

"After I got my degree, I worked for the university where I met Rich. A botanist and an edaphologist fit pretty well."

"I know what a botanist is, sort of, but what's an edaphologist?" Farrell struggled with the word.

"Specifically, an edaphologist studies soil influences on organisms and plants. Generally speaking, it's the study of soil."

"Then Tess's wild idea about feeling better here should have hit a nerve with you two," Farrell said.

"Oh, it did, believe me," Richard said. "What you call the Banner Effect, we call Living Up. It only happens to certain people. We're trying to discover why, and who gets chosen. It happens to you?"

"Yes. This is the first time I've been back, and I haven't had much sleep but I'm not tired. I've had a few injuries, too, and they healed fast."

"What kind of injuries?"

"Superficial. Scrapes and burns. They healed almost overnight."

"Can I see?" Richard Northby asked, leaning forward.

"There isn't much to see," Farrell said, but showed them where the scrapes, now healed, had been. The burns were healed, too, but his hair still had holes from the embers. Evidently skin healed faster than hair grew. He mentioned that and both Northbys nodded as if that was an important detail.

"Were you born in the hills or in Pazer?" Midge asked.

"Who were your parents?" Richard asked, almost simultaneously.

"This is supposed to be you helping me with Tess," Farrell said.

"We will," Midge said, scooting her chair closer. "This is very important."

"My father was born in Montana. I don't know anything about my mother." The Northbys rocked back in their chairs. "My father said she died when I was born, but I don't believe it."

"Why not?" Midge asked.

"I remember visiting the Cloud with my father when I was maybe four or five."

"You said six last time," Cat said, interrupting.

"No, I think I was younger. I remember a woman holding me and crying. It makes me sad when I think of it."

"You must not have thought of her often if you don't remember how old you were," said Richard.

"I didn't think of her or the Cloud at all until I came back. I've been here less than three days and I'm remembering."

"What did she look like?" Midge asked. Farrell felt Cat's eyes on him.

"I don't know. I see her with a hood and cloak, but isn't that what everyone wears in the Cloud?"

"We don't go in the Cloud," Midge said. "Cat does."

"Pretty common outfit," Cat said.

"Did Tessie know about your mother?" Midge asked.

"Of course she did when we were kids. I don't think there was much she didn't know, at least until she went off to college when I was sixteen."

"Did she know about you Living Up?" Richard asked.

"I didn't know about that until it was too late for Tess."

"Why'd you leave?" Richard asked.

"We know the answer to that one," Midge said, "Pearl threw him out."

"How about we forget about me and get back to Tess," Farrell said.

While Midge resettled herself Farrell noticed daylight fading, and with the dusk came the bugs. He slapped at an unprotected arm.

"Let's start with Simone de Beauvoir," said Midge. "She said tribes from hill countries are more warlike than those from the plains. Isolated hill tribes followed a shoot first and ask questions later approach to strangers. Tess started her research there. She had also read everything de Beauvoir had written on feminism and sociology."

"Why the feminism?" Farrell asked.

143

"Because all the power groups here are matriarchies, and apparently, always have been. Pearl, and before her Eleanora, to name a couple, and they leap-frogged the generation that had only male heirs. Even the Turners have their strong women. What's her name, Cat?"

"What was that?" he stalled.

"You heard me," Midge accused. "What do you call her?"

Cat rocked back and forth on his wheels, but said nothing.

"Cat, come on," Farrell said.

"Okay, okay. We call her Mother."

"Is that a name or a title?" Midge asked.

"Both, I guess," Cat said, and stopped the rocking since there was no way out of his spot. "The title gets handed down from generation to generation."

"What's her role?" Farrell asked.

"How about we get back to Tess! I can't discuss this. You aren't Turners!"

"But definitely a matriarchy, right?" Midge asked.

"Definitely. Men have other things to do. Now get back to Tess. I didn't push on your secrets, and from the looks of things you have secrets."

Richard tensed and leaned forward.

"Is that a threat?"

"No! What am I going to do? Make a run for it?"

Midge took the jug with the homemade wine and poured for everyone. When she finished, she said, "Tess told us functioning matriarchies were rare. She had gone to Pearl to get permission to use the family records which are the only meaningful local history unless the Turners have records and if they do, they aren't sharing. Tessie wanted to know if it was coincidence. She was pretty sure it wasn't. She said she knew there was a design here that was rigorously adhered to."

"She say what or how she knew?" Farrell asked.

Midge laughed and looked inward to what Farrell was sure was a moment spent with Tess, then the moment was gone. She then looked at her husband.

"She was under no obligation to tell us anything. I assume she told us no more than she thought necessary."

Richard picked up his shotgun and stood. "This is a farm and we have evening chores to do."

Farrell wasn't done, but he knew when he'd been dismissed. He thanked the Northby's for their hospitality.

"You get any help?" Midge asked, after Farrell had Cat inside the RV.

Farrell shrugged. "I have the feeling there's help here to be had, but I haven't heard it yet."

"Come back soon," Midge said, "but don't bring him."

He saw her standing on the porch staring after them as he drove away.

"They lied to us," Farrell said, from the driver's make shift seat as they journeyed through the falling dusk on the way back to Cat's. The heat of the day filled the RV and sweat ran down his sides. "Pretty much the whole thing was a lie. Any ideas why'd they do that?"

"They don't exactly confide in me," Cat said.

"I noticed. I thought the Grand Poobah had a free pass everywhere in the hills."

"Not everywhere."

"Why not at the Northbys?"

"Things have changed. The Nowhere put everybody on psycho alert."

"So why would the Northbys think you were a psycho?"

Cat ignored the phrasing, and said, "Not everyone in Banner is a Turner or works for your girlfriend. There are third party interests like the Northbys. Back in the day if you weren't one or the other or you couldn't survive in the hills. The Turners and Banners are now less like the Hatfields and the McCoys, and more like the Democrats and the Republicans. Lot of arguing but not much gunfire. That makes the Northbys independents with their own agenda."

The road twisted down the shoulder toward the valley where it would eventually drop them a mile east of the Nowhere. Farrell wished Zeke were open because a cold beer sounded good.

"I don't feel like the Grand Poobah anymore," Cat said. "There's a power shift and I don't know where it's going."

"I thought you guys held all the cards," Farrell said.

"Me, too. We had what everyone wants - at least where the gold is involved. We are the bank, at least metaphorically speaking, and power always follows the money. So, if it ain't us, who?"

"We have a ways to go," Farrell said, pointing at the road, "run it down for me. Start at the beginning."

"It's not hard because nothing's changed for a hundred years, allowing for some give and take."

Cat told Dewey his version of the history of Banner County.

"Politics in Banner are still being driven by the company owning everything," Cat said as he wrapped it up. "What I do know is that Pearl needs cash, and if she has a Plan B I don't know what it is. She doesn't have many options. She could sell a mill, but that would send a dangerous message to her customers and competitors."

"So take a guess about Plan B."

"Ask her."

On cue his phone rang. He pulled over and answered.

"You must be near the Nowhere," Pearl said.

"Yeah, just drove by."

"Would you meet me there in twenty minutes?" she asked. "Please? We have a trip to make and I'll drive."

"I'll see you in a few."

Dewey declined to give Cat details. He told Cat to listen to his tapes of the private conversation.

"Grumpy are we?"

Farrell slowed the truck as he made the turn into Cat's driveway. At the top he turned off the ignition and sat with his hands on the wheel.

"What am I doing here?" he asked, unsure if it were rhetorical, or if he was asking Cat or himself.

"Looking for revenge, that's pretty clear," Cat answered.

"What do I do if I find it? Start shooting people?"

"You're off to a good start. Three in two nights."

"That's exactly how many people I shot in the last ten years as a police officer."

"Too bad. You appear to have a knack for it."

Farrell got out and helped Cat into the house.

"You do know it isn't up to you, don't you?" Cat said. "If you stay, people are going to shoot at you. If you get the chance, you'll shoot back. I guess you could leave, but we've talked about that. You won't."

Farrell leaned over the sink and drank from the tap.

"You said you have an arsenal in the garage? What?"

"A couple of M-16's, six or seven 9mm Glocks, some explosives, and lots of rounds for the above."

"I use a .45. Rounds for it?"

"Enough to keep even you locked and loaded. Got some speed loaders, too."

"I'll lock the door on my way out."

"Say hi for me. Invite her to dinner. You could cook. It'd be a first."

The Nowhere's sign was off and the night was dark. He walked by the light of the stars and thought about Banner County. The violence and audacity of the crimes committed in the last two days meant the stakes possessed great value. In Banner with the tree market down, that meant weed and gold. Like Cat said, Pearl didn't have many choices. Farrell doubted she would sell a mill. It was tantamount to resigning from part of the business her family pioneered. It had to be gold and marijuana. As a working hypothesis that had serious drawbacks. Gold had been mined in these hills for over a hundred years, and even with the historic high cost per ounce he didn't see it as enough to bail her out. Had somebody found the colloquial mother lode? Had Thatch? It sounded like the stuff dreams were made of, not gang-style massacres and shoot ups. And whomever the bad guys were, they had money to support a significant payroll of men willing to die. Mercenaries didn't grow on trees. Where did someone go to recruit men like that? He had no idea.

Her S-class Mercedes sat in the middle of the parking lot. As he got closer he saw her leaning against the front quarter panel, her ankles crossed and her arms folded beneath her breasts.

"Sort of a James Dean pose," Farrell said.

She didn't move until he stopped five feet in front of her.

"I'm tired, Dewey."

"What's up, Early?"

She shook her head. "No one's called me that since you left town."

"Would you be happy if they did?"

She sighed. "No, it wouldn't be appropriate."

"I guess you're stuck with me."

She unfolded her arms and opened them to him. He stepped into her. The kiss lasted a long time and grew in urgency as more of their bodies pressed together. The kiss ended, but they held each other.

"So what's going on, besides the obvious?" he asked.

"Elsie said you both talked."

"We did," he said, rubbing her back and liking her head against his shoulder. His heart beat so quickly he thought he might faint. He held her tighter. "She told me the world's about to change."

"That's a little melodramatic but fair," she said.

"I've been away so fill me in."

"Give me a second to enjoy being held."

He looked down and reached for her chin. He tilted it up and kissed her again. He tried to think what he was doing and couldn't. A disconnect blocked rational thought and his body just held on. He sensed something of the same from her.

"Why changes now?" he managed to ask.

She softly pushed him away but still held on to his hand.

"I'm tired, but I'm scared, too."

"Of?"

"You. You weren't supposed to find the Northby's for days and that would be enough time for me to have a story ready. All I have now is the truth."

"Go on," he said, still holding her hand. He sensed her message was what frightened her.

"The recession has hurt. I've lost a lot of money. Really the company has been losing money for years, but the last five years has been a flood of loses. To make it worse, I have the State ready to break through the years of being kept out. Nobody is a better steward of their land than we are. This is all we have. We don't take care of it we're out of business. But our way is not the State's way. They will want to look at everything."

She dropped his hand and waved him into her car. When they were moving quietly through the dark, she said, "I've been looking for the next wood products miracle for years, but I don't see it. This business has not moved into the twenty-first century. Markets are not growing. To win market share, it's all about price, and I am suffering from a poor business model. There are much larger competitors closer to more lucrative markets and they're leaving me behind."

She turned on to the same road Farrell had taken a few hours earlier.

"How have you lasted this long?" Farrell asked.

"Banner Timber Products is the ultimate company town. We're the company county. I am a dictator, a benevolent one I hope. My people cut the trees, they delimb them, haul them, and process them into one of our core products. I can't lay people off because unemployment is still my responsibility and I don't believe in paying people to stay home. This is the downside of Eleanora's deal with the state. I pay for everything whether business is good or not. Times like now, though, a little help would be welcome."

"Maybe you should welcome the State and make them help."

"After you're here a little longer, you'll see why I can't do that." She drove at a pace that let her talk and keep control. "I have a problem with the Chinese right now. They love Banner County Douglas Fir. They say it has properties the same trees grown elsewhere don't. They want me to export logs. I've said no. It doesn't employ enough of my people, but they are insistent. People are going to want to know why I keep saying no unless I can find a way to get the cash flowing again."

"So what's so great about home grown Doug fir?"

THE WEIGHT OF THE JOURNEY BY KEN BYERS

She drove for a minute before saying, "Let me put the answer off for a few minutes. It ties into what you'll see at the Northbys."

"Plan B," he said.

She hesitated, but finally said, "Yes. It's fair to call it that."

Two minutes later she turned into the Northby's rutted driveway. She stopped lower on the hill than Dewey had in Cat's truck. She turned off the ignition and the headlights. They sat in the near dark of the star-filled sky until a flashlight came over the hill. Moments later Richard opened her door for her.

Pearl and Farrell stood with the Northbys in the middle of an extensive greenhouse set deep in the trees. They had walked a subtly lit path from the house into the forest to the greenhouse. Farrell wondered about the efficacy of the glass-enclosed buildings given the dense canopy hiding the greenhouses from aerial reconnaissance. Inside, the air was heavy with moisture, and plants with deep green spiked leaves grew more than seven feet high. Raised beds sat in neatly delineated rows with each pot labeled. He saw weapons stashed along the aisles. Just because the plants weren't in the forest, didn't mean they weren't valuable.

"The tobacco companies have been manipulating nicotine in cigarettes for years," Midge Northby said, "so why not manipulate THC? Richard identified differences in soil from different parts of the county and I studied the effects the soil composition had on what was grown in it."

""You could do that?" Farrell asked. "A botanist and whatever you said you are, Richard?"

"We are ideal. Her other degree is in organic chemistry and I have a lot of time in the field, which, in my case, is as important as time in the lab."

"What's happening with the soil trans-positioning?" Pearl asked.

Richard led them to a row of plants less robust than those on either side.

"Results support the theory," he said, his face alight with a scientific fervor.

"If the quality of Banner-grown anything – Douglas Fir or marijuana – is in the soil," Pearl said to Dewey, "what happens if someone drives a dump truck in and hauls it off? Will they be able to match our quality? Is the secret just the soil, or does it go deeper? That's why we're all here."

Midge and Richard beamed at Dewey like he was the answer to all their dreams.

"So what's the theory?" Dewey asked.

"Heat," the Northbys said, in unison. "Lots of heat."

"Under our feet, way under our feet," Richard said, and the college professor side of him stepped to a figurative lectern, "is the most geological active zone known to science – a triple tectonic plate junction."

"Not exactly known," said Midge, "more like suspected."

"Alright, suspected. We are on the North American tectonic plate – we *know* that – and it is being sub-ducted by the Juan de Fuca plate which is sandwiched between the Pacific plate which is diving under them both. All this plate movement happens on both sides of the Cascadia fault line, about hundred miles west of here out in the ocean. All this friction creates vast amounts of heat. And there is one hell of a lot of friction. The Juan de Fuca acts like a shim steadying the other two. That's why there aren't many small quakes along the Oregon coast. When there is an earthquake, it's a beaut. All this heat needs to reach the surface is a fissure. Welcome to Banner County. The Cloud is the proof. Heat and moisture creates fog. Because the fog stays pretty much the same, there has to be a uniform source of heat. *Viola!*"

"The heat filters up through layers of crust in the form of gases, then leaves deposits as it dissipates when it reaches the surface," Midge said. "We think there are vents like furnace ducts that carry the gas and heat through the whole area. It's these mysterious gases that brings us back to manipulating nicotine, or in this case THC – tetrahydrocannabinol – the active ingredient in the cannabis plant, better known as marijuana. The chemistry here is solid, if rudimentary. THC acts on the receptors in the central nervous system with a long list of effects. There are reasons to think that THC, in one form or another, has potential in fighting some forms of dementia, like Alzheimer's, and PTSD, plus some forms of

THE WEIGHT OF THE JOURNEY BY KEN BYERS

cancer. That's just a little disease name dropping." She stepped forward and touched Dewey's arm as if she feared he might be wandering under the assault of all her words. "Here's the really good part. All I just told you is based on research from conventional and synthetic THC. Cannabis grown here, in Banner County, and specifically within a hundred yards of this building, has a purer, more reactive, form of THC than anything under research elsewhere."

Farrell walked down one aisle and back on another looking at the plants in their organized beds with their legible tags and laminated sheets attached to clipboards hanging as if on the end of hospital beds. Even to him there were noticeable differences in the plants. He'd never worked Narcotics but he'd seen his share of weed grown in backyards and basements under banks of grow lights, but he'd never seen anything like the size and weight of the leaves protruding from these beds. Even without the potential of legitimate pharmaceutical applications, the illicit street value of the plants was in the hundreds of thousands.

"What happens if you just roll one of your own and light it up with this super weed?" he asked.

"Cannabis and its derivatives have never killed anyone," Midge said, "but you'll get a closer look at the cosmos than you've seen before."

"If you're lucky," Richard injected. "If you aren't it can make you sick to your stomach, or so lightheaded you can't stand. In some cases you just lie down and wake up a day later."

"Or you'll be so hungry you binge on anything at hand," Midge said. "That was where the medical marijuana movement started. Weed controlled nausea, and built appetites in chronically ill patients like AIDS victims. Then they found pain management qualities and wanted to know why. Next stop the central nervous system and its receptors."

"Pearl, who knows about this?" Dewey asked.

"Tess did," she answered. "The book was a cover. She was an outstanding researcher not only in anthropology, but in the related fields like history and forensics. Forensics became important when we decided we needed to know what the Turners have been eating for the last one hundred years. She'd been unearthing old graves and doing bone scans to determine how the composition of the Cloud affects people who live there. We made some concessions to the Turners to get access to the bodies."

"What kind of concessions?" Farrell asked.

"They control life in the Cloud, but down here with the rest of us, they have limitations. I made sure they could get to services they need without having to sneak around. That's worth a lot because they're having medical problems."

"What kind of medical problems?"

"The fourth and fifth generations of Turners inside the Cloud are being born, and the rate of problem infants is alarming. They can't exactly go to a hospital in Medford or Eugene, or especially to San Francisco without questions no one wants to answer. I'm helping bring people who can both help and keep quiet to Pazer."

"And Tess was sitting in on the diagnoses as part of her project," Richard said. Dewey saw Pearl's displeasure with his comment.

"Yes, she was," she said, testily, "but the health of the Turners always came first."

"Motivation aside," Midge said, "we know nothing about what happens in the Cloud. We suspect there is far more we don't know that would help if we could pursue the missing information."

"What makes you think so?" Dewey asked.

"Cannabis grown higher up the hill is stronger - no, make that different in lots of ways - than the same plant grown lower. The soil conditions are more dramatic the further up you go."

"I think," Richard said, "there is a giant fissure somewhere near the surface. It's probably close to the top and acts like a master vent. There is more gas than can escape so it looks for vents in the porous soil."

"How much gas are we talking here?" Dewey asked.

"No one knows," Midge said, "but it can't be too much. Keep in mind that however much there is gets absorbed before it gets off the hill. And it seems to be constant maybe for millions of years, or at least since the last major seismic event in this area which was a very long time ago."

Farrell threw up his hands.

"I surrender! I'm just an old cop with a bachelor's degree that doesn't help me a bit with this stuff."

"Oh, I'm afraid, Mr. Farrell, you are far more than that," Midge said. "You are exactly what we're looking for."

"What are you talking about?"

"All the Turners we've been studying have spent their lives here. We need one who hasn't."

Farrell saw Pearl Banner open her mouth and reach for Midge. He was still looking at Pearl when Midge Northby said, "You are that Turner!"

"Midge!" Pearl said loudly.

"What? Just a minute. Mr. Farrell, you're not just a Turner, you're ~ "

"Midge, shut up!" Pearl commanded.

" ~ you're Sophie's son."

Farrell looked to Pearl, who did not look back, so he asked Midge. "Who's Sophie?"

"Midge!" Pearl said again, moving toward the woman.

"Doesn't he know who he is?" Midge answered. "How is that possible? Everyone knows who they are. Sophie is the head of the Turners. The one they call Mother."

"What? That's bullshit. I know who I am. What's wrong with you people? You're all caught up in this Bannerland mumbo jumbo that reads like a Grimm's fairy tale!"

"I'm afraid," Midge said, ignoring attempts to shut her down, "that you are the one who is living a fairy tale, or at least a lie. There is no doubt as to your identity."

"Midge, shut up!" Pearl yelled, but by now Farrell had started for the door. He almost ran up the trail. He paced beside the car waiting for Pearl and refused to talk to her on the ride back. She tried twice, both times starting with "I'm sorry," then gave up. He got out of the car at the Nowhere without a word. He ran through the dark to Cat's. When he got there he found Cat with his head on the table next to the depleted bottle of Jack Daniels.

"Who is Sophie?" he asked, taking the bottle off the table and taking a drink without bothering with a glass.

Cat's Story of Eddie and Sophie

"Eddie Farrell, your father, was a child of the forest. His flowing gold hair and lithe body made him more of a sylph than a gnome, but there was no disguising his gender, and in his world if he was male he was a gnome. His destiny was to meet a sylph.

"Eddie was the son of Carl and Edith Farrell. They were from Montana and moved to Oregon to work for the United States Forest Service. They lived in a USFS ranger cottage on the outskirts of Merlin, but Eddie spent much of his time at a hut where the national forest met the Bannerland border. His parents were an independent couple who believed there was little reason to send their obviously very intelligent son to Grants Pass for a public education when they and the forest were capable of teaching him all he needed. Eddie could never be said to have had a classical education, but he knew how to read and write well enough, and there was little he didn't know about his father's part of the forest.

"His home studies put a pencil in his hand with paper in front of him often enough for mother and father to discover their son had a talent for drawing. He had a natural smoothness of line, and an eye for contour and color. He began to carry his sketch book into the forest and he filled one book after another with drawings that befitted the experience he earned. When he was fourteen he added water color to his charcoal and lead skills.

"He first saw Sophie before he began his water-color period. He had dabbled with water color before and no longer considered himself a novice, but he was hesitant to draw her and use a method he considered less than his best. In the end, it was the frustration of leaving her colorless on the page that forced him to the change. His first dozen attempts, there were many more he didn't count, fell short. On what he claimed to be the "lucky thirteenth" he got it right. It's the drawing of your mother that still hangs in the Cloud.

"Sophie, this mythical creature, and Eddie, her commonland outsider, as those neither Banner nor Turner were called, fell in love. It was one of

155

those loves that swamps reason. He was then fifteen. Sophie's age was unclear. Older, but by how much is unknown. She's been asked, but she never tells. Eddie was good with pencil and paper. He drew many pictures of Sophie. Some were good. He taught you the basics, and you learned to become even better at the art than he had.

"It's hard to tell this story and not make it sound like a fairy tale where the beautiful maiden and the fair prince fall in love only to run afoul of their respective worlds, but that's our story. For the first two years, no one saw them together. No real surprise because they only met deep in the trees. Their spot was a long way from anywhere. He had to walk or ride three or four miles from the hut to get to the place where they first met and it was even further for Sophie. What the spot had was a wondrous waterfall with a cave behind it. They made the cave their home, furnishing it with items they made out of what they found in the woods. He was good with wood, and she was better.

"Keep in mind much of this is legend. No one knows where this waterfall with a cave is. Sophie can still disappear whenever she wants for as long as she wants and no one can find her.

"They, Eddie and Sophie, knew they were playing a dangerous game, but they were careful. But as it always does, something happens and careful goes out the window. Sophie got pregnant. At first she thought she could manage it on her own, but that hope didn't last.

"They did have a kind of plan for the baby. Eddie would take it home as a foundling, but that would have been difficult especially as it turned out the boy looked so much like him. Sophie couldn't see how she could take the child back to the Cloud because her people would want to know who the father was. When it came out it was Eddie, both he and the child would be in danger for loving a Turner woman, and not just any Turner woman, if there is such a creature, but the Turner woman. Sophie would be the next Mother. That's Mother with a capital M.

"The power with the Turners always passed through the women beginning with Jessica, she who got pregnant herself at the loins of Frederick, or so the story goes. But it wasn't the wounded pride of her husband Jacob that led the Turners into the wilderness, it was Jessica. She chose the place to pitch their tents and decided how they would survive inside the Cloud. The Turner women aren't like everyone else. They have a different way of seeing things. One told me it's because they see more. I asked her to explain, but she said how do you describe sight to the blind. It might have been bullshit, you know, like the emperor's new clothes, but I've always chosen to go with it.

"Jessica knew when the second Mother was born. She told the elders she knew it with the first breath the baby girl drew outside the womb. Sophie was chosen the same way for her stint as the third Mother.

"That was part of the problem with her getting pregnant off the mountain. It had been decided when she did have a child it would be a girl, not to be the next Mother after Sophie, but the line needed a girl. Don't ask me why. I don't understand any of the Turner genealogical babble.

"The more immediate problem for the lovers was Sophie began to have a difficult pregnancy. She had started to show, she was in a world of hurt in the Cloud, and she wasn't talking. Things were bad when she managed to sneak away and reach the cave where she waited for Eddie. After he saw what was happening with her – what exactly is anyone's guess – he took her all the way to Merlin and his parents.

"Two gigantic armloads of credit go to Carl and Edith. They got it immediately there was trouble they didn't understand, and despite the mystery, they didn't waste any time. Carl knew all the locals, and because he was the one that issued national forest hunting tags, everyone knew him. He talked a doctor into coming to the cottage to care for Sophie and keep the patient off the books. Sophie spent the time leading to her delivery with them.

"The medical issues never came to light. The doctor's identity died with Carl and Edith a few years later when a log truck lost its brakes and wiped out their jeep on a mountain road.

"You spent the first year with your grandparents and father. The Turners circulated a story that managed to get off the mountain that Sophie had died, and after Carl and Edith really did die, there was no one to question it. It's not like the outside world had ever heard of her. Your father took you to see her a few times, but that's where the story ends. You think you're an orphan when Eddie dies in the fire, Pearl kicks your ass out, and as far as anyone around here knows, you aren't coming back."

The Fire

Parts of the forest in the fire's path had been clear cut at some time in the past. Clear cuts from decades ago had new growth that was easy prey to the flames, and the slash left behind by the loggers had long ago turned to tinder. It exploded when the fire ignited it. More recent clear cuts were less explosive, but still perfect fodder. The ground was so dry from the unusually long hot summer that the fire spread in the undergrowth minutes before it ignited the brush above ground. This is a fire phenomenon that requires creviced and cracked surfaces to catch windblown organics covered over by debris that lie in wait for the magic moment when they will explode into flame.

Experienced firefighters will tell you the most terrifying part of a forest fire is the noise. Imagine the cozy snap and pop of the winter blaze in your fireplace, and multiply it by thousands. When the wind is right, or wrong depending on your point of view, the noise is heard before the smoke is smelled or the flames seen. This happens in rough terrain that distorts and blocks sight and sound, terrain exactly like that found in the mountains where the Siskiyou-Banner Complex fire now burned and continued accelerating out of control.

Dewey Farrell

Eighty-four hours ago, as Dewey Farrell carried his fishing gear into the condo, he knew exactly who he was. He wasn't thrilled with the information, but there was no doubt. Thatch's call awoke his past, but there were no alarms, no foreshadowing of doom, and no thoughts of disaster crossed his mind. That all changed with Tess and Thatch dead on the floor of the Nowhere.

Farrell sat in Cat's driveway on a chair carried from the kitchen. His host had dropped his head to the table when he finished the story of Eddie and Sophie and refused to stir. Dewey looked at the stars and tried to empty his head. He mentally hovered over Tess, seeing her bloodied body, and wondered what brought her to this end. He wanted to know what had happened to her in the missing years. He wanted to know who killed them. Seventy-five hours ago that was the most important thing in his world.

Seventy-three hours ago he'd entered Pearl's home and threw open the door he'd slammed on his past. She instantly became an irresistible force in his life despite his vow never to return. Three hours ago his world suffered a direct hit. Everyone knew more about him than he did, and they were scraping the cornerstones of his existence.

Time for a change.

He had come here to help Thatch find his pot of gold and that was what Farrell was going to do. It had been the purpose in the beginning and would become so again. He had the bingo card and a clue he didn't have an hour ago. He knew there was a waterfall with a cave behind it and that it was only three or four miles into Banner County. That would fit with where B22 had to be.

It was time to catch that bus Fulsom had first told him to take.

Johann Prus

"Sir? There is communication from America in one minute."

Prus nodded at his executive assistant as he returned from the medical suite one floor down. His physician had reported on the latest scans and tests.

"There are still no tumors, no cysts, no growths on any organs to explain your symptoms," his private doctor said.

"Other than what you've told me for the last ten years," Prus said.

"Yes. You are not strong inside or out. If you had been born with a warranty you would have been returned," the doctor said with a straight face. They had had this exchange before. It depressed Prus and made the doctor nervous. It's never good to tell your only patient there is little that can be done.

Prus dropped into the chair behind his desk and picked up the blue cell phone. It was far too large to be stylish but it was secure with an encryption devise.

He was out of patience and running out of time with his plans for Banner County. He had found no weakness in Pearl Banner's shell. Yes, she had cash flow problems and her market position was eroding, but if she had sizeable gold reserves she could ride out the recession with no thought of selling it all.

Banner County now obsessed him. What was this cloud that hung over the center of the land? He'd been told it was a naturally occurring phenomenon because there was no technology that could produce what was there for all to see. Why were the trees bigger, the wood more sought after, the marijuana more potent? Why did some people live longer? Why did others enjoy robust health when they'd had none before? So many questions and no answers.

The phone finally buzzed.

"The event was successful," he heard.

"Details."

"Both the woman and the competitor are dead. We have the woman's computer. We do not have her paper files, but there are people on the ground who will continue to look. We have another event scheduled for tomorrow night."

"I want the computer brought to me immediately."

"We will land in San Francisco in thirty minutes. I will send the plane on with it."

"You flew in? Was that wise?"

"It was safe. There is a large forest fire in the region with a lot of air traffic."

"How close is the fire?"

"Thirty miles and predicted to get closer."

Prus looked out the window across the city to the sea where sunlight dappled the surface and gave it a brittle look. "It is a pity about the woman. She could have been a great help."

"Yes, sir."

"Make sure the plane leaves immediately with the computer."

He would go through Tess McPherson's research carefully. He had to know what conclusions she had reached. He was sure there were test fields and a research facility that must be protected at all cost if the fire became a threat. He would keep a watch. The fire could prove to be an ally, or it could threaten his dreams.

His hostile takeover had begun. It felt good to be in action although his chosen course spoke to his desperation. He felt like a dying man turning to voodoo, but even voodoo had more going for it than rumors and undocumented anecdotes of a fountain of youth. It would take twenty hours for the plane to arrive. The time would pass slowly.

Dewey Farrell

He got off the bus in Grants Pass a little after ten in the morning. He asked directions then walked two blocks to the Enterprise Rent A Car office. They didn't have what he wanted, but they sent him to a local guy that rented all kinds of off-road vehicles. His inventory didn't include what Farrell wanted, but his son did. Since dad had bought the Jeep, the son didn't have much to say about it beyond please bring it back in one piece because he loved that thing. It was a lemon yellow Jeep Wrangler with padded roll bars, glass pack exhausts, and a stereo with wrap around speakers. The canvas top was not to be found, but Dewey didn't care. It was guaranteed to go anywhere.

Before he left town he went to a sporting goods store and used a hefty portion of his available plastic balance to stock up on provisions. His last stop was Safeway for protein bars, bottled water, and food basics in case he had to fend for himself longer than he intended.

On the outskirts of Grants Pass he pulled the Wrangler to the side of Highway 199 and called Fulsom.

"Word has it you were on the bus this morning with your tail between your legs" the sheriff said.

"Some truth in that. I was on the bus. Now I'm not."

"Where are you?"

"Headed back, but let's keep that between us. Here's what I know. Tess is the missing piece. She was doing something for Ma'am that got her high in the sights of somebody, and they took her out."

"I'll pass that on. You got anything of value?"

"If we were face to face and I told you what I have and what I think, you'd kick my teeth in, or at least try."

"I'm not feeling real confrontational. This shit of knowing nothing is getting real old. The state guys don't like it either. They want to run off into the hills with guns a blazin' and carry home some guilty looking hides."

"Tell them about the bounty wars of the '30's. That ought to mellow them out."

Fulsom didn't laugh. "Let's forget we don't like each other for a minute. Do you know what's going on?"

"No, but I can't find a thing that makes it the same old Turner versus Banner thing. I think the bad guys are outsiders like I've been saying from the start. Somebody's paying them to come in and shoot people. I've talked to a lot of folk, and the name that keeps coming up is Tess's. She worked for Ma'am, and Pearl isn't talking."

"Great. What are you doing besides not leaving town?"

"There has to be a very big buck reason for all this."

"How big?"

"Like somebody wants to drive her out of business and take over. At least drive her into selling out cheap."

"She'd never do that."

"She would if she had to. Have there been any floods up in the hills in the last ten or fifteen years? Maybe big enough to change the course of the Salmon Jump's bed?"

A short laugh. "Nice off the wall question. Why?"

"Thatch found something. I think he found it because Tess pointed him the right direction and the river changed course to make it visible. If I can find it then we have something nobody else does."

"So you're looking for you know not what in a place you know not where."

"Sums it up. Buck, the shootings are going to happen again and people will die. I'm surprised they haven't already."

"Great talking to you, Dr. Doom, but I've been thinking the same thing. I've got men stationed around town and a few out at her place just in case."

"You don't have to cover her."

"I'll be sure and tell her you said so."

"They might burn her house down, but they sure as hell need her alive to negotiate her surrender. These guys like showy, so downtown is a good bet. Think Roseburg, 1959."

"I'll try to be sure no one parks a truck of dynamite in the middle of downtown."

A truck loaded with six and a half tons of dynamite and a blasting agent had exploded in Roseburg, seventy miles to the northeast, and leveled the downtown. The blast killed thirteen and injured 125 more.

"Stay in touch," Fulsom said. "Oh, to answer your question about the floods. About a dozen years ago we had record rainfall. The Salmon Jump went down instead of up for about three days before having a helluva surge. We didn't see much in course change down this low, but it had to make a difference up higher than I go. Make of that what you will."

Farrell placed one more call. Cat answered and said he had what Dewey wanted and would be home. Dewey turned off his phone.

The Wrangler was no dream in the corners and had a suspension like a truck that left Dewey shaken by the time he turned up Cat's driveway. The wheelchair and its passenger waited at the top.

"I heard you coming a couple of miles off," he said, surveying the bright yellow Jeep. "What the hell is that?"

"An ATV which I think stands for All Terrain Vehicle."

"What terrain are you headed for?"

"Any where I want."

"Free of Pearl, hey?"

"I'm done playing other people's games. What did you find?"

"I plotted the places where McPherson got shot at and a couple more where he was seen. They're all over the county, but you were right about the common denominator. Waterfalls, or at least rivers big enough to have a fall. But if you're looking for the magic cave, there isn't a waterfall for miles that hasn't drenched a bunch of people poking around behind it."

"You marked them on the map I gave you?"

Cat pulled the map out of the side pocket of his chair and handed it to Dewey as he asked, "Headed for the hills?"

"Time to use that free pass. Will you call it in?"

"Count on it." Cat pointed at the yellow Jeep. "They won't miss you."

"That's kind of the idea. One more thing. This is important. I know about the health problems in the Cloud. Tell them to find a recent blow down tree. The older and the higher up the hill the better. Tell them to cut ten three-inch slices near the base and take them to the Northby's. Do I have to think of everything around here?"

"No, you shouldn't have to, and that's a good idea. Sort of goes with growing up in the trees, eh?" He pointed at the Wrangler. "If you're headed for the Cloud you better have a top for that thing."

"Not standard equipment."

"Tarps in the garage and don't forget to restock on the ordinance. You seem to draw fire wherever you go, and you're not exactly low profile."

Dewey got what he needed from the garage, then climbed in and reached for the shoulder belt.

"Hey, man? Why not leave your cell phone here? It's no use to you up there, and if you leave it with me I can monitor your messages. Anything life or death comes up I can get word to you on the bat phone if you make it into the Cloud."

Dewey handed him his phone and gave him the password to his voicemail.

"You going to look for your mother?" Cat asked. "You look like her, you know. Not so much since you quit shaving, but you got the look. She's beautiful, and you're safe from that one, but you're her kid."

"Yeah, I'm looking for her. I want to know why I wasn't good enough for her."

The engine growled to life.

"It may not have been that simple," Cat yelled above the roar. "Besides, you're not the only one who isn't who they think they are."

Dewey left in the heat of the day under skies of a shade of burnt orange that without the fire would be no more probable than Cat's fairy tale of Eddie and Sophie. He drove alone over roads he'd traveled first with Cat and then with Pearl. He smelled the air and found subtleties beneath the omnipresent tang of forest fire smoke drifting northeast off the Pacific. He recognized smells from his childhood that he'd never identified, but remembered.

His childhood had ended with the face in the trees.

It began with his father.

Eddie was a single parent who taught his son the ways of the forest. The lessons gave Dewey a working knowledge of how to navigate through the tall trees that all looked the same to most people. As a teenager, the knowledge made him valuable as a circuit rider. He got paid top money by the weed farmers who needed a kid to ride a mountain bike between their patches. His job was to check on the drip systems fed by waterbed mattresses buried on the uphill side of their crops.

From time to time, he saw the Turners in their ponchos and wide brimmed hats as he rode the fringes of the Cloud checking the more daring patches that pushed the boundaries of Turner-controlled land. A couple of times he told his employers they were too high only to have his advice scorned, and later the patches were burned or buried. There was so much land Dewey wondered why the farmers pushed their luck.

Now he knew. According to the Northbys, at least, the higher up the hill the higher the quality, the richer the THC, the more the crop could be cut without sacrificing the high on the street, and the more cash to launder on Gold Night.

He turned the yellow Jeep Wrangler down the dirt track that would get him near the banks of the Salmon Jump River. From there he would start his journey upstream to find the place where he and Pearl fell in love.

Pearl. How they met was still a mystery. He was the kid from town and she was the heir to the throne. Eleanora held tight rein on her granddaughter, and the boy with no parents was not on the old woman's approved list. Pearl never sneaked around. She had too much pride, so opportunities to see each other were few. He didn't see her at school because she didn't go to the same school. She was home schooled with tutors brought in from San Francisco who taught at places like UC-Berkeley and Stanford. She had access to cars while he had his mountain bike.

No doubt he'd come to life with her, but it had nothing to do with Banner riches or forest lore, and everything to do with a boy and a girl. He was too young to know what was happening, and he only knew it now because it had never happened again. He'd fallen in love. He'd offered his love to her and it grew because she so unreservedly accepted it, encouraged it, and tended it.

He knew the second it changed.

It took months to reach sex.

Their love was consummated with the loss of their virginities on a rock. During the weeks that led to that moment, the sky was bluer, and the joy of life more consuming. With her in his heart, he pedaled the bike faster weaving through the trees, never using the same way twice, leaving no broken trail that led to their secret place.

After they swam naked to the rock that became their altar, fumbling led to discovery. They knew what went where, but precious little more. He had no one to discuss teenage hormones and desire with, and neither did she. They had talked about it, but didn't obsess over it. They both knew the day would come and it would be perfect.

The day came. She screamed when he penetrated her and he screamed when he reached orgasm.

They lay wrapped together, arms and legs holding them close. When his eyes finally opened he tilted his head back. When he did he saw a woman's face staring out of the trees no more than twenty yards away. She had long silver-blonde hair with blue eyes and flowers around her neck. He and Pearl yelled, then jumped in the water. They swam to where they left their clothes and dressed with hearts racing. They never returned to that sacred place.

The woman had looked familiar, but it took months for Dewey to put it together. He'd barely looked at his father's sketchbooks after Eddie died. Friends had packed up the house and boxes that held personal items were marked KEEP. Finally he looked, and found the sketchbooks with the drawings.

The face had belonged to his mother, but he rejected the idea. An imperfect memory and an idealized drawing did not mean his mother was alive. It was unthinkable. It would mean his mother had watched her estranged son make love to a girl who represented the evil side of her life. Turner and Banner. Romeo and Juliet. All he knew for sure was it was a woman's face staring out of the trees.

He hadn't cared about Banners and Turners, but at that moment something had changed for him with Pearl. Fate took control. He left. Now he was back and he wanted what he'd left behind. Before he could, he had to understand that moment. He needed a name for the face of fate. The need had brought him this far and he wouldn't quit.

Back in the present, he drove the Jeep as close to the river as he could. From there he picked his way down to the water. It was nowhere near where Pearl and he consummated their love, but it was as close as he could drive from this direction. He dropped to his haunches and stared across the jumble of rocks to where the river's weak summer flow murmured softly as it lazed its way down the mountain.

That day with Pearl had been much like this one. Hot and midsummer, but near their rock the water had been deep enough for them to swim, not like here where he would do no more than wade. They had swum in a pool fed by a waterfall coming off a high cliff.

A waterfall near where, if Cat could be believed, his mother watched him.

He picked his way across the rocks to where the river made its summer bed. Small plants made their homes in the silt, and the wood wedged tight by winter storms in the rocks was old and dry. Judging by the debris, the variance in the course caused by flooding had shifted the river north by at least thirty yards. A rocky spine divided where it had been and where it was now. He looked upstream. The river made a turn and entered a deep gorge. When the flood had surged out of the mouth of the rocks it had come with enough force to divert the channel.

He guessed the spot he shared with Pearl was at least three miles from where he stood. He'd never tried to drive the roads to meet her, choosing instead to ride his mountain bike zigging and zagging through the trees thinking only of her. On his bike he'd always worked his way down the sides of the hills – water always took the lowest route – and read the shadows cast by the trees to get him where he would meet Pearl. She got there over Banner logging roads in one of the company trucks to which she always had access. He wondered if the logging road was still there, but until he found the spot on the river he wouldn't know if he had found the right road.

It would be difficult to walk upstream until he found the waterfall because he would have to climb the gorge blocking him. The alternative was to find his old bike route and walk, but that had a whole set of problems of its own. With harvest this close, the hills were filled with paranoia, and he had none of the passwords, and was no longer a familiar sight. To make it worse he walked like what he'd been for so long – a cop. It was always open season on cops in the hills. Fulsom had good reason for not trespassing in what amounted to a free fire zone. Dewey didn't relish the idea of slinking for miles paying more attention to not getting shot than to where he was going. If he was stopped, it would not be by a

Turner, but by a weed farmer only days from raking in his investment. The law of the forest was to shoot first and bury the body.

He climbed back over the rocks and up the hillside to the Wrangler. He opened Thatch's map and spread it on the hood. The map wasn't detailed enough to pinpoint his exact location, but if his decades old reckoning and Thatch's rendering were close, he had further to go than he'd thought. There was about five miles of river to follow, and in the three hours of daylight before nightfall he wouldn't make it. He got his new equipment out of the Jeep, loaded his pack, fit his new sleeping bag into the pack straps, jammed his .45 into its new holster and set out. He didn't have hiking boots, but his cross trainers would get the job done.

The gorge blocked his way. He couldn't climb the rock face, but he could go around without going too far into the trees. Common practices could have changed since his day, but weed farmers didn't usually choose locations near anything like a river that would attract hikers or picnickers.

His side of the river didn't have a trail he thought he could climb so he crossed the rocks toward the water taking smaller strides because of the twenty pounds on his back. Fifteen minutes later he sat on a rock on the far side putting his socks and shoes on after wading. When they were on, he climbed.

By the time he reached the top of the of the cliff, he'd gone at least a half mile inland and much further into the trees than he wanted. He watched the ground for signs of recent activity, but saw none.

He read the terrain. He remembered the rules. Stay away from clearings. All plants needed light to grow and a clearing almost guaranteed a tended patch. Stay away from anything that looked like a lightly used trail. Not everyone up there was as conscientious as he'd been to remove traces of his passing. He'd climbed slightly since the top of the gorge so he looked for an offsetting downslope to get him back to the river. In winter he would have heard the water, but not now. He decided even though it might be a longer route it was smarter to get out of the trees, and headed toward the river. He found it when he stepped out of the trees and onto a five foot wide ledge looking down to the water. He stood on a point around the corner from where he'd started his climb that gave him a look upstream.

He saw more broken rock scattered over a wide debris field formed when the pent up water had burst out of its plug. Where the gorge narrowed, boulders of impressive size lined the walls. He wondered if there was a "Noah's Ark" tale among the Turners that talked of an immense flood that reshaped the river.

He looked for an easier path. Trails along the river were not the danger they were in the woods, and he set off carefully side stepping down hill and walking normally where it was safe to take a full step.

Another twenty minutes got him down the hill and on a trail. There were no signs of recent use, but Farrell moved cautiously. Weed farmers weren't the only danger this far into Banner County's back country. Along the river there was always the chance he'd cross onto a gold panner's "claim" although he rated the chance of that as remote. The river at this point would have been prospected to death.

The shadows in the gorge grew darker although the sky above still showed blue. He found a place to camp, and even though there was light left he decided to play it safe. He found a place that gave him a view of the stars. He recalled the many nights he'd spent in the woods lying on bare ground watching the stars. It was one of the things he missed the most from his childhood. As he ate an orange, he roamed the memories he'd marked as forbidden since Pearl had screamed at him to leave.

They came as a gradual unfolding. The sight of the stars, the smell of the forest; the sounds of wood aging and branches breaking, and the taste of food eaten alongside creek beds and berries picked off bushes loaded with its own harvest. Then came the specifics. Huckleberries were the ones he remembered the most vividly. They were bitter off the bush, but the best in a pie, so he'd carried a cloth bag on his belt to take them home where he and his dad made pie. Blackberries were the real find, and fortunately they were abundant. He remembered washing has berry-stained face and hands in a river many times, each experience approaching rapture with its submersion in nature. He took a deep breath and noticed the air smelled different here although he couldn't pin the smell down.

Thinking of the river sent him to its side where he leaned his face into the flow and drank deeply. He lifted his face, took a deep breath and put it back in to let the water flow around him. He knew he was back .

The Weatherman

Mitchell Ellers converted the Siskiyou-Banner Complex fire from off the USFS's charts to a top priority with one phone call. The National Weather Service has a direct line to the command center for the Western Region Fire Control of the USFS. He placed the call because he found no sign the Forest Service knew what was brewing far from any other action they currently fought. He asked for Colonel Bill Travis, the "Colonel" a throwback to the man's military career. Ellers had to fight to get through, but knew from experience the more fires on the board the longer he would wait.

This year the fire control center was in Reno, Nevada. It was there because it was centrally located to the decade's worst fire areas that stretched from New Mexico to Washington and Colorado to Southern California. The Northern Pacific Coast region had been pretty quiet for the last few years. The number of lightning strike fires through the high desert had remained high, but conditions alleviated by sporadic thunderstorms packing water with the lightening, and an improved system for fire spotting, had helped reduce their severity. Never long on equipment, the Forest Service had moved equipment out of the area to fight fires in other places.

Colonel Bill Travis opened the conversation when he came on the line with, "Mitch, I wish I could say it was good to hear from you. I would have been on the line sooner, but I had to take an antacid tablet."

"Sorry, Colonel, this *is* one of those phone calls. You've got a giant building momentum and I don't see any activity. MODIS has to have it covered."

MODIS, Moderate Imaging Spectroradiometer, provided detailed maps from two satellites that circled the earth and covered the entire planet every one to two days. The interval depended on the orbits.

"Where should I be looking?"

"About 42 degrees north and 122 degrees west."

"My view is thirty-six hours old," Travis said.

"You won't like what you see on the next pass from Aqua."

"You know what we're up against this year, Mitch."

"I do. New Mexico and Washington have spread you pretty thin. You're going to need the military on this one."

Ellers waited for a response but it didn't come. "Colonel?"

"Mitch, just give me the bad news."

"We're looking at a burn that will push a half million acres. Worse-case scenario is seven hundred thousand to a million given the terrain. Brookings, Oregon is probably safe. Cave Junction is in danger. If it gets east of the mountains, Grants Pass could burn. Banner could take it dead on. It's up to the seasonal winds. They will push the fire right along the crest of the mountains and it could go east or west. Colonel, you know I'm not an alarmist, but you need to get assets in the air right now."

"Is this official, or is this you playing fire demon?"

"I wish I could tell you this is official, but this is me and you know I'm more right than they are."

"Your track record speaks for itself. I'll get started."

Dewey Farrell

By the time the sun's light found the bottom of the gorge, he'd been on the move for three hours. Luck had been with him showing him paths that kept him close to the river. The gorge gave way to softer, rolling hills, and intense sunlight. His way had steadily climbed. Nothing high enough to excite more than a gentle cascade from the river, but his legs told him the way led up. Now that he could see more of the world, he felt the tug of familiarity. The rise and fall of a hillside; the shape of a rock face in the distance, or a breeze carrying forest smells of decaying tree and undergrowth.

The forest had deteriorated. The Douglas Fir Beetle left dead trees among the healthy. A fire would be cataclysmic. He took a deeper breath. He didn't smell the fires burning to the south. He wondered if it had been contained, or, miraculously, if it had changed direction.

He kept a steady pace, and had no sense of how much ground he'd covered. He reached a stretch where the rocks gave way to a dirt trail and made good time. At first, when he heard the sound of a waterfall he thought it was his imagination. Slowly it grew louder until he was sure. His excitement grew, then he came around a corner and found himself stopped by another rock face too steep to climb. He either had to detour around or cross the river. He chose to cross. He took his shoes off and tied them around his neck, then stepped into the surprisingly warm water. He tried to see where he was stepping, but unlike down river, the water was turbid and he couldn't see bottom.

Half way across he stepped forward. Instead of the rock bottom his foot kept sinking. He flailed his arms to recover his balance and failed. The water closed over his head while the weight of the pack pushed him down. He expected to hit bottom quickly, but didn't. Finally, he labored to swim up. When his head broke surface, he gasped and shook the water out of his eyes and blew water out of his mouth. He took a few pulls of his arms toward the far side. The second stroke took him out of the shadow and into the sun.

The noise of the falls grew louder. He tread water and turned to the sound. He looked up a narrow gorge where a lower fall dropped maybe fifteen feet. Behind it by several hundred yards he saw a much higher fall whose spray created a perfect rainbow in the sunlight.

"Like the pot of gold at the end of the rainbow," Thatch had said.

Farrell tread water while he stared in wonder. He saw how the flood had changed everything it touched. The top of the waterfall was now thirty or forty feet to the right of where it had been. Small things to the left looked familiar. He saw where a clump of trees formed a 'W' and below it he saw an exposed rock in the shape of a face with a long nose and one eye closed.

He swam the last few feet to shore and dragged himself out of the water. His new spot afforded enough room to dump his soaked pack, sleeping bag, shoes and supplies. He rested for a moment, then spread things in the sun with the hope they would dry before nightfall. He put on his shoes but not the socks. As long as they were already wet he would wade and walk as the river's edge allowed.

The lower fall presented the first obstacle. He climbed the wood wedged in deep crevices, and pulled himself up the slippery face of algae-crusted rock. When he stood at the top he searched the bowl created by the falls. The foliage for the first ten feet above the water was gone as if some giant weed eater had come through and hacked it clean. The general size of the pool was the same although the shape was more elongated than the oval he remembered.

He decided to assume he'd found the pool he sought. He waded into the deeper water and swam towards where his and Pearl's rock should be. He got out and crossed the jumbled rock to where the shoreline looked the right distance. He cleared the rock shelf as best he could, then dropped to his knees to push a few larger rocks aside. He surveyed what he'd uncovered. It was their rock. He sat cross-legged and swiveled to face the direction where he'd seen that long ago face in the trees. The hillside clicked into place like a jigsaw puzzle. Closer now he saw more than the 'W' and the rock with the big nose. In the one place where his memory said it should be he saw a spot of dark shadow on the otherwise field of green twenty feet below the 'W.' He saw the woman's face clearly in his memory.

He looked for a way up the cliff. If the woman, be it his mother or not, had a spot behind the falls she had to be able to walk to it in all kinds of weather. Now that the falls had moved thirty feet from where they'd been at that time, he should see a trail. He stood and walked closer picking his way over fallen trees and broken rocks. The fury of the waterfall in the past was now no more than white noise, and the drenching from the spray of the water hitting the pool was now no more than a mist.

"What am I looking for?" he said aloud. "The woman's cave or Thatch's stash? I don't think they could be the same. The woman, no, my mother, unless everyone is lying to me and why would they do that, still uses the cave and would have seen Thatch. He made it sound like a secret that he would only tell me. 'Tell them you're going to the pot of gold at the end of the rainbow.'"

He looked up but saw no rainbow. The sun still shown into the bowl but that would change shortly.

"The end of the rainbow," he yelled.

Three painful minutes later, after falling on the rock twice in his rush to get back to the river, he tread water where he had earlier. He looked up river. He saw where the perfect rainbow, confined inside the bowl, hit the hillside in the trees to his left, and into a jumble of rocks a third of the way up the cliff on his right.

"Okay, Thatch, here's hoping you're as clever as I'm giving you credit for."

He climbed and swam again until he reached the shore beneath where he'd marked the end of the rainbow. He saw no trail. Thatch would have been doing some kind of extraction from rock or water, or perhaps both, since gold was not found in lumps lying on the ground like in a fairy tale. It didn't take long to rule out access from below. Dewey wondered why he thought Thatch or his mother would have come from the river. He was doing this wrong. He needed to come at this as they would have. Now that he knew the location of the falls he should explore the top of the ridge, and for that he would need a piece of equipment he didn't have: a mountain bike.

Wading and stumbling up river had taken many hours. Going down would be much faster. He climbed down the lower falls, scooped up his still damp gear and stowed it. He walked several hundred yards downstream until he found a log he could move. He pulled it to the water, pushed it parallel with the current, and climbed on straddling it at the midpoint. His raft started downstream.

He got wet, but not dunked and had to push the log in places where the water was shallow, but he retraced his path in less than an hour. The yellow Jeep was where he'd left it. Another hour later he pulled into Cat's driveway and entered the back door.

"Didn't expect to see you so soon," Cat said, rolling into the kitchen. "You need something?"

"A mountain bike."

"And you came to me? How flattering."

"I came to the Grand Poobah, the man who can get anything."

The map of Banner County still lay on the kitchen table. Cat rolled to it.

"Where and when do you want it?"

Farrell examined the map before putting a finger on it. "Right there, and as soon as possible."

Cat pulled the paper closer and squinted. "Perfect place if you don't want anyone to know where you're going. Safe, too, since it's a lousy place for a patch. Eastside of a hill never as good as the west, but then you know that."

Two hours later he found the bike waiting for him. Mountain bikes had changed since he was eighteen and the purpose of a few of the knobs and handles didn't come clear until his fingers traced cables. He put the bike in the back of the Jeep and drove slowly up the old logging road.

The longer he was in Banner, the more he remembered. His memory had always been more visual than auditory or kinesthetic, but now it was like a camera with the lens being fine-tuned. He saw how much the forest floor had changed. With the forest canopy thick enough to block most of the sunlight, little grew. The canopy was unchanged in this part, but the floor now had crops of salal and Oregon grape in abundance, both plants that did not usually do well in deep shade. The ferns that thrived anywhere near water did not surprise him, although their lushness raised an eyebrow. The overall health of the forest had declined. All these plants would stoke a fire that would normally not find enough fuel low to the ground to allow temperatures hot enough to penetrate the bark of old growth Douglas fir. They also made it harder to make good time on his bike. The salal hid roots that could knock him off, so he carefully worked around the ground cover.

He pedaled uphill until he was higher than the falls, then veered to his right until he was well east of the river. On this course he would find the road Thatch had needed. It took an hour, but he found it. He had no doubt that it was the one he sought because it was high enough on the hillside. In Banner, you always let gravity do the work. Waterbed mattresses drip-fed weed patches from uphill, and tree falls were always above the roads for the log trucks. Many lumber companies in other parts of the West had relied on steam locomotives to haul carloads of trees out of remote areas, but not here. The terrain was too severe with steep canyons and hillsides for a route of no greater than a two percent grade.

When he found the ruts he sought, they had seen no recent traffic. Even so, he knew this was not an abandoned track. It had seen enough light trucks to bend the grass but not enough to eradicate it.

Farrell made good time as his bike flew along the open road. He quickly picked up the rhythm of standing to take the bumps, and rocking back to lift the front wheel to cross the rocks and roots.

When the road ended, he got off the bike and listened. He heard the hiss of the falls, but to his surprise he saw no foot path. Something had led Thatch this far, be it wealth or something so far unknown.

When they were kids, Thatch had loved misdirection. He would go to extremes to make Dewey think he'd gone one way when the opposite was true. Now, Farrell backtracked looking for a foot path off the road. He found it because Thatch was dead and couldn't mind his blind. The pulled up foliage Thatch had used to hide the entrance had turned brown. Had Thatch been alive, he would have kept it replenished with green. Dewey pushed it aside and carefully picked a direction that took him toward the water. The sun was still high, but nightfall wasn't far off. Dewey walked faster, determined to find the secret behind Thatch's phone call before the light was gone. Had it not been for the sound of the falls he might have stepped off the path into the air a hundred feet above the rocks, and to their right was the pool.

A cave would be lower. Dewey did not believe Thatch would climb down the face to get to his discovery, meaning there had to be a simpler way.

He found a log fall near the edge and sat where he could look across the pool below. This was not a place anyone stumbled upon. What had led Thatch here the first time? Tess seemed to be the logical answer. Something she'd discovered made her tell her brother. When she'd summoned Thatch, she'd wanted more than the company of family. She'd wanted help.

Farrell backtracked looking for something he'd missed. More slowly now he followed the steps of the McPhersons. He kept his eyes on the ground looking for a hole that would take him underground because there was no other possibility. The light was fading, especially under the forest canopy. Just as he was ready to give up for the day he found the doorway, not the hole, he sought.

The huge tree had fallen decades ago. Much of the trunk had composted to a reddish mulch, but at the root base itself the snaggly off-shoots ran in a dramatic pattern that caught his eye. The trunk was at least ten feet thick sending the higher roots more than twenty-five feet into the air. The tree had been a monarch fir, a tree so majestic it demanded the viewer's appreciation. He guessed its age at the time it fell at over four hundred years. He looked up and saw the hole in the canopy had not completely closed meaning the tree's fall had been within the last twenty years.

Footprints led to the partially submerged trunk. More dead branches leaned against the tree. Dewey pulled Thatch's camouflage aside and found the opening. He took a pen light out of his back pack, and flashed it inside.

The hole was cleverly designed so no one would accidently find it, but Dewey recognized it as the mouth of a cave. Now that he'd found it, his skin went cold and his breath went shallow. He hated caves. He closed his eyes and turned on the light.

With the light on, he followed the path into the ground. The way became steeper until he found steps cut into the ground. The way predated the siblings. Dewey guessed more than thirty years but less than a hundred meaning the way had been here before the tree fell.

He walked and side-stepped down the hole thinking of Alice's descent into Wonderland. The deeper he went the harder it was to breathe as his pulse rate climbed. After five minutes, the way became flat and the hole became a cave. Judging by the flow of fresh air he had found the back door of a larger cavern. Twenty feet ahead the cave mouth opened behind the waterfall. With fresh air and a large space, his pulse slowed and he breathed easier.

Emboldened, he stood with his back to the falls and shone his light into the cave's shadow. He saw a white-gas lantern against a wall and two large battery operated spots. Three cardboard boxes were stacked next to the lights. He picked up a spot and switched to it to save his flash. He glanced into the top box and found provisions of canned food and bags of chips and other non-perishables, including box of a dozen Snickers bars. Past the boxes lay a passage. A dozen steps later the passage opened into a chamber he estimated to be fifteen by twenty-five with a ceiling of about ten feet in the middle, dropping to four feet at its lowest point against the left hand wall. He saw everything from shovels and pics, to a gas operated compressor. A scuba mask and fins lay beside the compressor next to three compressed air tanks. He wondered how Thatch had carried everything in. Either Dewey had missed a trail, or seeing this stuff here helped explain Thatch's bulked up muscles.

A cot with a sleeping bag sat against the wall. Another cot stood on end with a rolled sleeping bag underneath. He shone the light, more slowly this time, and saw a tarp nearly the color of the walls draped over a five foot stack. Underneath he found three suitcases, an ice-chest, two stretch-wrapped cases of bottled water, a laptop computer, boxes of small tools with assorted screwdrivers, hammers, wire cutters, needle nose pliers, and a cordless drill with a set of bits. On top of the tools he saw a revolver, a long barreled .44. He checked to see if it was loaded. He smelled oil so it had been cared for. He set it with the tools. Next came five boxes with the flaps tucked in. He lifted the first box onto a higher stack and started through the contents.

Inside, the box contained books that belonged to Tess. There were three well-worn books on anthropology, one of them authored by her, an accordion file closed with an elastic band, loose papers, and at the bottom, a scrapbook. He set the box aside and moved to the next. This box belonged to Thatch. Dewey found a Dummies-like guide to placer mining, and a basic need to know about smelting. After what he'd learned at Gold Night, Dewey found it unlikely that Thatch had ever tried to actually smelt gold, but he understood why Thatch would want to know the process. Near the bottom he found two notebooks with yellowed paper. The writing matched neither Tess nor Thatch in a style that suggested they were very old. He set that box aside, too.

The next box held more old notebooks but these were written in a different hand than the ones in Thatch's box. He didn't look at them. When he got ready to replace the cardboard lid he saw Tess had printed words on the inside in black block letters: HOW WELL, NOT HOW LONG.

The third box overflowed with manila file folders. He read the names on the tabs. BANNER HISTORY, NORTHBYS, TURNERS, and near the back, a thin one that read FARRELL. He took two deep breaths, exhaling slowly, then pulled out the file with his name.

TURNER INBREEDING
(draft)
by
TESS McPHERSON

The problems of continued inbreeding are now obvious to the Turners. The problems include the advance of recessive gene traits that affect a growing percentage in each generation. Some of these traits have been hard to identify because medical care and evaluation has not been available in the Turner enclave. Until a more obvious problem became apparent, hemophilia, the other problems were dismissed with phrases such as "she's as crazy as her great aunt." In other words, nothing was done. Judging based on anecdotal evidence only, it is possible the practice of homogamy had been going on in the family well before the move to Oregon.

My primary challenge is a lack of documentation. Homogamy, the practice of marrying between individuals who are in some way culturally similar, has been practiced in the United States in isolated communities where eligible mates outside the social unit were limited, as well as a rigorously enforced endogamy where marriage within the unit was not only demanded but the mate carefully selected to fit preconceived norms. These communities resist documentation. Any documented studies I produce will be ground breaking in the field.

I have discovered no motivation for their inbreeding beyond strengthening the family even at the cost of losing some members. There are no records, not even in Frederick's notebooks, that suggest producing a line of long-lived geniuses was their intent. Frederick repeatedly said in his writing that it wasn't how long he lived, but how well. He had both, so his observation may lack appreciation for those who didn't.

My observations lead me to believe that there is more to Szondi's (Leopold, attributes needed) work than I have previously believed. Genotropism goes far in explaining the Turner collective consciousness. They do believe there is a hereditary hand in determining with whom to mate. The results of their practice have been astounding, and not all have been negative. They have an instinctual awareness of the needs of the collective unit and are dedicated to filling its needs. They adhere to a strict family plan.

Factors considered here are their extreme living conditions inside what they and the surrounding populations call "the Cloud," and a restricted diet that is low in vitamin C and other necessary components for what is considered adequate nutrition. The inter-marrying of their inner family, defined as the purest Turner bloodline determined by family records brought with them at the time of the migration, is total unless approved by the family elders.

The most dramatic manifestation of their genotropism is their maternal leader called "Mother." It is a role assigned for life and determined by the previous Mother. (I will need to get much closer to the family before there is any chance of obtaining documentation for some of the stories I've heard.)

There is a physical medicine element to this as well. The Banner Effect is present in some who are born in the mountains outside the family, and to a higher *percentage of members in the Turner family. It is manifested by vigorous living for more years, and by the few who have left and then return there is an almost immediate regeneration of better health and vigor. This is unprecedented in my knowledge. (When Dewey returns we will test him to see how ~ and if – he is affected.)*

Dewey Farrell is an important piece of this research. He is unaware of his ties to the Turners and does not know who his mother is and her role in the family. I still don't know how to approach him on the subject. I suspect he is unwilling to participate in a structured study.

Of equal interest is Pearl Banner. Like Dewey, she is unaware of her bloodline and has no idea of the role of her grandmother/mother. When Dewey and Pearl were young they were strongly attracted to each other, and I expect the same will happen when he returns. There is an undeniable expectation that Pearl and Dewey will mate successfully. Even I eagerly await the results. Of primary interest is whether their union and resulting child would be the first step in repairing the bloodline that has weakened since the child of Frederick and Jessica. Establishing methodology for tracking the next twenty years is paramount.

This will be a whole new branch of the research with no precedent outside of genotropism and Szondi's work. I will keep immaculate

It ended in mid-sentence. Like her life.

He sat on the ledge at the edge of the fall's veil dangling his feet sixty feet above his and Pearl's pool. He looked straight ahead into the void. In the near darkness with a new moon topping the ridgeline he felt suspended not only in place, but in time.

The memory produced a visceral reaction, a vertigo as if he traveled a worm hole. Now he felt the heat of summer at age eighteen; the sweat streaming down his back as he ran after a laughing blonde girl chasing her through floating dandelion fuzz riding on the breeze. The young man overflowed with energy and strength, his happiness filling him to the point where he thought he would burst. He did not run as fast as he could. He followed her more than pursued her, trusting she knew where to guide him. Wherever it proved to be, he wanted to be there with her. They reached the edge of the field and she darted into the forest, running harder now, but not to evade him, just to reach their destination sooner. He felt the need to erupt with joy and discovery and the sense they were on the course meant for them. The images faded.

Farrell, from his cat bird seat, wondered how they had known their course. Maybe it was a conceit of youth. A week ago while sitting in silence on Badger Lake, he'd felt like his life was behind him, but now he had a virtual new life in which he was youthful.

The magic of this spot on the ledge pulled him back in time again to his vision of the running girl. He had lost sight of Pearl when he entered the shade of the forest while his eyes adjusted. When they did, he saw her at the edge of where the woods opened to the river. She stood silhouetted against the light as she pulled her shirt over her head. Her white bra lay on the ground with her shirt when he reached her. She pointed at his shirt and he pulled it off. He unzipped his jeans as he watched her tug hers down, her white panties sliding down her hips with the tight jeans. In a moment they stood together naked, screaming with laughter. She touched his erection and then ran to the water, slowing the last few steps as she crossed the rocks and then waded into the river, the water climbing higher on her perfect body so full of youth and promise. He followed, acutely aware of his erection bouncing in front of him. She turned, saw him, and pointed at him as he neared. When the cold water swallowed him he lost none of his ardor. They rushed through the neck-deep water and crashed together, her legs coming around his waist, her arms around his neck, and her lips crushed against his. When the kiss ended they leaned their heads away from each other and yelled their joy to their tiny world of pool and tree-covered gorge walls. She kissed him again, her legs and arms locking even tighter while his hands held her buttocks.

"Now," she whispered.

Time jumped back through the worm hole, and now the moon stood higher above the ridge line. Clouds accumulated to the west stacked against the ocean side of the mountains. He heard distant thunder. A flash of lightening split the clouds and more thunder followed seconds later that rumbled through the hills.

He saw words from Tess's typed paper in the spray from the fall.

"Of equal interest is Pearl Banner. Like Dewey, she is unaware of her bloodline and has no idea of the role of her grandmother/mother."

What role had Eleanora played? What did grandmother/mother mean? Pearl knew who her parents were so this was no foundling tale. They had been absent and that was why Eleanora had raised the girl, but her mother came to see her. As he thought about it he realized what he'd thought about his own life was wrong, maybe what she knew about hers was wrong as well.

When they were young they were strongly attracted to each other, Tess went on, and I expect the same will happen when he returns. There is an undeniable expectation throughout the family that Pearl and Dewey will mate successfully."

Whose expectations? What family? Mate successfully?

"Of primary interest is whether their union and resulting child would repair the bloodline that has weakened since the child of Frederick and Jessica."

If Tess was right, Fredrick had impregnated Jessica Turner when he was eighty. What about the bloodline that resulted, and what would have happened to weaken it? Was this genetic problem infecting the Turner young, and if he and Pearl did have a child how would that change anything? The child would certainly not grow up in the Cloud. After a moment he added, "If I have anything to say about it."

Tess had closed with, Even I eagerly await to see the results.

More lightening beyond the hills lit the night. As he stood the thunder reached him. It was the drum roll that announced the next movement of a symphony.

He lay in the darkness of the cave where Thatch had slept. He dosed, but awoke chilled even beneath Thatch's sleeping bag. He heard a sighing from behind him, from down the tunnel that led to the heart of the mountain. The sound grew from a sigh to a whisper followed by a soft glow.

"Welcome to the end of the rainbow, Crash."

"Thatch?"

"More like Thatch's ghost."

"You're dead."

"Hence the ghost part. You were late."

"I'm sorry. I should have made it. I could have made it."

"Just as well, Dew. We'd be haunting this tunnel between worlds together. You remember I told you I'd be here if a cave ever scared you?"

"Yeah, thanks. What do you mean between worlds? Like dead and alive?"

"Just between. Dead is not omniscient."

"Thatch, I'm lost. I don't understand."

"Not lost. You found my clue, you figured it out, and here you are."

"What am I doing here? I hate caves!"

"You have to man up, Crash. You want me to tell you what you're doing, or do you want to figure it out for yourself?"

"Tell me."

"You don't mean that. How about a clue?"

"I do mean it, but I'll take a clue."

"When in doubt, go deep."

"What the hell does that mean?"

"Clues are just clues. You know what they mean when you need to know. Like maybe when your life depends on it."

"Not a big help. I feel like I've reverted to my Crash persona since I got back. Clarity would be appreciated."

"Crash is who you are. That you in the outside world was a shadow."

"Thatch, give me more. Please."

"You know you're doing the right thing. Stick to your course. Now go to sleep. You're time in the tunnel is about up for this visit."

"I'll be back?"

"Count on it. But don't worry, I'll always be here." The whisper faded. The last thing he heard was, "Go deep, Crash."

He awoke in the dark. His dreams remained as he emerged from sleep. He felt Thatch's Ghost nearby accompanied by a confusing montage of

Pearl, Eleanora, Zeke, Cat, and the Northby's, all giving eulogies for the siblings McPherson. He'd cried in his dream, and he remembered kneeling between the twin coffins.

Awake now and with the light on, he picked up Tess's papers he'd left scattered on the rough floor. He stacked them neatly without looking at tabs or cover sheets and replaced them in her box.

He would take Thatch's Ghost's advice and stick to his course.

Of the gear Thatch had left the SCUBA gear intrigued him the most. Why was it stored here almost a hundred feet above the pool? Granted, the cave was a good hiding place, but how likely was it the gear would be discovered closer to the pool? Likely enough to haul it up every night, apparently. Unless there was another explanation like either an easier way to get from here to the base of the falls, or another closer body of water that required underwater breathing apparatus, or a classic case of Thatch misdirection whose purpose eluded him.

He went back to the boxes and looked for either more batteries or a charger. He found the charger hooked up to the compressor that also ran a generator. He mentally kicked himself for not looking harder when he first got here. He started the generator, and lights came on. Even insulated, the generator was loud. He left it on long enough to complete a thorough inventory. Thatch had enough gear to convince Farrell the mining was sincere.

He set out to explore. The cave with the gear was the mouth of a more extensive system leading away from the waterfall. The floor was damp near the falls, but became dusty within a few steps. Wet feet had created a worn path into one tunnel, and Farrell followed it carrying the light. The ceiling gradually lowered until he walked in an exaggerated duck walk. He felt the weight of the earth surrounding him. He fought not to hyperventilate. Jagged snags erupted out of walls rough and porous with volcanic rock. He remembered other caves he'd been dragged into by Thatch as a kid with the same kind of rock.

His foot slipped and he almost fell. As he caught himself he realized his path down had steepened. He lowered to a knee and shone the light behind him. From this vantage point he saw he'd been going down since at least the last corner.

Five minutes later he emerged into cavern with a higher ceiling and pool of water in the middle. The pool was round and at least thirty feet in diameter. To his left he found marks that matched the compressor's runners, and a coil or rubber hose with quick connects at both ends. Thatch could have refilled his air tanks with the compressor and the hose.

The tunnel ended in this chamber and considering the wear on the tunnel's floor, Thatch or his predecessors had used it many times. He knelt and put his hand in the water. It was not the icy chill he expected, instead it was closer to lukewarm. He ran his hand through the water and brought it to his nose. There was no odor. Farrell stood and re-entered the tunnel. He timed his journey back. Eight minutes, and he was winded when he made it to the top. He estimated he'd gone down between thirty and forty feet, or about half the distance between the ledge he sat on last night and the pool below.

He raided Thatch's supplies and ate a can of cold chili chased with water from the falls that tasted cold and sweet. He sat on his ledge, and took a deep breath of the fresh air he'd missed in the tunnel. The day shone brightly on one wall of the gorge while the rest, including his ledge, remained in shadow. He could be seen from below but there was no one there to see.

He tried to make sense of his morning's discoveries. The pool where Thatch apparently had done his gold exploring was so non-descript that no one other than a scientist would be tempted to explore it. As far as Farrell knew, the McPherson siblings were not spelunkers. If they weren't, they were here for a compelling reason they'd learned from someone else. More fore knowledge. He thought it would be easier, and certainly safer, to find the 'who' than to dive on the pool alone looking for the 'what.'

The second tunnel led twenty feet and ended. The third was no better. The fourth forked. Farrell chose the fork on the left since it kept him closer to the falls. This one climbed and curved. After ten minutes it forked again. He shone the light on the floor but found no clue to make the choice more informed. For the first time he became concerned about losing his way. He patted his pockets and found his knife but the blade failed to leave a mark on the rock. Besides, if he lost his light he ran the risk of getting lost never to return.

He retraced his steps to the supplies and found sidewalk chalk to mark his way, he replaced the 9-volt battery with a new one still in its wrapper, and picked up his pack. He added three bottles of water to the energy bars already in the bag, checked his watch, and re-entered the tunnel. Twenty minutes later he came to an opening so small he had to take his pack off to squeeze through.

He would later think of that thin opening as the gateway from one universe to another. In this new cave, more passage than chamber, he found rock walls more brown than gray, and more solid than porous. The air smelled fresh rather than stale, and a soft breeze brushed his face. Ahead, he heard the whisper of the falls. He wondered if they were the same falls. He turned off his flash as the exterior light brightened. He saw scuffed cuts in the walls to mark a trail.

When he reached the cave's mouth, he saw he had climbed twenty feet since last he looked. He saw no way down the rock face, so he retreated into the chamber and looked for another way.

This time he found the passage on the first try as he followed worn dirt and rock whose smoothness suggested the passage saw regular use.

He reached a landing where the tunnel flattened. When he reached the mouth he found himself at river level. He looked around, saw no one, and stepped into the opening. The water was twenty feet from the shoreline. He picked his way across the rocks then turned toward the trees. His eyes went up the hillside then moved left to right. On his second pass he found an opening revealing a light colored rock. He took a breath. All that was missing was the woman's face.

He cupped his hands to his mouth and called, "Sophie!"

He waited a few seconds and repeated the call. He did it a third time then sat on the rocks to wait. Either she would appear, or if she didn't it was because she was either not here or didn't want to confront him. He scanned the bowl made by the cliff, the falls and the wooded gorge.

She appeared where he'd seen her all those years ago. At first he didn't believe his eyes. He was much closer this time. He saw the shape of her face materialize and become defined. It was the same shape as his. Her nose, finer and proportionately smaller than his, was still his nose. The color of her hair still blonde as his was his father's shade of brown. He saw silver streaks in her hair with no signs of gray although she would be in her early to mid-sixties. Their eyes met, then she broke away and disappeared. He raised his hand to stop her and prepared to yell, but before he could she came out of the woods and walked toward him.

"Why did you throw me away?" he asked, emotion filling his voice to the point where he could barely speak.

"Come," she said, and reached out her hand.

He took it.

Part III: Sophie

The Fire

Lightning strikes gave birth to the fire, and more lightning stoked it to a new intensity. Two strikes found a draw massed with dead wood from long ago floods that burst into flame within seconds. The canyon's rock walls reflected the heat, building it as the fire fed like a pride of lions on rich carrion. A gust of wind pushed the fire up the draw to where it reached living trees. The death throes of the living slowed the fire as it savored the toll it took on a part of the forest that had survived beetles, blow down, and centuries of smaller fires.

At the head of the draw the fire found a divide formed by a steep hill. The fire hung at the point as if deciding which way to go. Up the notch to the east lay Grants Pass. To the west lay Banner County.

The fire chose west.

Dewey Farrell

In addition to the flowers in her hair, she wore a skirt made of a lightweight material in a pale earth tone, and sandals. Dewey put her height at near six feet, and her body type as slim. It was his body. She wore her hair long braided in a single strand. She had greenish-blue eyes that reminded him of Pearl's. His were more blue and less green, compliments of his father.

"Come home with me," she said, in a rich, mellow voice.

"Where is your home? I've never been there," he said, his anger evident in both words and tone.

"You've been there," she answered. "You lived there the first year, then visited one other time."

"I don't remember. Why did you make me leave?"

There was a long silence before she said, "I'm sorry."

Her composure started to slip as her hands pulled at her skirt, and her feet shuffled. "It was the way it was decided."

"By you?"

"No, but I saw the necessity and . . . agreed."

"I had no mother."

She nodded, then lowered her face. "I had no son, either."

He walked toward her. "When Dad died, I . . . "

"Come home with me, son. Please."

She led him into the tunnel along a branch he had not explored. As they entered she guided his hand to a waist-high groove cut in the wall. Farrell felt nicks in the groove that felt like arrow tips.

"What are the nicks?" he asked.

"They tell you if you are headed toward the surface or deeper underground."

They walked for what Farrell thought of as an eternity. His fear of dark, enclosed spaces ate at his brain ramping up his need to scream. When he thought he could take no more, he literally saw the light at the end of the tunnel.

"Do you know that Thatch McPherson has a cave near yours?" he asked.

"Yes, I know."

"You did nothing to turn him away?"

"No, I wanted him there."

"Why?"

"He would bring you home. That was the plan."

Out in the open, they walked a gradual, but steady, uphill course through forests where the ground cover gradually thinned the higher they went. Eventually he saw only fir needles and cones at the base of the huge trees. He bellied up to one and spread his arms. They spanned less than a quarter of the circumference. Sophie waited patiently. When he rejoined her, she picked up the pace.

The light faded to gray as they entered the Cloud, and the temperature dropped dramatically. She led him to a hut stocked with broad-brimmed leather hats and duster-length coats. She put on a coat and handed him another.

"What is this place?" he asked.

"A way station where we leave the outside behind and enter our world."

"Doesn't the tunnel do that?"

"There are ways to get here without a tunnel," she said handing him a hat.

"What is this place?" he asked, looking around as he slung his backpack over his shoulder.

She straightened his hat then stepped away to admire him.

"The place where questions are born."

* * * * *

191

They stopped next beside a creek. She knelt and using a metal cup hanging on a branch, she took a drink from the rapidly flowing water. She refilled the cup and handed it to Dewey. He drank deeply and asked for more.

"It is best to have only one cup at first," she said. "Later you can drink as much as you wish."

"The water is different here?"

"Everything is different."

They walked up the hillside. A light mist filled the air. He saw no one, but he felt eyes on them. As the light gave out, two men wearing the same style hats and coats stepped out of the trees. They took off their hats and said, "Welcome back, Mother."

Sophie greeted them by name, but didn't break stride. Dewey saw them looking at him with curiosity.

Houses, some quite elaborate and all blended into their surroundings, appeared. Some fit the rising land while others sat in excavations to level the structure. Everything was made of wood. The gray of the Cloud, the brown wood, and the green moss that grew on trees, roofs, and in many places on the ground, made up the palette. The houses were widely spaced without fences.

Children ran out and waved as Sophie passed, and men doffed their hats and women waved like their children. Farrell saw the deference paid to Sophie, but there was nothing as overt as bowing.

"How many people live here?" Farrell asked.

"In this place there are two hundred and fifty-one."

"Then there are other places like this?"

"Yes, there are two more nearby. The ground can only absorb so much. We spread ourselves over a wide area."

"But it's all under the Cloud?"

"Yes. It is important that we live inside the Cloud. We will talk of this soon."

Their route took them between houses and always uphill. He saw bikes, and several times he heard horses, but didn't see them.

THE WEIGHT OF THE JOURNEY BY KEN BYERS

Sophie led him to a house larger than the others and built in a style reminiscent of a bungalow from the mid-twentieth century. No gutters hung from the sharply pitched roof; small windows on either side of the front door gave the house a symmetrical look, while a large porch, or gallery, extended across the front.

Three women waited for them on the porch, and Sophie gave them instructions as to a meal and a place for "her son" to sleep. The women evidenced no surprise at the mention of "her son."

Inside, he saw handmade furnishings with sturdy and well-polished frames, and thick cushions covered in a cloth with subdued colors. Electric lights plugged into the walls and lit the room adequately if not brightly. He smelled food preparation. One of the three women helped him with his coat and hat while another took his backpack and set it near stairs leading up. The first woman led him through the dining room and kitchen to a mud room with a hand pump and a basin. A clean towel hung above the bowl. He felt dirty after a night on Thatch's cot, the climbing through the tunnels, then the long walk up the mountain. He washed, and felt refreshed.

When he returned to the dining room, he found steaming bowls of stew, fresh bread, and pitchers of water. He explored the room while he waited for Sophie to return. Shelves to the right of the fireplace held framed photos, some quite old. He saw one of his dad holding a baby that must be him. He stared at it. He missed his father. He'd been a good man that had done all a single parent could do. What Farrell had known for years was that without a woman in the house during his childhood, he'd never adjusted to what he thought of as a female sensibility. He just didn't see the things Diane saw. The difference he summed as he saw big things and she saw small.

The next picture nearly stopped his heart. He recognized the same photo that he'd seen in the Banner library of Eleanora as a young woman with her humorless gaze staring straight into the camera. He kept looking and found one of an even bigger shock. The daguerreotype of Frederick and Eleanora mixed in with the Turner clan.

"We will speak of those shortly," Sophie said, from behind him.

"What's the tie between the Banners and the Turners?" he asked.

"Shortly," she said, and motioned to him to sit opposite her. One of the other women fussed with place settings and hovered until Sophie sent her away.

"How about now?" Farrell said.

"You asked me," Sophie said slowly, "why I threw you away. It pains me deeply you took it that way."

"What other way is there?"

Sophie stared at him. She looked so young. Older than he did, but not by much. Her steady gaze bore into him to where he felt she might actually be seeing inside him.

"What other way is there?" he repeated.

"I have practiced my story many times knowing this day would come."

She drank deeply from the glass of water next to her pitcher, then waved at him to do the same.

"You must drink much water while you are here. The water has the minerals and vitamins we miss by living under the Cloud.

"The world we live in here is isolated. It is structured with no room for deviation. There is a proven plan that has been in place for generations. We will not change it. I was born to assume a role here. My child would have a role, too. Part of my role was to give up my child and hope he would return to me prepared to meet his destiny. You have, and I am happy to see you."

"My destiny? That's it?"

"No, there is more, but it can wait. Our bloodline is thinning. Living under the cloud is not healthy. We need to reenergize. That is your role."

"Is my role to have a child with Pearl Banner?"

"Yes. It is important that it happen that way."

"Is Pearl a Turner?"

He knew he caught her by surprise.

"Why do you ask?" Sophie said.

"What did Eleanora do?"

"You have many questions."

"You said this is where questions are born."

"I did. Yours require more of an answer than I'm prepared to give. It is safe for you and Pearl to have children together."

"It has been arranged?"

"Arranged? No, not at all. Nothing has been signed and no one has been sold, or in any way indentured."

"But everybody's pulling for us to get the job done, huh?"

"Why are you angry about this? You are made for each other."

"You would know."

"Yes, I would. You have no idea how it thrilled me to see you both so happy."

"I saw you, you know, watching us."

"I know."

"Everything changed for me when I saw you. It's what made me leave."

"Yes."

He stared at her. "Like I was supposed to. Right?"

She slowly nodded her head. "Drink more water."

Farrell picked up the water glass, sniffed the contents, and then drank deeply, and refilled it.

"If you had been a normal mother," he began, "I would have grown up here, under the Cloud, found some nice girl, had babies, and you would be a grandmother. Fair to say?"

"I was never what you think of as normal," Sophie replied.

"Do you know the longer I'm here the better I can see in the dark," he said. "Not down in the tunnels where there's no ambient light, but outside. I don't know how the Cloud effects that, but I'm willing to find out. I'll walk out that door just like every other time someone lied or withheld since I got to Banner. It doesn't work for me, walking out like that. You don't learn things, but I do it anyway because I can't hit anyone or throw a tantrum about how unfair life is.

"I've lived a pretty normal life out there. Some unpleasant things happened. I loved my wife and she died. I was heartbroken, and shut the door on love. I had a job that I was good at, but when people didn't want me to do it my way I created a situation where they had to get rid of me. I guess you could say, one way or the other, I've been walking away from problems and disappointments my whole life. I certainly ran away from Pearl after I saw you. Now you tell that was supposed to happen."

"You had to leave and come back to discover who you are. It is your destiny."

He drank from his glass and felt the water inside him. He didn't remember ever feeling water before. The change, he was sure, was in him more than it was in the water.

"Sophie, I don't care if you want to tell me about who you are and what the truth is about this place or not, but either do it or I'm gone. If I leave I promise you I will not be back, destiny, as you put it, or no."

"You will not fare well if you leave. It will be worse than before."

"So be it. I will not be manipulated."

One of the women came in and said, "Mother, Martin needs to speak with you. He says it's important."

"Not now," Sophie snapped. "Tell him it will have to wait."

The woman bowed and backed out of the room.

"You have pressed me," Sophie said. "I am afraid if I tell you the truth you will call it more manipulation."

"Everyone has manipulated me. Cat told me stories that were only partly true at best. So did Pearl."

"You are told what you need to know. I not only want you to stay, but I want you to stay and do certain things. My story will guide you. Will you be able to hear the truth and get past your feelings?"

"I don't know. Let's find out."

The Weatherman

Mitchell Ellers stared intently at his monitor. The fire's coverage had increased by seventeen percent overnight. Fire's normally slowed at night as winds died, but there had been nothing normal about this fire from the beginning. Fires burning in the western Siskiyou National Forest tended to move easterly up the sides of canyons and long slopes leading to the higher mountains riding the breezes off the Pacific Ocean. Not this fire. It moved north. It was if the fire had a mind of its own. Big fires could make their own weather, but that homemade weather stayed in the heart of the fire and only occasionally reached the outer edge.

This fire rode different winds. Weather spotters on the ground in Crescent City, California and Brookings, Oregon reported winds out of the south, southwest gusting to twenty-five miles per hour. These were the winds that gathered momentum as they bled inland up the Klamath River valley, and, further north, the Smith and Chetco river canyons. The heat of the fire would suck these winds dry.

The long range forecast called for more low humidity, with highs in the mid to upper nineties, and no rain but possible lightning storms. As temperatures climbed during the day, the winds would become fierce in the late afternoon. The fire was already a killer leaving at least seven dead, five firefighters caught trying to climb out of a box canyon, and two campers that got lost and turned into the fire's path instead of away. In another of the fire's anomalies, winds aloft had carried smoke inland and not in the direction the fire would most likely burn.

The scenario grew ever more grim because of the fuel loads waiting in the fire's path. If fire breaks were ineffective the fire would roar at a sickening rate. It's advances would not be measured in acres, but in miles.

Ellers took these developments personally. Mother Nature was a heartless bitch. Banner County stood in the new path just as his vacation was to start. All these years of waiting and finally to have an entrée to the secret that drove his life, only to be have it snatched away by his other passion.

He leaned back in his chair, picked up his Coffee Rings cup. He'd waited too long and had too many questions to go away empty. He found the card in his desk. He dialed the number on the card.

Dewey Farrell

Sophie rang a small bell on a wood handle and the women returned to clear the table. On their last trip they'd brought cookies and coffee they poured from a carafe, then left.

"The story of the Turners and the Banners Cat told you has elements of truth," Sophie began. "It is the popular version most of Banner County knows. What little can be found in history books supports the story. Cat injected an alternative guess as to why the Turners left Pazer, but ~ "

"That's what good storytellers do," Farrell interrupted. "Misdirection. Most people can think of two things at once, but three is much harder. Please don't game me, Sophie."

"Like it or not, you are my son. You may not want to call me Mother because everyone else does, but it changes nothing. You have been the source of great pain for many years. Almost from the moment you were born. Had you been a girl things would have been different."

"Why?"

"To answer your question I must tell you a story."

"No," Farrell said, holding up a hand. "No more stories. All I get are what other people want me to know – not what I want or need to know. Just answer my questions."

"You won't understand the answers," she said.

"I'll surprise you. When I don't, I'll ask. Let's come back to the girl-boy thing later. How come if Frederick owned all the land he let the Turners build a rent free empire?"

"Because that's what he wanted."

"This Banner-Turner feud is a scam, isn't it."

"Scam isn't the right word. Frederick understood what the middle of nowhere meant, but his people did not. After the first few years, this was a virtual utopian culture with no outside threats. The families Frederick brought here were comfortable. They worked hard but felt no outside threats. Their attention wandered at work, production fell, and accidents rose. After the Turners became the bad guys in the hills, that all changed. People had to be vigilant."

"Did Frederick make Jessica pregnant?"

"Yes."

"How old was he?"

"He was seventy-two. She was twenty-two."

"Was Eleanora their daughter?"

"Yes. She was the first off-spring of a Banner-Turner mating. This is very difficult giving you nothing but short answers."

"You're doing fine. What was so special about her?"

"Other than she lived to be almost a hundred and possessed all her mental and most of her physical faculties until the day she died? Her abilities were apparent from the time she was two. She could reason by the time she was three."

"How did Frederick make her a Banner? Wasn't she born here?"

"She was born here and Jessica raised her. The Banner family was even more removed from the rest of the population then than it is today. Eleanora made brief appearances in Pazer as a child of the Banners. Remember, Frederick was dead as far as anyone else knew. He had set it up so two men knew the truth. They ran the company and propagated the story he gave them. Frederick had three children, none of them remarkable. They all moved away as soon as possible. What explanation that was necessary said Eleanora was the daughter of one of his sons who had subsequently died. The part about the dead son was true."

"How old was Eleanora when she started running things?"

"About fifteen, but no one knew she made the decisions. She did it from here with Frederick looking over her shoulder. Like I said, she was exceptional. At twenty-three she moved to Pazer and openly took over."

"Why then?"

"She had shown she could live outside the Cloud for long periods of time."

"What was Frederick doing all those years?"

"He was obsessed with the effects of the Cloud. Some people thrived and others – especially young men – died young for unknown reasons. He wanted to know why. He wasn't a scientist, but he kept notebooks on his observations and theories. He had boxes full of them."

"Where are they?"

"Tess had them. I don't know where they are and I want them back."

"Did Frederick's studies come to any conclusions?"

"They did with the help of a man named Peter Turner. Frederick met Peter Turner in London. Despite the name, Peter was Hungarian, or Magyar. There was probably Gypsy blood in his linage as well. Because historically, his tribe was feared and distrusted and nomadic, there was a great deal of intermarrying. This was a disaster for most, but some lines seemed to do well. Turner said he was taking his healthy relatives to America. Frederick later found out the Turners had gone to New Orleans. When Frederick needed people, he contacted Peter and here we are.

"The Turner intermarrying produced a line that had remarkable attributes and shocking weaknesses. When Frederick impregnated Jessica, the Banner genes filled in the holes and Eleanora was the result. She fascinated Frederick from the moment he saw her. By the time she was one he knew she was superior. He suspected the Cloud played a role."

"What does the Cloud have to do with it?"

"That was Frederick's other obsession. He was sure the secret had something to do with the water. He explored the mountain and many of its caves. He saw the steam vents and came to the conclusion they extended down to the magma level beneath the old volcanoes. The effects of the steam and running water solubilized minerals in the rocks carried by the water. He was not a chemist. All he had were first hand observations. He also had a friend that came with him to the mountains when he 'died.' Carl Wallace was a man much younger than Frederick. They also met in England and remained friends after they discovered they shared many of the same interests. Carl came to America not long after Frederick, and despite the difficulties of that age, they stayed in touch. Carl was alone and sickly and Frederick persuaded him to come to Oregon.

"Frederick wanted to see if the Cloud would improve Carl's health. He knew Carl was approaching the age when many of the men in his family died. He said nothing until Carl had been here for a year and felt better. There were several notebooks dedicated to Carl. He lived well beyond his family's normal life expectancy, but still died many years before Frederick. Frederick attributed Carl's longer life to drinking the water. In general, Frederick was convinced the water was a cure-all for just about everything. But not everyone."

"I've got the feeling we're getting closer to why I'm here."

"Yes. But let me finish this last piece on Frederick. Despite his work and diligent explorations, he needed a scientist to tell him if he was right or not. There were none he could go to. His research waited for many years."

"Tess McPherson."

"And Thatcher, too."

"Did Thatch lie to me? He said he'd found gold?"

"Is that what he said? He was to imply to you he knew *where* to find gold. A pot of gold like at the end of the rainbow. It was his job to entice you here. If anyone else would have called, you wouldn't have come."

"Why are Thatch and Tess dead?"

"Because events are proceeding faster than we thought they would."

"Why?"

"Tess must have gone too far. Someone found out."

"It was no coincidence the McPherson's took you in after Eddie died," Sophie said. "Their mother, Rachel McPherson, was a Turner. A cousin. She understood the problem and came to me with the idea."

"Promise me you will tell me about my father someday."

"I promise. He was the only man I ever loved. Things started to change very rapidly about ten years ago. Banner Timber Products suffered setbacks and Pearl had a money problem. She needed cash so it was decided to dip into our gold reserves."

"Who decided, what gold reserves, and who owns them? You said 'ours.'"

"There is a committee that administers all Banner interests not directly related to the management of the business. Remember Frederick owned it all, and Pearl still does. But the diversity of necessary skills is overwhelming. Banner is a political entity because it's a county. But Banner is also a well-known international forest products company. Here, the Turners smelt gold, we control the marijuana exports from the county, and now there is a whole new world of medicinal uses for our marijuana. That is what Tess must have let out."

Sophie leaned across the table. "In short, my son, we have gotten too big to hide."

"So there's never been a feud?"

"Well, there have been rivalries, but nothing like a real feud."

"What about that head hunting thing Eleanora was supposed to have started?"

"I said she was ruthless, not blood thirsty. There was another gold rush in the early years of the depression because looking for gold was better than a soup line. The head hunting story was spread to keep people out of Banner County and it worked."

"How'd the story get spread without real heads?"

"There were enough real heads to sell it. This has always been a dangerous place to live. People died, and when they did they gave up their heads."

"You talk like you've had a college education."

"I had very good tutors. Despite the age difference, Pearl and I were tutored at the same time. The world we could no longer ignore demanded my education."

"Have you ever left here?"

"Many times. As you learn more about us you will be amazed."

"Okay. Who's Pearl?"

"Pearl really is Eleanora's granddaughter. I thought you would ask who you are first."

"I thought I knew."

"You don't because we don't know. Eddie's linage is unclear. As far as we know it has nothing to do with Banner County, and you are free to have children with Pearl even if you are a third or fourth cousin from my side."

"Don't think I'm agreeing to anything, but why is it so important that Pearl and I have children?"

"Ah, the crux!" Sophie said, and drank from her water glass. "I'll do my best to keep this short, but be patient.

"There is far more written about Frederick, plus all his notebooks, than there is about Jessica. We don't know why the original blend of Turner and Banner was so potent that it turned out an Eleanora. She wasn't the only one either. Jessica had a second child by Frederick. A brilliant boy named Efram. Yes, your namesake. He saw how we could smelt gold using the natural gas that vents out of the mountain. Once he started working with gas he came up with other ways for us to use energy more efficiently. Granted, our needs are substantially lower per capita than in the outside world, but we are very good. Efram had seven children by three women. Jessica saw how important it was to spread his seed and arranged it all.

"Efram's contribution is every bit as important as Eleanora's, but together they accomplished a great deal. She helped educate him by bringing people to Pazer to tutor him, and kept it all secret. The way it was done became the model for Pearl and me. In return, his innovative designs on equipment streamlined the way her mills worked."

"What happened to Efram?"

"He died when he was thirty-six. Sixty years later when Thatcher saw what Efram had done, he was so impressed he wanted to file for patents. He said they would be very valuable."

"How would Thatch know?"

"He was an accomplished engineer. Once he was here, going through what Efram had done became his job, while Tess was doing hers."

"So I was a distant cousin to Thatch and Tess?"

"Yes, but distant. The McPhersons followed their instructions too well when I told them not to talk about me and the Turners. You left with no idea of who you were. But let's get back to Jessica."

"Just a minute. Efram died at thirty-six, and you said Turner men sometimes die young. Is that why I was sent away?"

Sophie stared at him and was slow to answer. "Yes."

"Am I out of the woods after being gone for twenty-three years?"

203

"We don't know. Tess was working on this when she died. We were going to call you home and wanted the answer when you asked the question. We don't have one now."

"I guess I'm sorry I asked. What were you saying about Jessica?"

"The Turners have Gypsy blood, and they also lived for several generations in Louisiana where magic and the dark arts are a science. Jessica came by her arcane skills honestly. They were a well-stirred pot of her ancestral learning that allowed her to see the world in ways others did not."

"What did she see?"

"The family called it seeing the future. She did not and never claimed magical abilities. To her it was rational. She saw how the effects of events – those that did happen, and those that might happen – would or could influence us. Hers was not an all-encompassing ability. It was confined to people. Natural events could only be deduced through the people."

"That needs some explaining For instance?"

"She did not foresee the effects of Efram's inventions because she had no framework for it. She foretold what Eleanora's contributions would be because they fell within the world Jessica knew well. She told Eleanora what she saw and the foreknowledge probably played a role, but the details would amaze you. Jessica laid out a plan for the family about who should marry whom that extends well beyond you and Pearl."

"You said if I'd been a girl it would have been different. If I'd been a girl how could I have had a child with Pearl?"

"But that's not the way it happened. When Jessica's plan varied there was always a reason. Since you were a boy it could mean that your genes would have an effect like Frederick's."

"So I'm a variation on the plan?"

"That's right, and there is a reason. We are facing problems and challenges like we've never seen including attacks on our people. We need help – a warrior's help."

Johann Prus

After Tess McPherson's computer arrived, he had to wait another twenty-four hours for the encryption to be broken and the files organized. He spent the hours resting, hoping to find the energy he would need to comprehend what he would read. When the call to action came, he found a remote hard drive attached to his computer and the data stored in three folders.

The first was called THC. That would be the research material on the pharmaceutical applications of the Banner marijuana. He was interested, but would read it later.

The second was called TOPOGRAPHICAL. He browsed the file names and scanned a few. Most of the information was new. Applications he'd never dreamed of flashed through his mind fed by information on what was under the so called 'Cloud.' The one point that did make him read was on the likelihood of substantial gold deposits.

The third folder was simply called HEALTH EFFECTS. He started there and read for hours. He saw repeated references to Frederick Banner's notebooks. He frowned at the first reference. He thought the man had died in 1900, but it was clear that he lived much longer, and lived in seclusion under this cloud. He remembered the small book with the notation it could have been written by Frederick Banner. It was clear that not only had he lived, but he'd been robust enough to sire children! Remarkable! When he read about Carl Wallace his pulse quickened. Supposedly there were notebooks in Frederick's hand devoted to this sickly man and his increased longevity because he lived under this inexplicable cloud.

He called his assistant. "Were boxes of notebooks found anywhere?" He was told no.

"I want to talk to the man in Banner."

"Roy Whitsett?"

"I don't know his name."

Prus glared out his window, thinking. "Have my plane readied for a trip to California. San Francisco most likely but, perhaps, further north."

It took nine hours for Whitsett to return the call.

"Nine hours is not acceptable, Whitsett," Prus said.

"I'm working," Whitsett said. There was no apology in his voice.

"You should carry your phone."

"I do, Prus. There is limited cell phone coverage and none where I'm working. What do you want?"

"Dr. McPherson makes mention of boxes of notebooks. Did you find them?"

"No. We looked at her house and where she worked. Nothing."

"Find them."

"That probably won't happen. They could be anywhere and I don't have the manpower to spare."

"You assured me you had everything you needed."

"I was wrong. I underestimated the situation here."

"In what regard?"

"Every regard. The terrain here is difficult, cell phone communication is almost impossible, and ~ "

"Why don't you use two-way radio?"

"They're line of sight, and they aren't secure."

Prus thought for a minute.

"I am coming. I will fly to San Francisco and enter the country there. Where do you suggest to land closer?"

"Stay home. You'll just be in the way."

"I will be there. Where should I land?"

"You don't know what you're getting in for, but if I can't stop you then land in Crescent City, California if the airport's open. The weather is often bad and the fires are close."

"Is it possible the notebooks could get lost to the fire?"

"Anything's possible, but there are a lot of caves all through the mountains. I'm guessing anything of value gets stored in them. Fires are nothing new around here, but this one apparently is bigger than they've had in decades."

"Search the caves."

"There are miles of them."

"I want those notebooks!"

"Well that's just too fucking bad! You have no idea how big this place is. Let's take care of our business first, and then you can hire a guide."

Prus fought his impatience, calmed his voice, and asked, "How are your plans coming? Why haven't you acted yet?"

"If we blow up the town we could set off a whole new wall of fire. You said you didn't want unnecessary damage."

"I no longer care about the town. Proceed – and, Whitsett? – find me those notebooks. Raid the cloud, do whatever it takes."

After the connection was broken, Prus stood at the window.

"Sir," his assistant said, "your plane will be ready when you arrive."

From here, sixty floors above the world, he was a king. Out there he was less. Only his conviction that he would beat death in Banner could get him to leave.

Roy Whitsett disconnected from his call with Prus. He hated standing anywhere in the open, especially here lit by the garish neon sign, but as far as he knew it was the only goddamn place for miles where his cell worked. His shoulder still hurt from the last time he was here. The bullet had entered and scratched the bone on its way through. He'd been lucky, he thought as he stared across the parking lot to the spot where he'd been shot. It wasn't the first time he'd taken a bullet, but it was the first time he could look back and say he'd been careless. It was also the first time he'd had nerve damage all because he'd taken too much time with the kill shots. Most of them weren't even necessary because the victim was already dead, but he liked it. Even savored it. He'd do it the same if he had the chance to do it all again. The shoulder would heal.

Less than a mile away, a man in a wheelchair took off his headphones. He reached for an old fashioned phone with a rotary dial and a Batman logo in the center. He placed a call that would take time reaching the person he

207

needed to talk to. He looked longingly at the bottle of Jack Daniels, then pushed it away. Not the time for his old buddy Jack. He thought of rolling a number from Banner's finest to dull the pain, but he couldn't afford to mess his head up right now. He needed to be a straight thinker, razor sharp, straight as a laser, all of that. He would have to live with the pain until the world got its shit together.

The Weatherman

His bedside phone rang at 0255. He answered on the third ring as he always did in these middle of the night calls. Usually they came in the winter when a cold air down the gorge met a wet Pacific front to threaten a foot or more of snow for the morning commute, or the gorge effect shaped up for an ice storm that would blanket the Portland metro in a layer of ice making that same commute even worse than snow.

"Mother Nature waits for no man," he said to himself, the phrase part of the routine he followed before he answered.

"You wanted to be called, Mitch," said Harry Long, the nightshift meteorologist. "It's bad news for southern Oregon. The winds picked up and shifted around to the southwest. That's going to push that monster north right through the Coast Range scorching everything in its path. God help those poor bastards. I'm going to harangue the USFS to throw everything they have at it before it's hopeless."

Mitch hung up and went to his office down the hall. If he left now he would be in Banner by seven or eight. He still had not heard back from his Coffee Rings sidekick, so he called again.

Those people in Banner were going to need the help of a fire demon, and maybe Farrell could get him to the right people. Maybe they'd be grateful enough to give him a tour under their Cloud when the fire was out.

He dialed the number, waited, then the call went to voice mail. After the beep, he said, "Farrell, Mitch Evers again. I assume you are in Banner.

The winds have picked up and pointed that monster fire right at you. It'll take twenty-four to thirty-six hours, but this is a potential holocaust scenario. Call me. I'm coming down to offer my services to the people planning how to fight this thing. If you know the right folks, it would move things along. When I get there maybe we can work together since I know you have strong feelings for Banner. Thanks. Hope to talk to you soon."

Dewey Farrell

Even in his fitful sleep, Dewey Farrell's mind swam with the revelations Sophie had heaped upon him. He lay in a bed upstairs, but dodged in and out of consciousness like a man playing hide and seek with another lifetime. Someone shook him and wouldn't stop. The trip to consciousness was like climbing out of a deep hole.

"Dewey, wake up!"

He opened his eyes enough to see his mother leaning over him.

"There is an emergency. Cat needs to talk to you right now."

He sat up. "Is Cat here?"

"No, but you can talk to him. Get up! Now!"

When he sat on the edge of the bed, Sophie handed him a glass of water. He drank it and felt well enough to stand and follow her.

"Tell him the horses are being saddled now," Sophie said. "We will take you to your truck."

He followed her outside. Along the trail marked with dim lights, he heard the hum of a generator. The trail led to a small house. Inside, a man offered him a chair and the handset to a black phone circa 1950.

"Dewey," Cat said, "the shit's hitting the fan, and we're just getting the word. There is a team of . . . I don't know what to call them, soldiers, mercenaries, something like that . . . in town. They're the guys that hit the Nowhere and Gold Night. Now they're going to blow up Pazer. I don't know when, but soon."

The words cut through the last of Farrell's fog.

"Slow down, Cat. How do you know?"

"I overheard a cell call placed from outside the Nowhere. The local guy is called Whitsett and he was talking to someone named Prus. It was an international call. This Prus guy is coming to the States. Prus must have Tess's laptop because it sounds like he knew what she was doing. He wants the local guy to find Frederick's notebooks. That mean anything to you?"

"If Tess had them I know where they are."

"Kisses for that favor. Hey, if that weren't bad enough, you know a guy named Mitchell Evers? He says he's a weatherman."

"I know him. He's the guy obsessed with the Cloud."

"He just called your cell. The fire is headed right for us. He called it a monster."

"He called me in the middle of the night?"

"He's coming down to lend a hand. What do you want to do?"

"Call Evers back and give him directions to your house. How long will it take me to get there by horse back then truck? Sophie says the horses are saddled."

"Three hours. A little more in the dark."

"Call Fulsom and Pearl. Fill them in."

"Okay. Safe journey."

He hadn't ridden a horse since he was a kid. He needed help getting up, but once up he stayed on. The horse needed no help from him. The ride through the dark forest was surreal. Images of bizarre shapes loomed out of the night and then disappeared behind them as they thundered by. All he had to do was not fall off, and he could do that and think at the same time.

"Here I am at forty-one," he thought, "and I know so little about my life that it's a miracle I've stayed alive."

He didn't feel ignorant, in fact he didn't feel any different than most of the people he knew. In his case, there was just more he didn't know. That was the upside. The downside was his ignorance came from people misleading and lying to him.

He didn't understand why it had been necessary. Was the likelihood of his early death that real a threat, or was Sophie overreacting? Pearl had to go along with it since she'd been the one who'd thrown him out, so she must have seen the treat, too. It was a tribute to his youthful ignorance that he hadn't caught on. In reality, he'd suspected nothing at all. Sophie said they needed a warrior and that was why they called him back. But they called him the day before the killings. They'd already decided.

It was like Banner County existed on a different plain. Everyone connected to the Turners and Banners believed in some kind of magic. The one part he could not deny was the Banner Effect. Here he was again with virtually no sleep for days, riding a horse through the night, trusting people he'd never met, and racing off like some kind of gladiator to do battle with armed mercenaries to save the kingdom, and he felt fine about it. He had felt up to it since he had reached under the seat for his .45 in the parking lot of the Nowhere and shot it out with killers. He hadn't hesitated. He did what had to be done. Was that possible? Could he drive over a line on a map that marked Banner County and immediately feel like some action hero? Apparently. He thought about the tactile feeling when he reached the top of the pass. At the time he thought it was his imagination. Now he wasn't sure. He found that his thinking had become clearer and more decisive since his return, but what wasn't clear was how he felt about himself. When he looked inward to unlock the secrets of his life, all he found was the weight of the journey.

By the time the riders reached the yellow Jeep, false dawn had given way to the real thing. Somehow his belongings had made the trip with him. He tossed them in the back and hit the road. It was a good thing he met no other vehicles as he drove like a madman down the hill. Here he was again racing somewhere to save the day. The last time, he'd raced and failed.

Start to finish the trip from Sophie's phone to Cat's kitchen table took three hours and fifteen minutes. A steaming cup of coffee sat on the table

THE WEIGHT OF THE JOURNEY BY KEN BYERS

and Cat, eyes red and hands shaking, said, "the whole fucking world wants to talk to you."

"Hit me with the highlights," Farrell said, after a sip of coffee that burned his mouth.

"The President called. He ~ "

"Cat!"

"Okay. It's been a long night. Fulsom says the Staties are willing to play nice as long as they get the collar. They're arguing over the best way to catch these guys. They'll probably fuck it up meaning Pazer is toast."

"Pearl?"

"She knows who this Prus guy is. Very old money, like the beginning of time old, and mega rich. He made an offer on the whole shebang - mills, town, hills, everything. She turned him down. The guy was pissed, and told her she can't afford to turn him down. Too bad for him, but he doesn't have a clue as to her hole card. She thinks he sneaked a peak, found the gold transaction she used to pay her taxes, and has decided to lay siege to Banner. She's mystified as to how he thinks he can do it. How do you invade a county, in a state, in America? It's the big question."

"It's not an invasion. Just good old fashioned intimidation. The shootings at the Nowhere and the attack at Gold Night are classic tactics. He burns the town down and drives home the point she can't afford to say no, no matter how much gold she has stashed. Scale aside, this isn't much different than a street gang intimidating merchants. Pay up or we drive you out of business."

"What do we do? Call out the county militia?"

"There's a county militia?"

"Well, no, but everyone has guns. Most know how to use them."

"Let's hold off on that and give Fulsom and the state guys a chance to work it out. I'm more worried about the fires. What did the weatherman say?"

"I gave him directions here. I'm guessing if you put on a fresh pot he'd be here about the time it was ready. Fulsom said he'd mobilize everybody for fire duty. Can't hurt."

Cat was again close on his time guess. The coffee had been done for ten minutes when they heard a car in the drive. Farrell went out and greeted Mitch Ellers. They didn't spend any time on small talk.

"My smart phone doesn't seem to work here," Ellers said.

Cat gave him the password for the his Wi-Fi network and Ellers accessed the latest news from the National Weather Service in Portland.

"Nothing good," he said. "The winds are still out of the southwest. They've moderated a bit, but that's morning for you. They're still predicted to gust into the fifty and sixty mile an hour range by 1600 hours and temperatures will move into the 90's by 1500 hours peaking near 100 by 1800. Just like every day for the last week."

"We've faced this situation before," Cat said.

"I know you have," Ellers said, "but the fuel load is worse this time. All the beetle kill. What kind of resources do you have? No one seems to know."

Cat took a deep breath and looked at Farrell, then said, "This is called dropping your shorts in public. If I answer that question you get an inside look where we don't like outsiders looking."

"I can keep my mouth shut," Ellers said. "It would kill me, but I could do it. I've been obsessed with your cloud for thirty years."

"When you live in the forest," Cat said, "you learn to respect fire. We have fire lookouts at the passes where the mountains could channel fires out of the south. That's the direction they always come. You draw a line from Crescent City to Pazer and go five degrees east, that's the fire line. I've told you that much as a tip to the fact we're pretty well prepared, but it's always a question of size and fuel load. Banner Timber is pretty sophisticated when it comes to fire suppression. I think you need to be talking to them."

"How about if we all talk," Farrell said. "Let's get Pearl, Buck, Mitch here, and you and me set up in town. Does Banner have a fire center?"

"Yes."

"Give me my cell and let's get moving," Farrell said.

Farrell called Pearl. When he heard her voice he said, "You said it was important for me to find out who I am. I've met Sophie and we've talked. Does that count?"

"It counts. You okay?"

"Overwhelmed, but it has to wait." He told her about the weatherman, and suggested they all meet at Banner's fire center. She said she'd set it up.

Less than an hour later they all stood in a large room in a portable double wide inside the grounds of the pulp mill surrounded by maps and computer monitors. Mitchell Ellers made himself at home immediately after the introductions, and started downloading weather maps. Next he established a satellite downlink to Banner's system.

"We may wind up being helpless," Farrell said, "but at least we'll be well informed."

When Fulsom came in, he nodded at Dewey and pointed toward the door. Once outside, the background noise of the mill pushed them close to be heard.

"That state cop, Hamel, called," Fulsom said. "He said they found cell phone records between Elizondo and Tess McPherson."

"I wish I could say I'm surprised."

"Well, I am. I don't see Ma'am mixed up with selling weed."

"Maybe Tess had something going on the side."

"Why do I get the impression this isn't coming as a news flash to you?"

"I didn't know that. I guess I'm not surprised by anything that happens here. What shape's the town in?"

"We're using the fire as cover for new walking patrols," the sheriff said, as a green semi pulling a large chip trailer roared deeper into the mill along the main road. Wood chips scattered out of the top netting and littered the side of the road. Farrell saw a man sweeping, but the passing truck undid all he had done. "We've told people to get ready to evacuate on a moment's notice, so all that's working for us. What isn't, is that we don't know what we're looking for."

Farrell leaned against the aluminum side of the fire center. The building had an unobstructed path to the satellites in the southern skies.

"If you wanted to burn down Pazer, how would you do it, Buck?"

"Depends on the time of year. Now with the winds out of the southwest I'd start the fire halfway between the pulp mill, right here, and the plywood mill to the south. The mills watch for fire. People in town aren't as careful. If no one's watching, it could get out of control real fast."

"What would you use for an accelerant?"

"What are my choices? Lot of accelerants out there."

"Let's make it hard. Anything, because money's no object, but you can't stack dead brush up because people will see it. Say, something exotic and hard to spot."

"Where would they get it?" Fulsom asked. "With the fires, not an easy place to buy that kind of stuff without getting noticed."

"That is the question. Where would they get accelerants?"

"If they're not above bodily injury," Fulsom said, eyes lighting, "they could take a driptorch off one of the firefighters trying to light a backfire. Portable and effective."

"I think you're right. That's what they'll do. Can you find out if anyone is missing a driptorch?"

"I think they'll wear the outfits the firefighters are wearing, too. Yellow hard hats, face shields fire resistant pants, that stuff. They'd blend right in."

"Doesn't everyone know everyone else?"

"Not on a fire this big. A lot of out of state fire fighters are working this one but they aren't supposed to come into Banner. We don't pay for outside help."

"That should work for us. Strangers get taken down first. Questions come later. What if you post people on the rooftops to watch the vulnerable spots in addition to the foot patrols."

They started to go their separate ways until Fulsom called, "Hey, Farrell. How'd you get Mitch Ellers to come here?"

"We drink coffee together in Portland. Why?"

"The guy's famous. He's got some kind of sixth sense when it comes to knowing what a fire will do. They call him the fire demon."

"He's been dying to come here for years. He wants to go into the Cloud."

Fulsom laughed. "He'd fit right in."

Inside the command center, Farrell saw Banner managers and Pearl grouped around Ellers. All of them watched a computer monitor.

"We need your best guess, Mr. Ellers," Pearl said. "It's too wide a front for us to protect it all."

"That's the problem, Ms. Banner. Your cloud affects everything. I don't even know why it never changes."

Farrell stood behind them and looked at a computer rendering of the fire zone with a red swath headed for them.

"I thought you had some kind of magic touch," one of the managers said.

"More like a lot of experience that adds up to educated guessing. I need more information here."

"Like what?" Farrell called from the back.

Pearl and the others turned to look at him.

"As detailed a topographical map as you have," Ellers said. "The fire will stay west of the Cloud because obviously there isn't much wind right there. Whatever holds the Cloud in place acts like a wall. That narrows the possible path." He leaned closer to the monitor, then used the mouse. "I'd say the fire will come through about here."

He pulled the broad, red arrow a little to the left and close to Pazer.

"Ms. Banner? Do you have helicopters or a spotting plane?"

"Both. Which do you prefer?"

"I hate helicopters, but it will give me the best look. Can you arrange it? I should be able to refine my estimate after a flyover."

After Pearl arranged the flight, Farrell motioned her aside.

"I may not be reading that map right, but it looks to me like the fire is headed right at the Northbys."

"You're reading it right. You thinking of warning them?"

"I'm going out there. I need to talk to them before it's too late."

She took his arm and led him out of the building. They stood in the shade of the awning.

"Dewey, what's happening? You saw your mother?"

"That's going to have to wait. The Northbys have had the slab the Turners sent them for a couple of days. I want to know what they found."

"With everything that's going on, that's the top of your list?"

"Sophie thinks the reason I'm here now is to watch out for everyone."

"That's what she said?"

"More or less. You have a job to protect your land, Fulsom's job is to uphold the law. Mitch Ellers, Mr. Fire Demon, his job is the fire. What's that leave for me?"

"Johann Prus, for God's sake!"

"Buck can handle it. If you were Prus, what would you be doing right now?"

"I don't kill people to get what I want, so I don't know."

"You would be sitting behind a desk telling people what to do. That's what he's doing, wherever he is. How much do you know about this guy?"

"Rich. He is an acquirer. I guess you could call him a man of the world. He's a citizen of Poland, but hasn't been there in years. He lives mostly in Dubai and other places where the weather is dry and hot. His health is poor for a man his age. He's under fifty."

"How poor?"

"I don't know."

"If it's death's door poor, it would explain his need to be here. He has to think he can find health like Frederick did."

"How would he know about Frederick?"

"Because Tess was indiscreet. Cat heard Prus tell his local guy to find the notebooks. He also said something about a woman on the research team. You know about that?"

"Yes. Tess had gone outside for help. I approved it. The issues are too big and too specific. The science swamped her."

"That's how the word got out, but something must have already had his attention."

Another chip truck passed on the inner mill road wafting stray chips in its wake. The man with the broom was still there sweeping. Farrell pointed at the man.

"He can sweep forever and not make any progress," he said. With the sound of more approaching trucks, the man jogged to a barrel and removed a wide-nosed shovel. "He sweeps up about as much as falls off the passing trucks."

"Are you saying no matter what we do it makes no difference?" Pearl asked.

The sweeping man hurriedly filled his shovel from a small pile he'd pushed together since the last truck.

"No. I'm saying you gotta know when to reach for the shovel."

"I don't follow. What shovel are you talking about?"

"Special things make this a special place. If we're to save it, then let's use those special things. Where does the water for the falls come from? It's too late in the year for runoff."

"There are obsidian funnels all through the mountain," Pearl said. "They're like tubes. Water is forced up the tubes when the rivers back up in the winter. When the dry season begins, the water in the funnels feed the rivers as the water level goes down. Efram - you heard about Efram? - found a way to plug the tubes and use deep caverns as aquifers. There are huge compressors that pull the water out of the aquifers to fill the tubes."

"How much water is there?"

"There's enough water trapped in the winter and wet springs to feed the river and falls through all but the driest summers."

"And those tubes are all over?"

"There a lot of them. I don't know if we ever mapped the whole system."

"Okay. Come on. Let's go in and talk to the Fire Demon."

Johann Prus

The jet was an hour east of Hawaii on a course for San Francisco when the updates from Whitsett came in. The fire had created problems. The additional precautions taken by Banner and the outside help brought in to fight the fire, made it difficult for Whitsett to execute his plan. The message said with the way the fire was going he didn't know if he needed to torch the town. The fire would do his work for him. Prus slammed his fist on the seat table. An incinerated Banner would be a setback.

"Did you find the research site?"

"Yes. I was saving it since it's the only good news I have."

"I want that facility even if the rest of the county burns. Wait until I get there, and we'll go together." He hung up and then asked his assistant, "Who do we know in forest fires?"

The Weatherman

Mitchell Ellers' head swam. He was learning about his obsession under circumstances he hadn't foreseen. He was also fearful that it could all be lost if the winds broke the wrong way. If he needed any greater motivation, he had it. He stared at the monitor. The forward wall of the fire moving northeast stretched fourteen miles. It would go where it wanted and burn no matter the feeble efforts of man.

"These are the two areas we don't want the fire to reach," Farrell said, pointing to the map at two points about ten miles apart. "What do we have to do?"

"Hope it rains, but it's not."

"Come on, man, you're the fire demon, or witch. What can we do?"

"Okay," Ellers said, standing and leaning over the map. "What do we have that isn't on that map?"

Pearl touched the map and ran her finger from under the Cloud to the southwest.

"There are underground obsidian funnels that can carry water near each of these spots."

Ellers looked at her, and his pulse quickened. "How much water?"

"I don't know the cubic gallons per second, but a strong flow after the tubes are filled."

"Can the tubes be tapped?"

"Yes," she said. "When you depend on the forest you live with fire."

Ellers stared at the fire's location on the computer screen. "That'll help. What else?"

"We are good housekeepers," Pearl said. "The fuel load is light. We have beetle kill, but to the south much of it has been cut out. The floors are cleaned to prevent fire spread."

"Okay, so the fire will slow with less fuel," Ellers said, "but it won't be as much help as you think, because this thing crowned long ago. It's moving through the tops."

They all stared at the monitor.

"We're going about this wrong," Ellers said, and picked up a black marker. "If we block the fire here and here and tried to turn the fire the way cowboys turn a stampeding herd, we might have a chance. That would point the fire right where you don't want it, but it also brings it to your water supply. Could you fight it?"

Pearl and her managers standing around the table looked at each other.

"We have one more thing going for us," Pearl said. She stepped closer to the map and pointed off the map to the east. "There is a natural fire break in the Illinois Valley where the placer miners left a rock field a couple of miles wide and about ten miles long. Fires have been stopped there before."

"That gives you a realistic shot," Ellers said, "but no one beats a fire this size. You have to draw a defensible line in the trees, clear your area, get water to it, and fight like hell. Most important is the realistic part."

They stood over the map until Pearl said, "Send this as email to the list I give you, lines and all, then we can make the call."

Ellers keyed instructions into the computer, then asked, "Who gets it?"

Pearl gave him a list. When the emails had been sent, Dewey and Pearl they left together.

"You still going to the Northbys?" she asked.

"Yes, You?"

"I have to go to the office first. Wait an hour."

"I'm not good at waiting. I'm going to Cat's then up the road. Meet me at the Northbys."

"Just give me an hour. We'll take the chopper and you'll save time."

Farrell spread his arms. "I'm a man of action. I'd drive you crazy pacing while you worked. I'll be there. Besides, bet you a dollar you ain't out of here in an hour."

Johann Prus

"You must be realistic," the forest fire expert who lived in Bavaria said in heavily accented English. "I have seen the weather maps and the news is not good. The winds will come back and the fire will move faster. Is the landscape hilly?"

"I presume so," Prus said.

"Then it will spread faster. Are the people fighting the fire good at it?"

"They are experienced. I don't know if they are good."

"You have two choices. First, put your faith in those fighting and hope for the best, or, two, take action and remove what you value from the fire's path."

"No magic?"

"No magic. What is this cloud on the map? It's always there and seems out of place."

"The cloud is my problem. Will it impact the fire?"

"Without knowing details I would say yes. Under the cloud the air and the ground will be cooler and have more moisture. The fire may go around, or it may burn off the cloud."

After he broke the connection, Prus considered the choices. They came down to life or commerce. He had to be sure the secret to renewed health and longer life lay under the Cloud. If the cloud evaporated there was no guarantee the ground would have the same properties, the ones he so badly needed. The commerce element remained chancy. If he didn't have the cloud he would need the plants with the elevated THC. Plants could not be moved in a helicopter. Data could. He called the flight deck.

"Change our course. I want to go to Crescent City, California. Do what is necessary for permission to land there."

He waved at his assistant. "Send a message to Whitsett. Confirm my arrival in Crescent City."

Dewey Farrell

Cat gave instructions over the old fashioned phone to the Turners under the Cloud. When he hung up, he looked at Farrell.

"We're in over our heads here. We've never had to fight a fire that far out." He rocked the wheelchair with his hands. "It stretches our supplies line, just like Hitler going to Moscow. But that isn't our biggest problem. We're going to be very visible to the outside world. Turners don't do that."

"Clear choice, though. Reveal yourself and get the help, or lose it all."

"Yeah, it sucks."

"Sophie told me the Turners had gotten too big to hide. Maybe this is the coming out party. Try to keep her in the loop."

"I can do that," Cat said, to Farrell's back as he walked toward the door. "Where you headed?"

"Thunder Cap Road. Me and everyone else."

Farrell steered the yellow Jeep without a top over the familiar roads. As the smoke grew heavier breathing became more difficult and his eyes began to sting. The blue sky showed signs of yellowing around the top of the surrounding hills to the south and west announcing the fire. Nobody had offered a guess about how long before the fire reached the Northbys. He wondered how they would feel when they learned the land to their south would soon become the "line in the dirt" for the fire fighters. Outsiders would be coming from the west while the Turners would be coming from the east over paths and roads only they knew.

When he turned on to Thunder Cap Road he picked up speed and nearly missed the tight turn into the Northbys rutted drive. As he parked he heard helicopters to the south. From the sound there was more than one. He looked up expecting to see a Banner Timber chopper hovering with Pearl, but neither machine had the distinctive logo. He checked the clip in his automatic and stuck it in the back of his belt, then got out. He climbed the gate, and walked quickly passed the house and down the trail toward the greenhouses. By the time he got within fifty feet, Richard Northby stood in the doorway of the first building holding a shotgun.

"We thought you might be joining us," the edaphologist said. "We got a message from Sophie. She said tell you everything, but I don't know if we have time for everything."

Northby led Farrell into the humid, smoke-free, environment of the glass house. Tables with one plant to a container made twin rows on either side of a central aisle. Moisture dripped from the ceiling. Midge Northby stood over a table of small plants all in fiber pots. She looked up and pointed at the pots.

"Biodegradable," she said. "I'm sorry for the insensitivity I showed last time. I didn't know what I was doing." She looked at her husband and reached for his hand. "Spending all my time here with Rich, well, I've lost some people skills."

"How much time do we have?" Farrell asked.

"One of those gadgets over there will beep when the smoke reaches a certain level," Richard said. "It gives a warning, and then becomes more insistent."

"Let's get to it," Farrell started. "Why does it matter who I am?"

"You, we think," said Midge, "are the missing part of the Turner/Banner DNA that, for some reason, has mutated over the last two or three generations."

"How could you possibly know my DNA?" Farrell asked.

"When you left all those years ago, you left clothes and toiletries with the McPherson's. They sealed them in plastic. Tess got what she needed from a hairbrush. Then, we did a DNA analyses on the Turners. Even Sophie. Simply put, you are the son of Sophie and someone else who has no shared DNA with the Turners. That makes Eleanora your grandmother."

"Sophie's her daughter?"

"One of several. We can't figure out how she could disappear to have kids and not be missed."

"How can Sophie tell me it's okay for Pearl and me to have children?" Farrell demanded. "She's my first cousin!"

"No, not really," Richard said, to deflect Farrell's ire from his wife. "Eleanora is not Pearl's grandmother."

"Then who the hell is she?"

"Eleanora," said Midge, jumping back into the line of fire, "is Pearl's mother."

"That's ridiculous!" Farrell shouted. "Eleanora would have been in her seventies when she conceived. How could that be?"

"We know nothing beyond the anecdotal about the effects of living up. Obviously, that plays a role. When you said you were feeling stronger, younger, and healing faster since your return, we were thrilled. That was the first real evidence that you are who Tess claimed you to be."

"I can't accept this. Nobody would believe that Eleanora is Pearl's mother. What about menopause? How could she stay fertile all those years? Did she have a period all that time? Why would she want to, for God's sake!"

Richard held up his hands in a mock surrender. "We agree! The answers are to be some of the most exciting aspects of this research."

"It's one thing for Frederick to be fathering children, but Eleanora?" Farrell asked. "Don't tell me Pearl doesn't know."

"She doesn't," Midge said. "We don't think it's a good idea to tell her."

"But it was okay to tell me and belittle my ignorance?"

"This is not mere discrimination. Pearl can suffer no distractions. Especially now. You, on the other hand, dealt wonderfully with the information. You charged into the mountains and did precisely what needed to be done. We knew your nickname."

"I don't understand. What's wrong with doing it like everyone else? You have kids, they have kids, and bring the grandkids by to play on the floor."

"Is that how you did it?" Richard asked, quietly.

"Christ, this is confusing!" Farrell said. "If Eleanora is her mother that makes Pearl my aunt and Sophie's sister."

"And what's wrong with having a child with your aunt?" Richard asked. "It used to be done all the time. Keep in mind that society and heredity do not abide by the same rules."

"It's got to be against some kind of law."

"None that I know of, and even if it were it wouldn't be applied here."

"Okay, even if it's not against the law, what about the other part? The genetic issues?"

"We don't think there's a problem," Midge said. "It's far more likely the offspring of you and Pearl would repair the flaw in the Turners."

"'Think there's no problem,' and 'far more likely' do not inspire faith. How do you even know that much?"

"Tess compared your DNA with Pearl's. She needed some outside help to do the projected mapping of the child's DNA, but it was done."

"Very exciting," Richard said.

"How good is that projected mapping?" Dewey asked.

"Better than reading tea leaves," Midge said. "Nature is not precise, but the mappings indicated your children would repair the line."

"So Thatch's talk about finding a pot of gold was just talk to get me here?"

"I'm not so sure," Richard said. "He came here because Tess asked. Once he was here he did his thing until she told him to call you. By that time, she didn't know he'd already tried."

"To call me? When?"

"Maybe six weeks ago."

"He didn't leave a message."

"He chickened out. He was sure you didn't want to talk to him. When he heard your recording, he hung up."

"I didn't know. Why was he talking to you?"

"We were kindred spirits of a sorts. There aren't a lot of formally, well-educated men around here. He needed somebody to talk to, you know, a deep voice that would bullshit with him, help him feel normal."

"What did you talk about?"

"Initially, pretty general stuff. Nothing personal. Then it started to change. He asked what I knew about maps of any caves near the fringe of the Cloud. He wouldn't be more precise. I told him I'd never seen any, but rumor had it there were caves everywhere. Then he said, sort of out of the blue, if there was any gold around here it would be near where the Cloud starts. He never said why. From that time forward the only thing we ever talked about were caves and water. He was good at asking questions without tipping his hand at what he knew. About a month after he first brought up the maps, I asked him if he'd found any. He said he didn't need them, and winked. It was a cat that ate the canary kind of look."

Farrell could see it. Thatch saved it for his I-know-more-than-you-do moments that he enjoyed and Farrell had hated.

"He said a couple of days before he died he was ready to call you because he had something to say you would want to hear," Richard said.

"But Thatch came to Banner because of Tess," Midge said, "and Tess came because Pearl asked. Tess was supposed to find out what was wrong with the Turners. The book was a cover. Tess used our lab because our work was the logical place for her to start. She thought the Turner health problems might be connected to whatever gave the plants their astounding properties."

"Why?" Farrell asked.

"Two miraculous occurrences in the same place ought to have some connection," Midge said. "She had done DNA comparisons on generations of Turners. Fortunately, the Turners are as obsessed with genealogy as the Mormons. They are also practical. If Tess needed a sample, Sophie made sure she got it, even when it meant exhumation. Tess started with Frederick and Jessica, then went to Eleanora. From there she spread out. Direct descendants, then cousins, and so forth. She found what she called the 'magic mix' in Eleanora."

"Here's the really interesting thing," Richard said. "There was nothing remarkable in Frederick's DNA. Jessica's was more interesting in that she had different strains in hers, but in Eleanora - Frederick and Jessica together - there were mutations. Tess didn't like that word. Too negative. She preferred to call it changes. No matter the name, Eleanora's DNA had surprising changes."

"When Tess saw that," Midge said, looking across the room, "she stood right over there. She had this expectant look on her face. She said she didn't see how there could be that much change. Every child's DNA is 99 point something the same as the parents, so what happened?" Midge held up her hands. "Dewey, don't think I'm expert in any other science than botany, but she knew my limitation and kept her explanations simple. She wanted to brainstorm together. The idea we kept coming back to is that there's something in the air, ground, water, or maybe all of it, that goes right to the gene level."

"This is when the microscope gets put aside in favor of a walk in the woods," Richard said. "To have that much change, the outside world had to contribute."

The Northbys exchanged looks and stepped closer together.

"We knew this was a special place," Midge said. "It's what brought us here in the first place."

"We didn't come here to grow pot and get high," Richard said. "It's what our friends thought, but we came to figure out why the pot others grew here varied so much in quality. Quality not being fewer seeds, but the potency of the tetrahydrocannabinol, the THC."

"Before we came here, we heard about this mind blowing stuff from Oregon," Midge said. "Some guy had dropped out of Cal for the street life on Telegraph. He went to Oregon in May and come back in October with a ten pounds of weed that was the talk of the street. Everybody wanted to try it. Supposedly, one joint could lift a whole party."

"That was an exaggeration, but four or five lightweight hitters on the same joint was not," Richard said. "We tried it, agreed with the street talk and decided to find out why. We're still here. But the point is not all of the marijuana grown here is of equal chemical composition. Where it is grown . . ."

A beeping came from one of the machines.

"We need to step this up," Richard said. "Take my word that all things in Banner are not equal. The secret is the water."

"Sophie told me. I have questions, but I guess they'll have to wait."

"Yes. Places, like where we are right now, and others that sit in canyons or gullies, get enough runoff to build soil-rich deposits of minerals and materials that started out as gases and have been absorbed. When I can publish the soil science this is Nobel quality stuff. Nothing like it has ever been seen. The net effect is super-saturating. Sort of like you find the components of the soil you'd expect to find, but they're on steroids."

"Including the people," Midge added.

"But not all of the people," Richard said.

The monitor gave two beeps close together.

"Tess was making real progress when she was killed," Midge said, speaking faster. "We don't know enough about what life under the Cloud was like for the first Turners and Frederick, but it impacted his chemistry. How it changed is speculation. But Jessica descended from a polyglot mix of Eastern European bloodlines that, at least by myth and rumor, included some pretty exotic ancestors. The idea Tess played with before she died was that Frederick and Jessica figured out they were special."

"Tess had Frederick's notebooks," Richard said, "but she hadn't read them all. She hoped she'd find an answer there."

"Are they safe?" Midge asked Farrell.

"From the fire?" Dewey asked. "Yes."

"We don't have time for distraction," Richard said, and as he did, the beeper sounded twice again. They all looked at it. "In the realm of science, the amazing and unforeseen usually happen through wild coincidence. Often the coincidence happens after the planet goes through massive upheaval. It's like Nature shuffling the deck. There is no record of when the Cloud was formed. The tree slices the Turners sent were helpful. The oldest was over three hundred years, but the rings indicate the Cloud had been there all that time. There's no reason to think that it hasn't been here a hundred thousand years. Maybe more. It hasn't changed. The soil and mineral content of the area hasn't changed, so all the erosion has left us the best of the best. We do know the land has never been cultivated prior to us. If it had, there would be evidence."

"So it is, what it is?" Farrell asked.

"Exactly," Richard said. "Nature resents copycats especially when it comes to the biggest prizes. It spent all this time refining what we see here, and complicated it enough to make it impossible to replicate in the lab. We made some progress. Even discovered some things along the way, but more with the Doug fir seedlings than the pot. Sure, we can make changes, add some stuff, but bottom line, if you want the benefits, you have to live and grow here. When it comes to people living there is a price for those who aren't blessed."

"For every one like you," Midge said, and pointed at Farrell, "there are four Turner men who will die young. Before they are sixty."

"Sophie didn't want that to be me. That's why I got run off."

"We wondered about that," Midge said.

"Turners dying young weren't so obvious until about eighty years ago when people started living longer," Richard stated. "Not true for the majority of the Turners, especially the men."

The beeper sounded with five beeps close together.

"I have another question," Farrell said, and waved around the greenhouse. "You're Pearl's Plan B, right?"

"Plan B?" Richard said. "I guess."

"We're proud of this," Midge said. "The implications for our work are far reaching. Richard talked about Nobel consideration for his work in soils, but what we're doing in medicine in a field that has until lately been overlooked, is truly revolutionary. We looking at brand new ways of exploring the brain. New ways to treat brain disorders from PTSD to Alzheimer's to cancer. THC provokes a response in the brain that can be mapped. That's mainstream research. And it all starts right here."

"What was the marketing plan? What was Pearl's role?"

Midge and Richard exchanged looks. "Talk to her," Midge said.

"No, let's talk now. What was Pearl doing to sell dope by any name?"

"Nothing."

"Because she didn't know," Dewey said, and paused. "This was all Tess's doing. Right?"

"She didn't say a word," Midge said. "Tess was afraid Pearl would veto the idea. Tess couldn't wait for Pearl to make up her mind, because she said she was tired of studying the past. She wanted to do something that was happening now, and something somebody like her would study a hundred years from now. She figured Pearl would go for it if she handed her a completed plan that was already working and bringing in big bucks."

"What do you think happened?" Farrell asked.

"She knew Hector from Berkeley. He must have talked to the wrong lab."

"How did you two feel about Pearl not going public? Wouldn't that snuff your dreams of Noble prizes?"

The Northbys shared a look and stepped closer together.

"We're not proud of this," Richard said, "but we agreed with Tess. Pearl didn't need money or notoriety. She has the gold. She has it all."

Farrell heard a chopper landing. He ran for the door. By the time he reached it, he saw Pearl as she jumped down from the chopper.

"The fire's less than five miles away!" she yelled, as he ran to her. "It could explode up the draw any minute!"

She handed him two red canvas bags and carried two blue ones herself.

"The red bags have a new fire suit with a face plate and an aluminized shell to reflect the heat," she said. "The blue ones are the standard pack with the aluminum sheet for emergencies. Get the Northbys out here and lets go."

The Bell chopper could carry five plus the pilot who sat ready to go. The open side door beckoned as an escape route from the fire and the need to tell Pearl of the betrayal of Tess and the Northbys.

"We can't leave yet," he yelled. "Come on. Bring the bags."

She protested, but he kept going and hoped she came in his wake. Inside, he led her down the center aisle of the greenhouse, marijuana plants on tables on both sides, and saw the Northbys where he had left them. At least they hadn't tried to run out on the truth.

"Come on, this place ~ " Pearl started, but the smoke detector beeped four times. "What's that?"

"Smoke detector," Richard said. "After five beeps it goes to a steady tone. Then we run."

"Why wait? The chopper's right out there," Pearl said.

"You may not want us, Pearl," Midge said.

"Why?" Pearl looked from face to face and Dewey moved beside her, a bench loaded with plants between them.

"This is our fault," Richard said. "We showed Tess our THC research and she saw an opportunity. She tried to set up a deal to sell the finished compounds to pharmaceutical companies. Word got out."

"Why would she do that?" Pearl asked, her anguish apparent.

The fire detector beeped five times.

"She was tired of the past," Midge said, talking faster. "This was her chance to do something memorable."

"She did," Farrell said. "You said you showed Tess the research. Was that it, or did you give her copies?"

"Copies," Richard said, as the detector went to a steady tone. He bent over to pick up one of the fire bags, and as he stood his gaze traveled over Dewey's shoulder. "Get down!" he yelled as the tone stopped.

Richard dropped the bag and came up with a gun as Dewey ducked and pulled Pearl down after him. Two gunshots sounded very close together as the tone began its warning anew. He saw Richard take both to his chest and fly over backward into a table full of plants. The momentum of his impact sent the table crashing to the floor.

Midge screamed and threw herself on Richard's body. She scrambled to pull the gun from his hand as the tone grew more insistent. Dewey crawled beneath the upright bench to the Northbys. He felt Pearl following him. When he reached Midge, he held her back from leaping up and seeking revenge.

"Stay down!" Dewey demanded, then sneaked a peek. Three men stood near the door forty feet away. All had guns. He recognized the one in the middle as the man he'd shot in the shoulder at the Nowhere. The men spread out and moved cautiously closer. Dewey raised up and fired at the man to his right.

Farrell had been unlucky at the Nowhere when sweat fell in his eyes, but this time he got the shot off and hit his target in the chest.

"Nice shot, but you won't get another," the man in the middle called. "Two choices. You die by fire, or by gunshot. We're okay either way. In case you're thinking you can shoot the rest of us and fly your chopper out of here, that won't work unless one of you can fly. We took the liberty of shooting your pilot."

The smoke alarm turned to a horn and drowned out anything else the man had to say.

Midge felt her husband's wrist.

"There's a pulse! He's still alive," she said.

Dewey looked under the tables. He had no shot at their legs with all the supplies stacked on the floor. He stuck his head up and drew shots from both men. They had moved closer, but were taking their time. He thought of the Nowhere and the deliberate pace of the kill shots. Even with the fire, the shooters chose to relish their prey's last minutes.

Midge pulled on his arm.

"There's an escape hatch in the glass two rows back to your left. Use it. Find Tess's notes. It has everything we worked on for all these years."

"Come with us," Pearl said, to her.

"I won't leave him," Midge said. She looked around the greenhouse, reached for a spiked-leaf plant on the floor. "Without him, without this, what's the point? Go. Promise me! Find Tess's notes and don't let us be forgotten. We can save lives with this research. It's the only comfort we have left."

Pearl looked at Farrell, then said to her, "I promise."

"You'd better," Midge said, tears flowing. "Richard experimented with your seedlings. They were all he had for comparison. The notes are in the books. You want to see them."

While the women talked, Farrell reached under the table and grabbed the fire bags. He raised up, saw the men closer than the last look, then fired shots at both by sticking his hand up and hoping as he pulled the trigger.

"Come on, Pearl. We have to go!"

Dewey and Pearl crawled to the wall searching for the escape hatch. They found a plywood board over an opening used to shovel in topsoil. Farrell pushed and it fell back. He and Pearl scrambled through, crawled over the mounds of dirt, and ran for the woods.

From inside the greenhouse, Farrell heard two measured gunshots.

The Fire

The northeasterly edge of the fire found the gap in the mountains that would take it directly into Banner County. Firefighters to the east and west stopped mini-advances searching for the fuel to gain momentum, leaving the main body of the fire to move north. The fire needed more than wind. Without a glutton's array of fuel, the wind would thin the flames and eventually make it easier to stop. Fire, in that regard, was like any advancing army.

But the gap in the mountains had a plentiful supply of both beetle kill and downed limbs that storms had washed into the bottom of the gorge and beyond the reach of humans attempting to pick up after Mother Nature. The narrow opening slowed the fire, allowing it to build heat and energy as flames struggled to get through. Finally, when they did, they came with the fury of roaring dragons.

The fire screamed with passion as it raced up the draw.

Then, the unexpected. The leading edge met a wall of water that turned flame to steam. The fire had a greater supply of flame than the enemy had water, but then it met a second surprise - no fuel. The enemy had cut a fire break. The fire pulled back. It probed the walls to its side. Each time it got started on a hillside the fuel ran out. The hopes of exhausted firefighters soared.

Then the fire found another escape. A narrow gorge with rich ground cover and windfall. A gusting tailwind gave it a boost. The fire escaped. It's roar sounded like laughter to the firefighters who witnessed the break out.

The Weatherman

From his seat in the second Banner chopper, Mitch Ellers had a view of the fire more dramatic than he'd ever seen firsthand. His fire work usually came through computer monitors. What the sterile monitors could not provide was the smell and the sound. Even the chopper's blades could not drown out the roar of the fire consuming every combustible in its path.

His excitement grew steadily grown as the plan to herd the fire into the canyon seemed to be working. Each time the fire tried to break in a new direction it failed.

He asked the pilot to take him higher. The chopper climbed a thousand feet. From this perspective, Ellers could see the fire's front threaten Banner County. Smoke climbed thousands of feet in the air. It climbed so high the authorities now directed non-firefighting aircraft around the plumes. Through the smoke he saw flames. They, too, formed a wall. The last satellite imagery he'd seen had put the hottest spots at more than six thousand degrees Fahrenheit. Observers in planes reported small firestorms with swirling flames creating hellish patterns of orange and purple that exploded without warning into the deepest red imaginable, and then to white.

To the east and north he saw the Cloud. It stood as a solitary sentinel primed to protect all it covered. Unless the fire could be contained, the showdown was less than a day away. He struggled to find condolence. If he could not see beneath the Cloud he would see its historic demise.

He looked for terrain features that might help fire fighters stop the fire before it destroyed the Cloud. He pointed out at a ridge line to the pilot.

"Sorry, sir," the pilot said. "That's a no fly zone."

"Says who?" Ellers said, surprised.

"Ma'am says, and what she says goes."

"Ma'am?"

"Ms. Banner. None of her people go near the Cloud. Right here is closer than I 've ever flown, and I'm not going closer."

Ellers swept the area with his field glasses.

"There," he said and pointed. "Two choppers on the ground. They're in your no fly zone and one of them has the Banner logo."

"That's her bird. She goes anywhere she wants. I don't recognize the other one."

"Can you radio her and get permission? I need to get closer."

Repeated efforts to raise the other chopper failed.

"I don't get it," the pilot said, as they watched the Banner chopper lift off. "She's not answering."

"Let's go after them and see if they need help," Ellers suggested, not willing to give up.

"If they do, we got no help to give," the pilot said.

"Can't you call in her position?"

The pilot called the fire control center and asked if they had been contact with Banner One. They had not. They radioed in its position and that it had not responded to radio calls. The pilot asked for permission to fly closer to the Cloud.

After a long delay, the response came, "It's your ass."

Dewey and Pearl

Dewey and Pearl ran deeper into the trees until they were sure they were not being pursued. Smoke made breathing difficult. When they stopped they both dropped to a knee.

"They killed them both, didn't they?" Pearl asked.

"Yes. How close do you think the fire is?" Dewey asked between deep breaths.

"We'd hear it and feel it if it were close. Tell me what's going on."

"Blame it on Tess. I'm guessing that Prus guy found out and that's when he made his first overture to you. When that didn't work he figured he could take you by force. Tess started this and paid for it big time."

"Her notes that Midge said we need to find, do you know where they are?"

"Yes. Can you get us through the trees to our pool?"

"Our pool?"

"That's it. The cave where the boxes are stored are above the pool. Sophie's cave is near there, too. If those guys found the Northbys, they might know where the stash is, too. If we can get there, maybe we can stop them."

"I can get us close unless the fire makes us go in a big circle."

"We have these," Dewey said, and pointed to their packs.

"They won't do much more than keep us alive if get we get caught in the open. There are no coolers and no air supply."

She took the lead and kept a strong pace. He admired the confidence she exuded with every sure step. He tried to put his feet where she put hers. It made for an uncomfortable, choppy stride for his longer legs, but he accepted it as preferable to falling and risking injury. He kept up, but the pace began to wear.

She stopped near the tree line on a steep side hill. She pulled her pack around and unzipped. Inside, she found a bottle of water and drank deeply. He did the same.

"You know how to put one of these suits on?" she asked.

"No."

"The gloves and booties are in the bag's side pocket next to the water and the matches. Put the suit on first, zip it closed. Make sure the headgear is tucked into the neckline, then go to the pocket. Boots then gloves. And, Dewey, don't wait too long. It's not as easy as it sounds."

"You start, and I'm right behind you." As he drank the last of the water, he asked, "Do you hear that?"

A distant roar from over the ridge grew louder.

"Keep the fire above you," Pearl said. "It would follow us uphill."

"I remember the rules. My dad drilled them into me."

"I'm sorry, Dewey. Where was he killed?"

"Not far from here, I think. You know how it was, no one said much past 'I'm sorry.' I wonder if this high tech suit would have saved him."

"Let's hope it saves us," Pearl said. "Come on, let's go."

They cleared the tree line and jogged across a clear cut. The angle of the steep slope grew higher when they reached the trees. Smoke billowed over the hill above them. Pearl coughed.

"Down," she said. "Use that creek bed to move to the next hill."

They ran down the hill. She jumped and used the side of her foot to brake. Dewey tried the same move and fell. He rolled and tumbled down the slope. He kept his head away from the ground and trusted to luck. He felt a sharp pain in his right knee, but it was the knock of a rock rather than the tear of a ligament. Pearl caught up seconds later.

"Anything broken?"

"Pride. Let's go."

Their way slowed at the bottom of the trough formed by the heavy rains of winter and spring. Pearl stopped, and looked up. Dewey did, too, but there was no alternative other than to slog along the creek bed.

"Bad spot to get caught by the fire," Dewey said, stepping on a branch that snapped under his weight.

"You lead. You can break this stuff up better than I can."

He stamped on branches that he could crush making the way easier for her. He kept his head down, picking his steps carefully.

"Oh, no!" Pearl cried.

Dewey looked up. A wall of flame came around the corner with long tongues of flame leading the way.

"Go back!" Dewey yelled.

He turned and saw another curtain of flame closing the other end. He looked around, then pulled her in the direction they'd been headed until they found a rocky shelf going up the hill. He picked up a desiccated bush lying on the bottom that still had dried leaves. He scrambled in the pack to find matches. He got them out and struck the first cardboard match. His hands shook and the fire went out.

"Backfire?" Pearl asked.

"Not much of one, but I don't see another choice," he said as he struck the second one. This time it burned and he held it next to the leaves. They caught, wavered, but Pearl fanned it and the flame stayed lit. They raked combustibles with their hands into a pile, and when the fire got started they grabbed short branches and sticks and stuck the ends in the blaze. After their staffs ignited, they ran around their shelf starting fires to clear as much fuel from around them as possible.

When they had five smaller blazes started, Pearl opened her pack. "Now," she said.

She got her smaller body into hers well before he did. She had the suit and the booties on while he was still trying to get his feet down the pants leg.

"Sit," she demanded.

With her help, he got his feet through the legs. He leaned back and zipped while she removed the booties and gloves from his pack. He got the booties on, stood, and then they checked each other's suits. The heat in the narrow gulch drew sweat from every pore.

Before Pearl pulled her hood over her face she looked at Dewey.

"I love you," she said. "I have since I first saw you in the forest."

"I love you, Early."

They kissed, pulled their hoods down, and put on their gloves.

The Weatherman

Ellers watched the two helicopters disappear into the Cloud. His brave pilot who had put his job on the line this far, said nothing further.

Ellers watched the fire as they circled. He used binoculars looking for places where there was no fuel. As he searched he saw two people on a slope trudging into a slit in the hills. He trained the glasses on them and recognized Farrell and Pearl Banner.

"There's your boss!" he shouted, and pointed.

"Who's got her bird then?" the pilot asked, fighting buffeting from the winds.

"More important," Ellers said, "they can't see the fire over the ridge. They're running into a trap! Any way out?"

"No. No place to set down, and too much turbulence to hover."

Ellers watched the flames crest the ridge. Farrell and Banner must have seen their danger, because they stopped. The two pulled silvery clothing out of a bag.

"What are they doing?" the pilot asked, and moved the chopper back as the turbulence threw them around.

"Fire protection suits," Ellers said, as he watched. The two raked a pile of debris, then Farrell bend over it. "Their burning the fuel to keep the fire off them!"

He watched as Farrell and Banner tried to burn a hole to hide in. Next they put on their suits.

"Oh my God!" Ellers yelled. "They have to turn around!"

Dewey and Pearl

Dewey hoped the flames would leap over them and move on because of their little backfire, but it was a longshot. Pearl pointed at a narrow runoff crease in the creek bed partially shielded by the rock shelf. He pointed at her, then down to the spot. She lay down, then he covered her with his body.

The hoods had faceplates, but their first job was to save their lives. Allowing sight was a distant second. They didn't need to see to know the distance to the fire. The heat built to a screaming agony inside the aluminum shell, and sounded like the gates of hell screeching open. The sides of the gulch bounced the fire noise back and forth. Individual sounds disappeared into the cacophony that threatened to swallow them.

Dewey imagined every molecule outside their suits screaming its demise as the fire consumed it. He felt Pearl under him. He saw a shallow notch in the runoff bed that had eroded dirt from underneath the rock. He rolled so he could push her into the overhang. He got her as deep into the small crease as possible then sealed her in with his body.

The fire swept over him, then lingered as it danced on him.

He imagined the inside of a rotating cement mixer. He felt the noise of shifting cement, the buffeting as the drum turned, and the battering of small rocks hitting him as the fire exploded around him. His body anticipated spontaneous combustion. Heat soared beyond the endurable into a white world of senseless pain that filled the inside of the aluminized shell like a ripe tomato ready to burst. He couldn't breathe. His only thoughts were of hope and how much he had to live for.

Then the fire passed. He was sure it had been gone for many seconds before his ears stopped ringing and he could hear the silence. He felt Pearl moving, and knew she, too, lived.

He knew the ragtag impurities of his life had been burned away. Only the miraculous and angelic remained. He knew this to be a state of mind that would take time to appreciate, but appreciate it he would. No evil could possibly have made it through. There would be new expectations for his life now. And new abilities. He wondered what they would be.

Pearl pushed against him. He braced himself before he moved preparing himself for the pain of singed skin rubbed by the suit. Moving demanded breathing. He discovered there was no air. He ripped the hood off and gasped, forcing a racking cough from the smoke of smoldering remains that filled his lungs. He tried smaller breaths and was rewarded by air filled with smoke, but air nonetheless.

He pulled Pearl to her feet. As he helped her out of the mask he warned her to take small breaths. She ignored the advice and coughed and gasped as her knees gave way.

"Try it my way," he said, slipping a hand under her arm and holding her steady, but he suspected they steadied each other.

"We're alive!" she marveled.

The Weatherman

Ellers and the pilot watched as the fire swept unbroken through the gulch. It stopped for seconds over where the two had gone to ground inside their fire suits.

"They don't have a chance," Ellers yelled, feeling a sense of failure as the figures disappeared..

"Look!" the pilot yelled. "They're alive!"

As if the earth opened and two aliens emerged from the depths, two silver beings stood like exclamation points against the charred backdrop. When they ripped off their hoods, Ellers and the pilot cheered. Seconds later the silver-clad survivors trekked toward the edge of the burn.

"Come on," Ellers said. "Let's get the word out about where they are. Maybe it's not too late to help."

"They'll get help, but not from us," the pilot said, and pointed out the windscreen. "They're headed for the Cloud."

Dewey and Pearl

They stood. He imagined how they would appear from afar, perhaps from the air. Two silvery humanoid creatures standing in a sea of smoking black punctuated by small fires sucking the last lick of fuel out of a dead hillside that had lived only minutes ago. He looked at her face streaked with sweat, and he was sure tears. A fierce, defiant light burned in her eyes that his own no doubt contained as well – the look of death stared down.

"I can't stand this suit another second," she screamed, and tore off the gloves.

"Leave it on until we clear the burn," he said.

"Why? You think it's going to flare up again? There's nothing left to burn!"

"Let's see what's waiting around the corner. If I take this thing off I'll never get it on again."

241

They walked, hood in hands, toward the burned out end of the gulch. Smoke from areas where the fire still thrived blew over them in gusts both blinding and choking them. Farrell imagined the landscape rivaled the devastation of a nuclear bomb blast, or the arid terrain of a distant planet.

At the mouth of the gulley they turned into the crossroad of two worlds. To the uphill, the fire had raced up the grass and scrub trees in seconds leaving blackened sticks and wilted ferns in its wake. To the downhill, green slopes and new growth existed.

"How could this happen?" Dewey asked.

"The vagaries of nature. How are we alive? We should have been baked in those suits. They weren't designed for fire that intense."

"How do you feel?" he asked.

"Different." She kicked the booties off, unzipped the suit and waved him closer so she could lean on him while she removed it. "Very different. I can't put words to it yet. You?"

"Purified, but I don't know what it means. I think I lived because I'm supposed to do something."

"What?"

"Something with a purpose. I can't take the credit alone for living through that." He went through the same process to get out of his suit as she had. "I guess I'll find out when the time comes."

Their clothes were soaked as thoroughly as if they'd jumped into water.

They stood shoulder to shoulder looking down the living hill, the burned out side at their backs. The smell of the devastation hung heavy in the air. He took her hand.

"We'll feel better when we reach our pool," he said.

They started walking. He followed her as she cut across the side hill toward a ridge line he recognized from his journey up the river. Their way appeared free of fire, but how long it would stay that way they didn't know.

"Do you think my pilot is really dead?" she asked, taking a quick look over her shoulder.

"Unless they needed him, yes. They like killing people."

"Dan was a good man. He had a family. I knew them. This will be hard."

"There are hard times ahead all over Banner County."

"There's something I haven't told you," Pearl said. "There is a GPS locator on board my chopper that leads to my landing spot above the falls. It's the last place to land a helicopter before the Cloud. I always use it."

"Why would they go there?"

"It's what Prus is after."

"What? How do you know?" he asked.

"Kind of a long story," she said, as they walked. "Frederick published a monograph in 1912 under a *nom de plume* theorizing the effects of living under the Cloud. Eleanora tried to buy up all the copies, but she no doubt missed some. One of the big three theories Frederick put out was the possibility of reversing the effects of premature aging. Prus is dying of old age at forty-seven."

"You know him, for Christ's sake?"

"Know? No, but he's hardly a secret. I researched him after he made an offer to buy me out."

"What about the other three theories?"

"One was the benefits of inter-marrying to propagate the dominance of strong family traits. Frederick wrote it long before gene research, so this was pretty heady stuff. The other was that there was no such thing as recessive traits. Heredity uses everything. The less noticeable traits hold subtle influences that determine who we love and who we would be most successful mating with."

They stopped talking while they moved along a narrow path where a misstep would send them down the hill. When they reached safer ground, Dewey asked, "I thought that was called natural selection."

"Frederick foresaw a sort of un-natural selection where the family intuited how to best preserve itself. Twenty years later a Hungarian psychologist named Leopold Szondi theorized what he called a 'familial unconscious' as part of his encompassing theory. He called it genotropism."

"I've seen that name, Szondi. It was in Tess's notebooks in the cave. She thought his work was worth looking at with the Turners."

"Eleanora thought Szondi had seen Frederick's monograph, but I read Szondi and I don't think so. Even with the problems of the 1930's, if Szondi had read it, he would have shown up on our doorstep. Frederick didn't use his name, but a motivated researcher could have figured it out even with Frederick supposedly dead. Things were different then. Death was no guarantee of the end."

"This is how the Turners figure out who is supposed to have kids with whom?"

"It's part of it, but only the Mother knows the whole process."

The discussion of family moved them toward dangerous waters. Farrell didn't want to talk about Sophie, and he didn't want anything about Pearl's parentage to come up.

"How much further?" he asked.

"Two steep miles. I'm tired and need water." She stopped, and tugged on the shirt stuck to her skin with sweat. "And this is killing me!"

"Where's our path take us?"

"What do you mean?"

"Brambles, whippy branches, poison oak? If there isn't we can take our shirts off. I've seen you in less."

"We have to have a plan. If Prus or his men follow the GPS coordinates, it takes them near the upper entrance to the tunnel."

"The entrance through the tree?"

"You found it?"

"Yeah, but I had to look for it. I guess, like looking for the author of the monograph, if you're motivated you'll find what you're looking for."

"Do you know how to get to the cave from the pool?"

"Sophie led me, but I was thinking about her, not where I was going."

"Could you get us close?"

"Yes, once we're there. But it took me part of two days to get up the river to reach the pool."

"I'll get us to within a half mile before we have to use the river."

"Let's do it. Between us we can make it."

He pulled his shirt off and tucked it into his belt. She looked at his chest.

"You've changed," she said, then unbuttoned her shirt. She didn't look at him as she took it off.

"So have you," he said, as he looked at her.

They started walking, him bare chested and her in a sweat stained white bra.

The Fire

During the week the fire had grown into the monster that now ravaged the Coast Range in both California and Oregon, it had profited from every whim and breeze of nature. Whenever a junction presented itself, the fire went the way of the heaviest fire load even if the fire load was out of reach at the time of the choice. Inanimate objects don't suffer from luck, and there were reasons why the fire took the course that promised the best fuel, such as a moist breeze from the ocean that was the reason the fuel existed in the first place.

The fire rode the gusting winds swept the blaze skittering along the tree tops in a devilish dance that carried it miles in minutes. The fire's speed ran it passed the fire lines and all resources lined up against it leading to wide spread calls for evacuation in Banner County and all the way to the coast in places like Gold Beach and Port Orford.

As the advancing fingers of the fire probed Banner County, it met adversity for the first time. Promising fuel loads led into box canyons where the fuel was quickly exhausted and the fire burned itself out. In other places the fire roared around a hillock and met itself on the other side, the first to arrive depriving the second of the necessary fuel. They burned against each other and then were snuffed like a child blowing out a candle.

Part of the obstacles were bad luck; a trip up a blind draw, or a probe onto a barren hillsides that led to fuel-less dead ends. Others were part of the Turner's fire preparation. Substantial firebreaks had been kept clear of fuel from the days when Placer mining cut great swaths across the land near the southern boundaries of Banner County. These rock strewn scars were technically in Josephine County, but no one there wanted to tend to the useless property, so the Turners, always mindful of their history, did. They knew the great fires always came from the southwest and saw the slag fields as allies in their battle against the purges of nature. Most of the Illinois River Valley had been heavily mined at the beginning of the twentieth century, and coincidentally this acted as the first line of defense to protect the Cloud from a head on assault. That left the flanks, but with the frontal attack under control, the Turners concentrated their homemade technology on the edges.

The most serious challenge to the firefighting supremacy of the Turners came on the western slope of their mountains. This leg of the fire came within yards of blowing past the defenses near the Northby's greenhouses. If the fire had breached there, there was nothing left to protect it before it stormed in on Pazer.

The order had been out for several hours to evacuate the town, but no one left. In one hundred and forty years no one had ever left and the current residents were not to be the first to give up. Instead, they went out in force to fight.

Dewey and Pearl

They hadn't spoken since heading for the river. His fire-induced dry mouth left his tongue and lips swollen and cracked. He tried every trick not to think about being thirsty. He knew Pearl was as bad off as he was. His chest hair was the first to note a change in the wind. Instead of the blast furnace drafts that had made them cringe with each gust, this new breeze cooled against his skin.

"You feel that?" he asked.

"Yes, thank god. We're almost to the river. Can you do another ten minutes?"

"As long as it's no more than ten."

The last two hundred yards included climbing down the rock face Dewey had chosen not to climb on his journey upriver. They climbed down, testing each step. He went first, then steadied her with one hand while hanging to a rocky outcrop with the other. Several times he held the belt loop in the back of her pants while she leaned forward to see a path down for them.

"I'm fading here, Pearl."

"Five minutes."

"Your ten minutes was up a half hour ago."

"Think about tearing off your clothes, jumping in and feeling the river close over your head."

"If I tear off my clothes I might not be thinking of the water."

"Then you're not in that much pain. Come on, we're almost there."

When they reached the bottom, they both sat on a rock and stared at the river. It wasn't much. No more than twenty feet across, but there was a steady flow, and it promised relief. They searched for the inner strength to make it the last thirty feet. He took deep breaths and noted the absence of smoke at the bottom of the river's gorge. He stood and reached for her. He noted the dirt streaks on her face, the rivulets of sweat down from her chin that dropped between her breasts, then disappeared. He felt an attachment to her he knew he would never lose. It had nothing to do with love, at least in the classic sense. It came from the shared journey, the quest, the road home. What it lacked was the sense of completion. This was not the end of the road. It was the first step on the next leg.

Hand in hand they walked with shaking legs to the water. As they neared it, he let go of her hand. He dropped his gun and his shirt on a rock, then took her hand again. They stepped closer to each other, then, hip to hip and hand in hand, they waded into the river. They kept going until they stepped into deep water, and sank below the surface. The sensuousness of the feelings of water soothing him penetrated his every pore, and nearly drove him to rapture. He parted his lips to let water seep in to his parched mouth. Slowly his body bloomed to its pre-fire state.

He felt no need to swim to the surface and breathe air. The oxygen in the water seemed to give his dehydrated body what it needed. Pearl hung, arms outstretched in a crucifix-like cross, in the water above him before slowly rising to the surface. Dark spots formed in his mind and before his eyes, and he followed her up. He gasped as he broke into the air. He opened his eyes after he shook off the water.

She stood near him, water to her neck. She reached for him. His feet touched bottom and he walked toward her, found her hand and waded closer until they were eye to eye. He pulled her into an embrace. Still clinging to each other, they looked up river. They heard the falls around the bend.

They retrieved their shirts and walked on. She knew ways he had not found that kept their path out of the water. Once they could see the falls they kept in the trees to avoid a watcher stationed above the fall.

"Where did Sophie enter the tunnel?" Pearl asked.

Farrell took the lead. It slowed them down because he didn't know where to step. She tapped his shoulder, and said, "Point."

Less than five minutes later they pulled limbs away from the entrance.

Johann Prus

He'd always blamed his dislike of leaving his crystal towers on his health, but that wasn't the only reason. Power was an illusion, and he hated to feel powerless which is how he felt each time he ventured out. Only the 'powerful' knew the extent of the illusion. The world was big. Huge. Biggest of all was nature. Winds destroyed what any man might own, seas dismantled seaside mansions and castles, and fire consumed any structure and its contents no matter how grandiose.

But at no time had he felt as insignificant as when he saw the fire. He'd seen the smoke for over an hour without knowing what it was. It seemed to reach to the heavens fed by an inferno whose appetite for destruction beyond his comprehension. His first sight of the angry orange flames made it clear what he wanted mattered not at all.

He marveled at Whitsett and his hard men who made their plans and talked of success, and how they would spend the money Prus had transferred into numbered accounts. Not once did they speak of fear or death. Prus thought them naïve. Perhaps no mere mortal could kill them, but one look out the windscreen should convince them they were not up against a mortal.

Prus believed in results. Process often bored him. When Whitsett said he discovered the site of the lab, Prus didn't ask how. Their chopper had flown wide of the fire to avoid the working helicopters dragging monstrous sacks from their bellies filled with water or fire retardant. Their pilot ignored radio hails to identify themselves and to get out of the fire zone. Their one close brush with disaster was with a lumbering World War II relic that swooped out of a canyon almost in their face, the last vestiges of reddish-orange powder trailing out of its bomb bay doors. Their pilot swerved to avoid the falling fire retardant, but the chopper bounced on the wake of the bomber's passing. Prus breathed easier when the pilot landed next to another helicopter whose rotors idled. He saw the Banner Timber Products logo on the fuselage, and his pulse quickened. He focused on his goal.

When Whitsett shot the Banner pilot, Prus felt nothing.

He waited while Whitsett and two of his men went into the greenhouse. Their instructions were simple. Remove all paper and any computers. Plants and equipment were in the hands of fate and the direction the fire chose to take. He sat in the left front seat of the chopper as the numbness of purpose slowly faded, and feelings unclear and mysterious seeped in. They, he, was here to win a longer life. Many had died, and more soon would, for him to win his desire. This is the way it had always been. The insignificant, the powerless, the poor, the masses, often died on the altar of another's ambition. It would always be this way.

Surrounded by fire, heresy slapped his face. What if that wasn't the way of the future? What if the coin of power was no longer money and what money could buy? How often had he said in the last few years what he wanted most could not be bought with all his wealth? If what he found this day proved to be a longer and more virile life, it would be his not because he could buy it but because it was bestowed upon him. It would prove the coin of the realm had changed. More startling was that this coin could never be his to own. Nature defied petty ambitions.

In a previously unknown moment of omniscience, he foresaw the choice he would face would be the lingering end to his gaudy life with its trappings and illusions, or a longer life of simplicity and an adherence to disciplines he'd never considered. He had not yet set foot in this place that had haunted his dreams, but he already felt the change transforming him on the simplest and most elemental level.

He remained only vaguely aware of gunshots from inside the greenhouse, and when Whitsett and one fewer man than went in came out, they climbed aboard the Banner chopper. Whitsett laughed shortly after they boarded when he found a GPS setting he said would lead them where they would find what they sought. The pilot took off and flew a course east of the leading edge of the fire.

When Prus saw the Cloud for the first time, he caught his breath. When he could speak, he said, "That's it?"

"That's it," Whitsett said. "How do you plan on owning that?"

Prus did not answer but saw the futility of such an idea.

They flew over a gorge with a magnificent waterfall at one end before landing near the fringe of the Cloud. The stands of giant trees suggested they had lived as long as his family had ruled. The idea added to his sense of insignificance.

"The doctor's research should be in a cave near the falls," Whitsett said.

Dewey and Pearl

"Do you know what a whisper line is?" Pearl asked, before they entered the tunnel. "In cave systems like this there are places where the fissures in the rock meet, like the center of a spider web, and carry sound. It's use is limited because you can't tell where the sound came from and sometime you can't distinguish what the sound is, but it is helpful if you want to know if you're alone."

"How far to one of these whisper lines?"

"Not far."

"Can we be heard, or is it listening only?"

"Two-way, but if you're thinking of having a conversation, that doesn't work. Whoever is at the other end of the line has to have an ear against the rock in just the right place. Even so, it's best to talk out here."

"Then let's have a plan. Prus, or at least his mercenaries, have to be near. He knows the magic is in the Cloud. I doubt he's told his goons the real reason he's here, so he may have left them near the mouth of the cave. How good is Sophie's early warning system? Would Prus be able to reach her without her knowing?"

"Not usually, but the fire may have all the watchers busy. I thought Cat was going to do that."

"Just covering our asses here. Could Prus find his way to her on his own?"

"Maybe. There's been no reason to be careful for a long time, so there's probably a trail."

"You think he could find his way?"

"Yes. I'll go and warn her. Can you manage here?"

"If I don't get lost, and if they're here at all, I can cause some problems. Guide me to the whisper line and then point me in the right direction."

"I don't feel good about this," Pearl said. "You have no weapon. They do."

"I've made it this far. Nothing's going to stop me now. Besides, we don't have a choice. I have local knowledge on my side, Early. The caverns and tunnels are small so there's no way they can gang up on me. Just do what you need to do with Sophie and I'll manage."

They walked into the black hole of the tunnel. She placed his left hand in the groove as Sophie had, and made sure he could distinguish the directional nicks. Farrell counted steps so he would have an idea of how far they had traveled. One hundred and thirty-one steps in, she stopped. She placed her hand on his head, then guided it to the wall. She whispered, "Use your hand to find the slit in the rock then listen."

He heard indistinguishable noise. From the rhythm he guessed voices. He stepped back.

"There's someone here," he whispered.

"Stay uphill and to the right. There are only two forks. Be careful."

"You, too. Say hello to Sophie."

He heard her walk away, then started uphill. He couldn't quite reach the other side of the passage, and worried about missing the fork. Every five steps he stopped to feel across the tunnel. He found the first fork more by sensing it rather than by feel. He stopped and felt the wall above the hand guide for the fissure of the whisper line. He didn't feel it and moved on. He tried again one hundred steps later, and this time felt it. He pressed his ear to it, but heard nothing. He knew he'd been right the first time. He needed to get to the notebooks He walked faster.

It was his haste that made him miss the second fork. He discovered his mistake by walking full speed into the end of a tunnel where no end should be. The impact knocked him to his knees. He berated himself for his carelessness. As his head rang his claustrophobia crushed his chest.

"Thatch!" he whispered. "Here I am in the cave again and I hate it. How about some help, Mr. I'll-Always-Be-Here-For-You?"

"Not until you really need it," said the voice in his head in Thatch's most obnoxious tone.

"So, here I am lost in the blackest cave in the world and I don't need the help? I can't wait until I do!"

"It's going to be a doozy."

"How do you know these things?"

"Does it matter?"

252

"No. Where the hell am I?"

"Twenty strides back and hang a left." Twenty strides later he found the fork he'd missed.

"There, I helped you," Thatch said. "Stop whining."

Farrell found the groove in the wall and walked uphill. He felt the ceiling closing in. He'd reached the small opening where he'd gone from one world to the other, and listened for the fall. Faintly he heard the whisper of water cascading past the cave mouth. He squatted and, without his pack, slipped through it easily. He felt his way uphill.

It startled him when he saw light ahead. The mercenaries had found Thatch's boxes. He stayed in the shadow where he could see the chamber. The boxes of books were unstacked and the flaps were pulled back, but they were still there. He saw no one, and moved slowly into the chamber. Carefully, he stepped to the next chamber with its ledge next to the falls.

"What took you so long? We didn't think you'd ever get here."

The voice came from the tunnel that led to the surface. The man Dewey had shot in the Nowhere's parking lot stood with a gun in his hand. The killer stood tall, but leaned toward the shoulder Dewey had shot. He held the gun with the other hand.

"Who are you?" Farrell asked.

"Good question. Is it literal or philosophical?"

"Literal, but I'm in no hurry."

"No, you aren't. You have all the time left to you in this world. My name is Roy Whitsett, but you can call me the Angel of Death. Others have."

"Roy works for me. Sounds friendly."

"Seems like all I do is offer you your choice of deaths, my friend," Whitsett said. "Very creative last time, but now we'll try to be good to our word. Here are your current choices. You can die being helpful, or you can die refusing to help. I guess you could say you'd be dying to help." He laughed, and another man laughed behind him, although Dewey could not see him. The gun wavered and a grimace slipped across Whitsett's face. "No way to undervalue a sense of humor at a time like this. Speaking of, this is one of those moments you see in movies, when the villain, me,

253

has the drop on the good guy, you, and instead of shooting him and getting it over with, he bullshits with him giving the hero a chance. I guess I'm challenging you to take a chance. You have nothing to lose."

"Some challenge. You're armed, I'm not. You have your buddy behind you and he's armed, too. Not very sporting."

"Ahh, you want sporting. Not going to happen, but I don't need any help." He glanced behind him and said, "Holster it, you might hit me. Now, friend, it's just me with a gun and you without. Here are a new set of choices. I can shoot you now. Boring and no fun for either of us, but less for you. You can help, and then I shoot you later. Interesting for me because I get to watch you wonder when you're going to die, and it gives you a few more minutes to live. Neither have much sport, I'm afraid."

"There's a third choice," Dewey said.

"Pray tell."

"I do the totally unsuspected and disappear before you can pull the trigger."

"I seriously doubt that. I'm pretty fast on the trigger even if this isn't my normal gun hand. Some asshole shot me in the shoulder." Whitsett's eyes grew big feigning surprise. "Oh, my gosh, that asshole was you."

Thatch wiggled in Dewey's head. "This is it, Crash. Time to go deep."

"Would you shoot me in the back?" Dewey asked.

"I'm not above it. I'd shoot you in the balls, if I felt like it. I like shooting people." His gun hand drooped, but he pulled it back. "You could have bought a few minutes by answering some questions, but you frittered it away."

"I don't think you can hit me if I'm moving."

"Right." The hand that held the gun shook. "You want me to count to three? Forget it."

"How about one?"

The hand wavered.

"One, two, three!" Dewey yelled.

On one he began the turn in the direction that required Whitsett to move the gun the furthest. By two, he had leaned low and dashed away from the killer. He crashed into the wall that sent him ricocheting in a new direction. He heard a shot and felt the chips of rock hit his head.

On three, he jumped into the veil of the falls. He disappeared into the plunging, frothy water as he rode gravity down.

"Thatch!" he screamed, "I'm going deep!"

He dropped, arms wide, feet together, enduring the battering inside the cascading torrent. As he raced down, he pulled his arms tight to his sides. His feet sliced the roiled surface of the pool. The deeper he dropped, the less turbulent the water. The sound of the falls faded. He looked up. A ball of light backlit the splash of the water above him. He stayed buried in the pool, experiencing a similar sensation of "airlessness" as when he floated with Pearl. The drowning would not happen; being shot would not happen, not this day when he survived his trial by fire and came out cleansed.

"You made it, Crash," Thatch said.

A vague form with arms and legs shared the water, then beckoned him to follow him down. "It's all here, Dewey. All your hopes, dreams, all you've ever wanted. Follow me."

"Not yet."

"Don't leave. We have unfinished business. I told you I'd make you rich."

Dewey Farrell started a slow swim to the surface.

"You have. You got me here."

"No. Really rich."

"Another day, old friend. Thanks."

After he broke the surface, he waded into the rock overhang behind the falls. Unless someone wanted to jump in after him, there would be no pursuit. He wasted no time. He splashed close to the rock to keep out of sight in the unlikely event someone watched from above. He came out dripping near the trees. He ran through the undergrowth, re-entered the tunnel, slid his hand into the groove and walked quickly through the darkness. He knew how far he had to go, but overestimated how long it would take his adrenaline-rich body to cover the distance. When he hit his head again, he saw stars. He shook it off, then pushed through the small opening and back into the tunnels that would take him face to face with Whitsett.

He had no idea how much real time passed between his plunge to his assumed death and his return, but when he entered the storeroom there was no one there. He found the box with the revolver. He pushed off the safety. Three of the five boxes with books and papers were gone. He listened for voices from the next chamber. When he heard nothing, he decided the men were either in the tunnel or on the surface.

He knew the way, but still let the grooves lead him to the surface.

He saw the light from the flashlight before he heard the man carrying it, and stepped into a notch in the rock. The advancing man walked with his head down and never knew what hit him. Dewey stepped into him and hit him with the butt of the gun. The man dropped soundlessly to the floor. His flashlight shattered, and again the tunnel went dark. Dewey felt the wall, then pulled the man into the notch. He went up.

When he saw daylight, he climbed the last few feet cautiously. He peered over the top, and saw no one, but heard voices coming through the trees. He dropped behind the downed tree.

"That idiot was supposed to have the next boxes here by now," he heard Whitsett say. "Take the light and find him. Between the two of you get those boxes up here. I want to get out of here."

"Where's Prus?"

"Fuck him if he isn't back," Whitsett said. "I hate this place."

When Dewey was alone, the man who liked shooting people peered over the edge probably looking for Dewey's body floating face down in the pool far below.

"Looking for my body?" Dewey asked, from thirty feet behind him.

"Well! Aren't we the resourceful type. I wondered when I didn't see a body."

Dewey stood so he could keep the gun pointed toward Whitsett, and see the other man if he came out of the tunnel.

"You want the same deal you gave me?" Dewey asked him.

"Get shot in the back or jump?"

"Okay, not quite the same deal. The jump is a little tougher, but you're a tough guy."

"You're flirting with the same mistake I made. Better if you just pull the trigger."

"I don't like to shoot people."

"I killed your friends."

"It's late for confession. I feel a little melodramatic counting to three."

Whitsett stared at the gun steady in Farrell's hand.

"How about giving me a minute? I'd like to suck in the beauty of the moment. I've planned how I would die since the first man I killed."

"You want me to make your death better. Die according to plan? No. Thanks for the incentive. I'm going to avenge my friends and shoot."

He raised the gun and fired as the man stepped off the edge and fell silently to the rocks one hundred feet below. The only sound was the crunch of the impact. Dewey felt sure he'd missed, but he was glad he'd pulled the trigger. The gun dangled at his side as he walked to the edge. He dropped to a squat and looked down. Whitsett's broken body lay on the rocks sixty feet from the edge of the pool.

"Okay, Thatch. That's part of the promise."

The voice inside his head stayed silent.

Johann Prus

Prus would not be waiting for Whitsett at the chopper. The data and writing they would bring him no longer mattered. He had something far better. He would experience what was written instead of reading about it.

When he stepped out of the chopper, his feet sank into a carpet of fir needles cushioning his steps, giving him the feeling of floating above the world, above the mendacity of his former life. He walked unerringly to a path that wound through the immense trees towering above him and his dreams and his accomplishments. These giants that had outlived his family did so never moving from this spot. They drank in the world that came to them taking only what they needed. He wiggled his toes to see if he still stood here thinking these foreign and, until this day, heretical thoughts. He walked ahead slowly drinking in the wonders around him.

Daylight faded, fog filled the space between trees, and mist dampened his clothes. He felt no surprise nor threat when two men in wide-brimmed hats and long leather coats flanked him on his journey deeper into mystery. They stopped at a hut where they handed Prus a hat and coat. They walked uphill, and though it was more exercise than he had known in years, he kept pace. The first houses he saw so closely fit their surroundings that he was among them before he saw them. Few people lined their way until they reached a large house with a sweeping gallery. A blonde woman with flowers in her hair and a flowing gown of a white that shone in the mist, greeted him with her arms spread. To her right stood another woman. This woman had shorter, darker hair, but flowers were still woven into it. Instead of a gown of shimmering white she wore denim. To his amazement he recognized her as Pearl Banner. He removed his hat and bowed with a sweep of the arm holding the hat in a courtly, old fashioned manner.

"Come in, Johann Prus," the blonde woman in the gown said. "My name is Sophie. You are expected."

"Expected?" Prus asked, surprised again.

"We are not completely isolated here," Pearl Banner said, as she held the door for Sophie then Prus.

Prus marveled at the entry of dark toned wood that sparkled in the low light. Sconces lit the rooms softly in a manner reminiscent of modernized Eastern European castles. They never quite provided enough light to see clearly, but suggested more than history awaited in the shadows.

Sophie led them to a table with eight chairs. Three of the chairs were pulled out, two on one side and one on the other. As she passed, Sophie pointed Prus to sit on the side with one. In the middle of the table stood a large glass filled with a clear liquid reflecting bright sparks of light as if fireflies swam there. The only other thing on the table was a crystal bell. He stood behind his chair until the women sat facing him.

"The glass contains our water," Sophie said, pointing to the glass. "It is the reason you are here."

"You have come alone," Pearl said.

"Does this place speak to you?" Prus asked them, bewildered by their foreknowledge.

"Oh, yes. It has spoken to Pearl and me since we were conceived."

"Does it speak to everyone?"

"It speaks to those who listen. What does it say to you?"

"That it isn't how long I live. It's how well."

"What does that mean to you?" Sophie asked.

"It means what I had is not important. There is only . . . here. Can you help me understand?"

"When did you know this?" Sophie asked.

"The moment I saw the Cloud. Any thought of ownership disappeared. Help me know more."

"I will tell you one thing. It may not help. The Turners have a familial consciousness. We know it is there, but not how it works. It tells us what we and it needs."

"I would like to know more," Prus said.

"Perhaps you will," Pearl said, and looked at Sophie.

"Understand, Johann Prus," Sophie said, slowly, "you may leave now but not later."

"I did not come here to leave," he said. "Is this the way you welcome all your guests?"

"We don't have guests," Sophie answered.

"Why am I so lucky?" Prus asked, leaning forward, watching the faces before him.

"You interest us," Sophie said. "What happens to you will help us understand ourselves. That is why if you stay you may never leave."

"What is to keep me here?" Prus asked.

"The water you will drink. Our water gives life to some and death to others. If you live, you will need the water."

"Do you know now if I live or die?" Prus asked. "Is there a secret?"

"Do we know? No. Is there a secret? As in potion? No. The water here is different. None of us can live in the Cloud without drinking a great deal of water every day. But we do not know how it will affect you."

He reached for the glass.

Pearl held up her hand.

"Drink the whole glass. It will help you toward what you seek, or," she paused, "you will die very soon."

Prus retracted his hand and stared at the glass.

"I will drink it," he said. "I have little to lose."

"Then understand this," Sophie said. "As far as the outside world will know you are dead. Do you understand?"

"Yes. Am I a prisoner?"

"Of your own devising. If this place gives you life it will take it away when you leave."

"I see," he said, and reached for the glass.

"One moment," Sophie said, and rang the bell. A woman with a file folder entered, and handed it to Sophie. "These are papers you will sign before you drink assigning your assets to a trust administered by capable people in San Francisco. Your wealth will no longer be yours."

"How will the world know I died?"

"You will fade from memory. Without wealth or notoriety, few are remembered for long."

"I am the last of my line. It will not be easy to separate me from my wealth."

"We are adept in such matters," Pearl said.

"If I live, will we speak of this again?"

"Perhaps," Sophie said, looking at Prus carefully before sliding the papers toward him. "If you live you will have other responsibilities."

He signed all the papers after a quick scan It didn't really matter what they said from his side. He did notice they were professionally prepared and dated with this day's date.

"How did you know?" he asked.

"The way we always know," Sophie said.

"Tell me more," Prus said.

"You are in no position to give orders. Not now or ever after, be it a day or years." She pointed at the glass on the table. "Have you decided?"

He stared at the glass. He considered the events that had brought him to this moment. He remembered various objects he thought of value in his gaudy life.

He remembered the girl whose nipple he'd pinched and how he had arrogantly assured her he would own the answer to pain and a long life. He wondered if he'd been right. He looked at the glass. It all came down to this. Not sitting high in a glittering steel tower shining in the sun, but far from all he'd known in a wood house and shrouded in a cloud,.

He reached for the glass. He toasted the women, and drank deeply.

Dewey and Pearl

They swam in their pool. Their naked bodies sparkled in the afternoon light that reached the water through the throat of the gorge. In the weeks since the fire's containment, the air had cleared of most of the smoke although a haze remained that made for magnificent sunsets.

They danced in the water. An observer would call it a mating ritual of dolphins because of the way their bodies brushed against each other, then flashed away only to repeat the movement in some more intricate variation. When their fingers brushed for the first time, a signal passed between them. Their moments apart shortened, their touches became more insistent, intimate, and intense. The first time they kissed they floated stretched apart in a straight line, heads back so only their faces touched. Each succeeding kiss brought their bodies lower in the water, closer to each other.

No words were spoken.

When they finally pressed the fronts of their bodies together they became one, and slowly sank below the surface until the need for air forced them to kick their way to the top.

When they emerged from the water and climbed upon their rock, their glistening bodies touched wherever possible. When she lay on her back, she opened herself to him. He knelt between her legs and leaned forward. She held him tightly, pulling him into her, and when he touched her as deeply as possible, she raised her hands over her head and cried out with the repressed joy of two decades. Their bodies moved in a rhythm that brought them closer to what they both knew was a destiny neither time nor place could deny them, and that both now accepted.

With their orgasms they ignited a new chapter, and when they finally rolled apart, hips still touching, it was as a book opening to a new page.

THE END

Book Two
in the Bannerland Stories

All That Glitters

Coming in October 2013

"I can't explain you," Dewey Farrell thought to Thatch's ghost who shimmied and shined in the pool beneath the falls, the thunder of the water's impact diminishing as they sank deeper.

"How bad do you need to?" Thatch thought back, the words forming in Dewey's head fully and finely tuned.

Dewey stalled his descent after twenty feet slowly feeling the oxygen deplete his consciousness, but neither minding nor worrying. "I guess I don't."

"There you go, Crash! Let the world come to you, don't try to control it. Play it heads up. Live it full. Banner County doesn't let you define it. It defines you!" The light ripples danced in the water, stars popping in Dewey's eyes. "Might want to go up, Crash, but you come back soon. There are miracles down here beyond your wildest dreams."

15141912R00152

Made in the USA
Charleston, SC
19 October 2012